Published by Odd Tales Productions
Email: oddtalesofwonder@gmail.com
Cover Art © 2017 James Bezecny

Also from Adam Mudman Bezecny:

Devil Skull Takes London
Dieselworld
Words from the Inner Circle
Tail of the Lizard King
The Monogram Monograph

Adam Mudman is the editor of *Odd Tales of Wonder Magazine*, and has had short stories featured in *Nebula Rift* and *Tales of the Shadowmen*. She also runs the film and book review blog *Adam Mudman's A-List*.

Deus Mega Therion

CHAPTER I:

The sun hung low over the desert, but soon the cool sands would be alive with fire. The flames that burned here would none other than those of Hell itself. And the lightning would come down and decimate the enemies of the Adversary. The demons themselves would break free of their chains and dance here under the full and too-huge moon, and a new era of darkness would reign over this foul land.

The demons in question had their instruments. In the center was the Burnt-Face Lady, the Phantom of the Opera, the Crispy Mistress, with a voice from Hades and a bass to match. On her right was the Fissure Man, the Ice-Cold Man—his guitar, a Flying V, was as cruel and merciless as he, and black like the stars he came from. And finally, in the shadows, at the drums, was the Thinker, sometimes called the Brains of the Beast.

Their cry was coming. Their vast scream that would sweep over the sands to the fertile plains of man, and bring the cities of the New Babylon to the ground as naught but ashes—

But immediately, there was a feedback shriek. The Burnt-Face Lady tipped forward—she had been clutching the mike stand, and one of the techs tripped over the mike cable.

"Nik!" Alex shouted. He threw his guitar to the ground and took her wrist before she fell. It was only a two foot drop, but it was dark, and the sand was crawling with scorpions. In fact, he couldn't resist the thought that maybe a scorpion had stung the engineer. But then again, this particular engineer had wrecked this particular session about three times already—nearly set the torches off by mistake, which would've cost him both his hands. Either due to the flames or due to Alex finding a way to a kitchen knife.

Once Nikola was back on solid ground, he asked her if she was okay.

"I'm fine, Fissure Man," she said, using the name as casually as she'd used his birth name. "I think it's time to fuckin' pack it in, don't you?"

"I'd say so," he said. "Damn jackass. He's getting himself fired immediately."

"We should count ourselves lucky we've *got* a crew, Fissure Man, given the circumstances."

"Ugh. Don't remind me." His smooth voice was broken by tiredness and financial anxiety. "Well, album two'll kick ass. We know it will."

"Still needs a title, though," Cedric called over. He didn't need to call. The stage was tiny and so he was literally two yards from them. "I mean, we already used up the self-titled magic with *Jagged Skull...*"

Alex Fischer-King retrieved his guitar and started unplugging it. The engineers were grumbling about how they'd be hauled out here to do nothing. "Yeah, that was a little stupid of us. Well. Maybe for the rest of the night we'll just get drunk and throw things at the wall to see what sticks."

"We did that every night it took us to get out to Nevada," Nikola Shorter said. "And the three nights before that. Man, I'm sick of beer. And scotch and vodka, for that matter."

"I'm just gonna turn to hard drugs," Cedric Frost replied. The other two could no longer tell when he was joking at this point.

Five thousand bucks remained from the treasure trove seized from the release of Jagged Skull. And Jagged Skull themselves were already deeply in debt. Most of their equipment was on borrowed money. But the majority of the crew would stay on for a while longer, even perhaps after the funds ran out. These kids were stupid, the crewmen said frequently, but they could easily go places if they had the right assets at their side.

"Just as long as those drugs stop you from chatting about some of your notions," Alex said to Cedric. "For the last time, we're Jagged Skull, not some pseudo-philosophical shift of that name, like…"

"…like 'Mick Jagger's Skull'? Because metal is the antithesis of the flimsy hippie shit the Stones played in the '60s? Lest ye forget, Mr. Ice-Cold, that it was from my pitching that name that you derived 'Jagged Skull' to begin with. Yours is the shift, not mine."

"Whatever. And stop calling me Mr. Ice-Cold. That's for the fans."

"And Nik, apparently. Well, you can call me the Brains of the Beast all you like."

Nikola had to struggle to avoid replying. Indeed, it was going to be another night around the campfire, probably on lands they weren't supposed to be on, with Cedric J. "Frost" Flatow, relative of the pop singer and rabble-rouser from twenty years ago, who pathologically hated hippies, government officials, and probably many others ranging from conscientious objectors to homosexuals. Which was rather silly, actually. Metal as it stood today in '88 was a hideout for the weird and different. There were the glam metal people, filling the scene with LGBT folk. And of course, there were the nerds, bring in the mysticism of this rising "power metal," this subgenre so concerned with mythology and fiction. It had its religious elements even as it did its best to spit in the face of pretensions a lot of faiths had, even if most of its inspiration came from late-night D&D sessions. In any case, metal was a fortress, a haven, and being a bigot within it was a little contradictory.

Whatever. He was on triple-secret probation, and Nik and Alex were ready to replace him the first chance they had. But there was a scarcity of drummers in these parts, or indeed, in any parts. Ones who were good at drumming but also intelligent, hygienic, and capable of carrying on conversations without fantasizing about beheading Communists were depressingly hard to find. And they wanted one who wouldn't insist on "testing" an increasingly garish series of wigs to attempt to create a replacement for the industry's popular corpse paint. Fortunately, Alex had plans. Tonight, he would be the first to speak, and he would use his time wisely. A phrase had struck him in just the right away as he probed his errant thoughts for any seed of a good album title, and he fully intended to let it grow.

It was his favorite part of the process. Music was a living thing, a flower blooming with motion and emotion. He took pride in his work and he would starve for it. And he was happy that he found that kinship in his concept of music—of metal—in Nik and sometimes in Cedric. Nikola considered music to be more like a natural sound that existed in parts of reality that people couldn't normally hear, exposed by singing or stimulating an instrument. Cedric Frost had never stated his opinion on how music was shaped.

The crew and the band split into separate camps, as they had a tendency to do. That was by Cedric's request. There was a pair of brothers on the crew who were the descendants of a family named Sanders. Apparently a Colonel Frost, an ancestor of Cedric's, had been, in Cedric's words, "...mercilessly gunned down by the Yankee bastards at the heroic sacrifice known as Pickett's Charge." An ancestor of the Sanders brothers, apparently possessing a similar rank as Cedric's forefather, had been the one to land the blow on Colonel Frost. In fact, upon learning of this ostensible family tie, Cedric had tried to kill both men. That merited introducing singular-secret probation at the least.

As they sat around the fire, Nikola went into her second beer of the night—her fifth for the day. Much of Jagged Skull's profits had faded away on beer, and yet it had been such a success because of the drink. Most of the beer made it into her mouth. Losing some of it through the holes in lips, and the cavities in her lower jaw, she needed all five of them to get the buzz of two. Once album two was out, she had sworn she would look into getting plastic surgery—though it would be to patch the holes in her head, not to restore her appearance. The Burnt-Face had to stay. It was part of her charm now, her mystique, and she wanted to keep it even while still wanting just to drink. The lost liquor was dripping down onto her shirt, which she'd been wearing for five days. Through the white fabric, that was the white of the skull that took up most of the space of the *Jagged Skull* album cover, one could tell that she wasn't wearing underthings. Only Cedric bothered taking notice, and he did so like a coward. She was extremely attractive, and to devotees of the genre, her face never stopped being a turn-on. To Alex, she was the perfect friend, and Cedric left her alone because he disagreed with popular opinion on her injuries.

They had done a home tour at First Avenue in Minneapolis, and around that time there was a group of religious extremists who managed to keep their origins vague. They seemed to be Christians but it could have just as easily been a UFO cult. It didn't matter who they were, because during the concert this extremist group decided to reveal that their solid steel water bottle wasn't full of water, or even vodka. It was full of hydrochloric acid. She was left burning and screaming on stage, but the damage stopped at her chin, ears, and hairline. Her hair kept growing fine, but her nose was a lost cause, and her corneas were scorched so her eyes appeared red, though her optic nerves let her keep on seeing, somehow. No eyebrows were left, of course, and her teeth, charred brown, were always exposed. Her cheekbones poked through a little bit.

Of course, in order to survive, Nikola Shorter needs to continually inject herself with antibiotics. Alex knew he could trust her not to mix anything else in those syringes of hers. The poor girl was pockmarked all over, though—she also had diabetes, and had to give herself insulin shots. It was no big deal to her, though. She never wanted to live past fifty. She was almost thirty now.

A shame, Alex considered. She could play bass like an expert for three or even four more decades if she hung onto that practice regimen.

She had taken on the name "the Crispy Mistress" in an admittedly rather embarrassing reference to that British sci-fi program that should've been canceled years ago—Doctor Who, Alex remembered it being called on the evening PBS broadcasts. A central villain of the show called the Master once went through a phase in his life where he fought Dr. Who in the form of some sort of hideous burnt corpse, Nik said. The fans of this show called him "the Crispy Master" to differentiate him from the other two versions of the character seen in the series. Having seen some photos in books of this character, Alex saw a little resemblance. They had done a song in reference to this version of the character on Jagged Skull, called "The Keeper of Traken," after an episode he appeared in. If there was an issue with that they had done a demo for a re-record called "The Keeper of Nekart," which was an equally solid name.

Above all he wanted to be nice to his friend and if she found kinship with a fictional character, and used him as a crutch, that was fine by him. Even if that character was a villain.

He had his own crutches. And when he felt like Nik and Cedric's respective states of sobriety were suitably shaken, he decided to start his discussion.

"So you know that I've been researching the occult, in order to try to invoke success for the project," he said. At once, he took on a smirk, which Cedric ignored and which to Nik was a sign that he was about to starting spoofing Cedric.

"Yes," Nikola said anxiously.

"Yes," Cedric slurred drunkenly.

"Studying the long history of the intimations between the paranormal and the music industry," Alex elaborated.

"Of course," they said in unison.

"And how in the '40s and '50s, racist white folks started perpetuating stories of black jazz and blues musicians selling their souls to the Devil to get musical success and charisma...particularly charisma over white women. A belief a lot of white folks carry on to this day for other symbols of black expression."

Cedric was, as ever, tellingly silent.

"Well, eventually, those same suburban white folks, once they became suburban, hated music derived from black people's music. Again, they said that deals with the Devil are involved. Elvis' hips call forth demons of lust. Lennon said that people were turning away from religion and suddenly the Beatles were devil-worshipers—and there were the stories that there was something evil about Harrison being a TMer. Didn't help the Beatles that they put both Aleister Crowley and Cyrus Sincodemius on one of their album covers…"

Nikola laughed and waved her hand at Alex. "Dude, you're starting to babble—like one of those conspiracy theory idiots you see on some of those bootleg 'documentary' tapes we keep finding."

"I'm trying to create an atmosphere of…cocky mystery, Nikola. Like we do on stage. Sexy, but unknowable."

"Right, like sexy means anything to *you*," Cedric chimed in mockingly.

"Anyway," Alex said, smiling jovially. "I was *going* to talk about the Rolling Stones, and their whole occult thing, especially with *Sympathy*, but you know already. There are all these accusations flying around hither and thither about backmasking and frontmasking and all of that…" And Nikola was enjoying the warmth of friends, as well as the warmth of alcohol. "…and so I figured, why don't we be the rock-and-roll-slash-heavy-metal group that actually makes a pact with legitimate wizards?"

"That doesn't sound like a good-and-slash-or practical idea," Nikola said.

"Yeah—what've I told you about believing in paganism? You wanna wake up the Athenians?" Cedric said.

"Oh, God, no," Nikola moaned, as she realized there would be no zipper on the maw of "the Thinker." Alex's parody had awoken the real thing.

"No, think about it," he said. "The Athenians were the ones who killed Socrates. And as I've said before, Socrates' great wisdom came from his strong faith in Christianity. Though the faith had no name yet, the universal creed of Jesus Christ was…"

"Stop, Cedric," Alex implored.

"…was carried back in time by the Holy Spirit. Now to backpedal a bit, Socrates was one of the descendants of the virtuous Minoans, who were wiped off the Earth by a vast conspiracy of witches such as that which Margaret Murray writes about—more populous in these paganistic times are these believers in Babylonian faiths. These Minoans were the earliest Christians, like I said, having received Christ through the Holy Spirit before He incarnated on Earth. But the Babylonians, who worshiped devils like Belphegor, they were jealous of the Minoans, and…"

"*Cedric, stop.*"

Alex was under the impression that once upon a time, these bizarre tangents were, like his own impression of Cedric, meant to be parodies of people who truly believed in conspiracy theories. But Cedric seemed to be buying into the stuff now, almost against his will, as if his wits were going with the years. There was a certain insincerity about his claim of being twenty-six. There had been one time when they had decided to take peyote together. They had all decided partway through the trip—Alex's first and last—to gather all of their identification in case one of them had a medical emergency. Cedric, for some reason, had his birth certificate handy. Alex half-remembered that he apparently always kept it close so he could prove he was 100% American, as if that mattered. After the trip, wherein Alex had vomited himself into oblivion after making absolutely zero progress on *Jagged Skull*, he discussed what he'd seen with Nikola.

"I saw it too," she said. "Did...did that certificate really say 'Born 1896'?"

"I had a nightmare once," he admitted, "where he was pulling his hair off—his apparent real hair—and it was just another one of his wigs. Underneath were a few thin gray tufts. Then he peeled at latex and makeup on his skin, and underneath were thick flabs of skin oozing down, and wrinkles so deep the shadows of them changed his skin tone. And his skin already looked like beef jerky. He was grinning, like a skull, and his white, nearly-blind eyes were staring at me..."

Nikola didn't reply. She had a thing for older men (and women, for that matter), for indeed many of them were handsome and very devoted, but it wasn't her thing if it was clear that they had had something eat away at them over the years. If Alex's vision was true, and the creature below some layers of thick-caked makeup and bunches of wigs was ancient and decrepit, then she would find him reprehensible. While some of the elders she'd been with had had those lines from smiles, oftentimes it was guilt or hatred that cut into a man in the way Alex said he'd seen.

"But I didn't even get to connecting Jesus to Mithras," Cedric continued, "and Mithras' bull to the Minotaur, to prove that the Minoans were..."

"I do not care. Please, show some respect and allow *someone else* to propose an implausible idea for once," Alex said.

"I stand with Alex. Let the man speak, for God's sake," Nik said.

"Fine. What's your spiel?"

"One of those magic books I got at that garage sale in Wyoming mentions something that sounds right up our alley, in that it's fucking brutal," Alex explained. "There was a myth in that talked about some sort of thunder-spirit who had once ruled the Earth, destined to take on a mortal incarnation on our world. He would return, like King Arthur, or..."

"Or Our Lord and Savior," Cedric interjected.

"Yeah, or Jesus. Anyway, this child would contain the fury of nature within him. Thunder, to the writer of this grimoire, was an idea of nature in motion, in dance, which would be embodied in this creation..."

"Creation?" Nikola asked.

"The spirit's new body would be created as the result of a magical ritual," Alex confirmed. "The wind, the rain, the power within them would be like the music of the gods. That's actually what the book said, and I believed it. This...'Thunder Child' is powered by music."

"That seems awfully convenient. So much for the ban on applying overly complicated ideas to things, by the way," Cedric said. "I feel like there's more going on here, though."

"It's true. The Thunder Child story has a special relevance to me, and not merely because the phrase makes me think of the Captain Marvel comics from when I was a kid." Then paused. "Hey, what do you guys think of doing a song about Captain Marvel?"

"Shazam is honestly not the most brutal word," Cedric said. Nikola nodded.

"Okay, that's fair," Alex said. "Anyway. Shazam or not, I came across this grimoire, the *Codex de Novem Milia Spectris Malum*, and the account in it...*after* considering *Thunder Child* as the title of an album. After the ship from *War of the Worlds*."

"That's a pretty decent coincidence," Nikola said. "That means I love it."

"I don't really care," Cedric grumbled.

She ignored him. "Do you want to do this? I mean...what exactly do you mean, Alex...? Are we going to try to find a real-life wizard, and have him teach us the secrets of calling forth whatever's in this grimoire?"

"It may be the beer talking, but yes," he said. "Sometimes success—especially in the arts—comes at tremendous risk. If all else fails it's a great story to tell on tour circuits."

"If we get another one of those. This inspiration session was a fucking bust," Cedric piped up. "Look, I will go along with this seeking-the-sorcerer thing, but on one condition. You have to do something for me."

"Oh?" Alex asked.

"You have to help me fulfill...a lifelong dream of mine, we'll call it."

Nikola immediately scooted away from the drummer, and reached towards her bass as if she was preparing to club him with it.

"It's not perverse, I promise!" he said. "What I want is a supplement to what you want. This Thunder Child will...endow us with magical music power, right?"

"I believe so. But like I was getting at, now that I'm saying it aloud, I really am starting to think it might just be a good tour story—"

"No, no, listen, I'm a believer in the unlikely, as you guys have probably seen. I will own up to it. And I want to play some goddamn heavy metal, the heaviest in the world, just as you guys do." The words, especially "goddamn" and "guys" seemed weak in his mouth. "History may hold an answer for us, and that answer is in the 19th Century. If either of you are fond of fucking whoever you like to fuck—you'll like it."

"I guess I'm not interested then, regardless of who's involved," Alex said.

"You're just confused, I keep telling you, man—everyone likes to fuck and I know you're no exception. Look, in the 19th Century there was a great composer. If you truly know music, Old World music, the predecessors of our creed—"

"Get on with it," Nikola said, with Alex echoing a second later.

"There was Franz Liszt."

"You had all that buildup just to talk about Liszt? What do you think my degree's in, you asshole?" Nikola cried.

"Hell, I haven't studied music a single day in my life outside out of just practicing the shit I make up, and I know who Liszt is," Alex said.

"Well, then, surely you know about Liszto…"

"…Lisztomania?" Nikola finished. "Yes, Liszt became what we'd call a pop star today. He was supposedly really attractive, as well as being a prodigy, so his fans would mob him and steal his clothes, coffee grounds, cigar butts…"

"Yes! But the important thing, Nik, is that since no one had seen it at the time, everyone thought it was a mental illness. Now, we've been through Elvismania and Beatlemania, and this stuff is normal to us. But once, Lisztomania was the stuff of legends. No one was more brutal, or more typifying of metal, as an idea and as life, than Franz Liszt."

Nikola was largely weirded out, and frowned, even with her lack of eyebrows. "I can see the appeal in that, I guess. But imitating the 19th Century kinda defies the whole 'metal fighting against conformist culture' thing. I mean, we're called Jagged Skull because with my face, I'm the fucking avatar of Death Himself, and that's five across the eyes for people who let their fear of death infringe on one's right to express oneself with taboo or deviant topics. Those topics are facts of life…"

"…facts of life, yes." Evidently Cedric felt he owed Nikola a final interruption. "A wizard, Alex, will know a thing or two about such antiquated subjects, if they're the real deal. Liszt and Cagliostro and all them, to say nothing of Crowley and Sincodemius…"

"Well, you know, we are truly in luck then," Alex said. "I have been exchanging letters with a man who lives in a small town in Vermont, called Astaroth. His name is Edward Tamaron, and he claims to have ties to an occult group known as the Incomputare. I know nothing about them. But in any case, he says he is the worshiper of an entity called Ska, and he wants us to come out to…do a private performance for him."

"I mean, some of our demo songs were in that Italian women-in-prison movie from five years back," Nikola said. "The one that I think was part of that Mrs. E sexploitation series…"

"I'm nervous," Cedric said. "One, he should pay us, to cover the air fare. Two, he should pay us for the performance, in advance. Three, I don't trust a town named after something worshiped by the stinking Babylonians, much less a place in Vermont—haven of a bunch of liberal hippies. Four, and lastly, I don't trust a man who claims to worship a demon named after a music genre."

"I've heard of Ska before, in the same book about the Thunder Child," Alex replied. "A *very* ancient demon, supposedly."

Nikola realized she was getting tired, as the two men were clearly trying to out-pretentious each other. Normally she sided with Alex even when he was being pretentious. Frustration clouded her mind. "If we're flying to Vermont, pay or no pay," she said. "I need some sleep if I'm gonna make people bleed out of their eyes.

I guess it's nice to have an objective again, instead of just listlessly looking for inspiration..."

"Ha! You acknowledge my words! You said 'Liszt'-lessly!" Cedric declared.

She didn't kill him, though she wanted nothing more. Instead she stormed to the van, to sleep in the back seat, shivering in the chill of the desert.

CHAPTER II:

With nothing more to do, they drove to the North Las Vegas Air Terminal and booked flights for themselves, the crew, and the equipment, to a small airport in Brattleboro, Vermont. Rented cars could take them there to Astaroth, and from there they would find Tamaron at his quarters. He apparently owned an expansive apartment complex wherein he housed his servants. He called them the Order of Draco, which made Nik at least laugh.

"That's pretty awfully generic, wouldn't you say?" she asked Alex. "It just means 'Order of the Dragon.' Sounds like a Walgreens-brand Satanic coven."

"Or a Dungeons and Dragons group."

"It's got the metal feel to it, in any case. I mean, the metal horns—" And she made the iconic gesture. "—were introduced to the world by Dio, who was introduced to it by his grandmother, who knew as a ward against the Evil Eye. But people who don't work with us say it's a Satanic thing, when I don't give a shit about religion and I never will. People say the same thing about D&D, even though it's just a game. One I happen to enjoy. Like metal, D&D's a place where you can hide, if the world doesn't like you for being a geek...like Satanism, actually, from what I've heard of it."

He grinned. "There was that movie we saw in Canada about a D&D session gone wrong. *Skullduggery*, was it?"

"That movie was amazing."

It was. Now, Alex was closing his eyes, and trying to enter what he called a "meditative state." Also known as the mental equivalent of huffing into a paper bag. He hated flying, but he evidently saw so much promise in Tamaron giving him a Thunder Child—and the Thunder Child fueling their fame in turn—that he was willing to fight back this fear. She didn't quite feel up to it, and neither did Cedric, probably. They were pretty hungover. Nikola had thankfully been able to sleep last night without having more to drink. Last time she'd been to a doctor he said she'd been pushing it, liver-wise.

All the same, they passed an uneventful flight—and all three of them struggled to keep themselves composed enough to avoid vomiting on the passengers next to them.

Several hours later, they touched down, and at once it was night. The shock of stepping off the plane—jet lag—was the final straw for their collective nausea. Their dignity stayed intact, even if the things that Cedric stored in his digestion were worthy of being wiped from memory by the brain's natural defenses. The sights they saw on touchdown via his nausea were rendered dream-like, just like their glimpse of his birth certificate.

It took them an hour to regain composure, and at the end of it they went to McDonald's. Feeding nine adults was a lot cheaper if the executive parties chose to eat at McDonald's. Cedric remembered how painful it was to have an empty belly, and he suppressed his beliefs about McDonald's' use of mind control in their food. Alex tried to remember that what would follow this—his eating a burger, that is—would not be worse than some of his previous illnesses, like dysentery, or some of drug experiences, like the peyote trip. Nik liked McDonald's. It reminded her of her first date with Charlie, her fiancé.

Despite Alex's gastrointestinal fears, it was sparking inspiration in him, too.

"Eating this—and traveling—reminds me of my childhood," he confessed.

"Makes sense to say such a thing when we're looking for a wizard. You're just afraid of the real world, that's all," said Cedric.

"No, there is a sort of magic to it," Nikola agreed. "I mean, my dad—he tried to fix the mark my grandfather left on our family by changing the name a bit to 'Tesler' instead of, well, y'know, my namesake. I still say it would be worse if we had been Edison's descendants, but whatever. When my mom said that Tesler was too obvious he switched it again to more opaque 'Shorter.' My dad would take me on road trips to try to get me interested in geography and not science, like grandpa. And we would eat tons of fast food, and he would tell me ghost stories..."

"Incidentally, the town of Astaroth is supposedly haunted," Alex said.

"Why didn't you say so in the first place?" Nikola asked.

"Of course it's haunted," Cedric said. "It's named for the demonic perversion of an already corrupt source. Ishtar, to Astaroth, the demon of Deuteronomy."

Alex read Deuteronomy, and didn't remember that. Lots of emphasis, however, on the prevention of Moloch sacrifices. Another instance of magical children, like his Thunder Child, this time on the side of evil—the children were magic because they were killed.

"Ishtar was Babylonian—" Cedric began again.

"Yes, we know," Nikola said.

There was an awkward silence, which continued as they got back on the road.

Two rental cars were needed, as it turned out. That was only natural given the size of their party. While they had taken the car with Cedric earlier to maintain their image, Nikola and Alex "accidentally" jumped in one car and left Cedric to ride with the crew. They'd done it before. He would suspect nothing. Triple-secret probation would remain triple-secret.

They didn't gossip about him. They mostly slept, and tried not to take Cedric's words personally. If they wanted to enjoy this road trip by way of reverting to mental children, that's what they would do. And slowly, they left the hard world of civilization behind. Montpelier, the urban center, was soon to be left back behind a barrier, and they would have entered a new realm. Out here there were empty fields, both barren and overgrown, and thick forests. The drive jostled them, and they did not sleep well. Through the night they passed through the dark thicket, where the road was so narrow that if another car along they end up in the ditch. In some places the sounds of nighttime insects, along with the hoots of owls and even the cries of wolves, nearly deafened them, and the silent crewmen in the car possessed an almost unrecognizable sense of dread. Other times, the trees were as quiet as they, and that was even worse.

Eventually they came out into open fields, with no signs of life in sight. No farmhouses, no distant lights from towns or villages. Even the smallest villages had all-night businesses these days—they would have seen signs of those. Nikola spent a full five minutes awake, and found herself missing the feeling of entering a gas station in the middle of nowhere at midnight. She had heard some people talk about how those places were like alternate realities, parallel universes, or maybe they just seemed like such because of the nostalgia of childhood wanderlust.

Of course, for her, there was a sense of danger. It always seemed to be the ugliest of men who cashiered at these late-night establishments, and they were always men. But now, with the socialization of an adult, she realized it was more than these people were downtrodden, beaten. Exhausted by capitalism. In any case, it was entirely possible that these cashiers, who gruffly handed back some much-needed candy, were sociopaths or serial killers. Or cultists.

The thought of traveling through the night to meet with cultists calmed her enough so that she slept again.

When she woke up, she had the Star-Spangled Banner in her head for some reason. She turned and saw that Alex was still sleeping, even as the purple and gold fingers of sunlight reached for them.

They were coming through a valley now, and she could feel the pressure change in her ears as they descended. The valley was surrounded by tall, rocky hills, which to Nikola seemed almost like guardians, or toll-booths. As they passed into this ring of hills, there was another forest, and deep within that forest was what the map said was another valley. Filling the cup of this inner valley were the houses and roads of Astaroth.

Of course, Nikola and Alex, being young, were happy to stumble across "quaintness." That was what they always looked forward to the most. They hoped the store contained an antique shop—there would certainly be no end of bizarre and forbidden books hidden in such a place, waiting to be bought with their cool city money. Actually, a self-respecting antique shop, even in a small town, would stock goods that were generally well outside their remaining disposable budget. Kitsch would have its great victory over them.

Besides, they were here on business. As bizarrely gorgeous as this place was, they had to meet with that wizard. That served to distract them further—both of them were now thinking about the Yellow Brick Road, with Astaroth being the Emerald City. However, when they at last came up the town, they found it was brown instead. These were old-style brick structures, like one would see in the Cities back in the '30s, which could still be seen today in towns like Stillwater, though there were also plenty of worn-down wood houses. The paint on these had long since faded, and it was possible that they were abandoned, or that the inhabitants were too old to repaint.

"I bet this is a place where you can buy human skulls!" Nikola screamed then. In this case, it was a metal scream, scratchy, anti-vocal. Alex had his guitar near him and began to play some quiet but harsh notes. "The legions of the dead are the ones behind those doors!"

But she didn't continue.

"Fuck," she whispered.

"Still having mental blocks?" Alex asked.

"I am."

They were silent for a while.

"You know, it *is* okay..."

"It's not okay, Alex. This is our livelihood, and if I can't keep producing content, soon I'll be below even Cedric. Sales aside, if we don't get this new album put together we're fucked, and it'll be entirely my fault."

"I just wish my writing was a little better, Nik. I can do a few songs but you know they won't be that good."

"And every time Cedric tries something, the Third Reich—"

"I know. But we'll figure it out, Thunder Child or not. We have unlimited imagination."

"Yeah, but sometimes, that's a *handicap*. I mean, consider that song, 'In the House of the Beast,' from *Jagged Skull*."

"Okay."

"Do you think we conveyed the concept well enough?"

"What, that it's about a gay guy who goes to an estate sale for a dead man who turns out to have been a first-generation Nazi?"

"Yeah."

"I think we did. We did it as best as we could. Hey, music's not like fiction. In a song you can't go into a lot of details. And a lot of it is throwing imagery at the wall just because you like it. You like how it sounds, how it gets under your skin, like the feel of a good woman. Not like I would know or anything." And he laughed.

"No, I getcha. Thanks for using a simile relevant to my life," she said.

"You do the same for me when it comes to it. Now, are you worried about telling a good story? Do you feel it isn't well-composed?"

"Both."

"Listen, friend, it's our first album. You can't predict the mistakes you'll make while just in the theory phase. You've got to set it out there, and let it dry, and then you'll seen where all the cracks are."

"I suppose you're right. So *Thunder Child* should be a fix for *Jagged Skull*?" she asked.

"Nah. Let it be its own thing. There'll be time to celebrate the past later."

She grinned. "You're right. For now, the present is much more inviting...and mysterious. Is that morning fog?"

"It is. It's covering everything, and could be hiding anything."

The entire valley was shrouded in this thick mist, and it came up so suddenly—it seemed to flow from the center of the village, as if the town square had been paved with dry ice. As the cars slowly drifted into this fog bank, Nik rolled down the window and looked up. There was a long road that led up the far side of the valley, along the narrow edge of a cliff, with no railing. But after crossing such a pass there was a tall house, well-painted and yet still ravaged by dozens if not hundreds of years. It was too tall, and it was windows stretched too high, as if fingers had come down from the sky and tugged it up just a little. She knew at once that that was where they were headed.

"Okay, getting a few ideas even now..." Alex said. "Can you feel it?"

"A little," Nik replied. "Just wish it was a little stronger..."

"Once we make it up there, it should be fine."

But then, the driver turned back to face his passengers. "With all due respect, Mr. Fischer-King, I'm not going up there. Not if there's no railing."

"Please do it. I will give you overtime pay."

"Not even for that, sir. These vehicles are rented. If they're damaged it's a tremendous loss to our firm."

"I will sign a contract for that overtime pay if I have to." And he paused. "Please do it. Listen to the other car. You can hear it even from here."

Evidently, the driver of Cedric's car had raised similar concerns, for now they could hear the beefy folds of Cedric's voice as he screamed angrily at the man to keep going.

"Be very glad we're not like him," Nikola said. "And we're really sorry. Those guys we'll pay triple."

"Nik...!" Alex hissed.

"It's a deal," the driver said then. "Up we go, I guess."

They both felt immensely guilty. Especially because they could still hear Cedric hollering.

The driver was cracking, even though he wasn't in the condemned car. "Is he—always like this?" he asked.

"Cedric once mentioned signing up for one of those gag home video shows that he felt were about to become popular," Alex replied. "Once, while drunk, he had suggested filming himself slicing his fingertips off, or slicing off the front of his corneas, and sending those in."

"What?"

"He also wanted his erect dick to be the album cover to *Jagged Skull* before we decided on the more obvious skull design..." Nik said.

"...calling it 'the real Tower of Babel,' incidentally," Alex added.

"And he shot down a good song we put together called '*Beowulf*' because he claimed, well, that Beowulf was actually a piece of poetry from...a certain historical region of modern-day Iraq that he tends to bring up a lot."

"And he specifically hates Babylonian stuff because...?"

"He calls it 'pagan.' It's sort of...a new world order sort of thing for him. Those sorts of conspiracies are pretty popular these days, aren't they?" Nik said.

"He hates Ancient Greece most of all," Alex added. "To the point where he doesn't even acknowledge people when they mention it. One day, when he was tired enough to finally cave to my questioning, he explained that Antiochus IV was a Greek. He was the one who installed the 'Abomination of Antiochus' on the Throne of God in the Book of Maccabees, in the Bible. And the Abomination in question, historians say, was Zeus. He considers Zeus to be the ultimate evil in the cosmos, besides the Babylonians.

"The story of the Thunder Child is related to Zeus, but I couldn't say that to his face. After all, he was fond of attempting to reclaim the Cross of St. Peter from the 'real evil-doers' in the metal community—by promising to apply Peter's punishment to those who would worship 'false gods.'"

"That's a real shame," the driver said. "Because I worship Satan, and I don't think there's anything wrong with my doing that."

"Nah, that's cool," Alex said then. "If it's based on Milton's Satan, and taking on a sort of optimism with the Rule in Hell thing, along with rebellion against absolute authority, then I think that's a good thing."

"That's me in a nutshell," the driver replied.

They were quiet for the rest of the trip, but only because they all focused on the road. Alex, a believer in the powers-that-be, hoped his will would guide the automobiles on their journey. The crawl to the ledge of death was agonizing, and Nikola squeezed her eyes shut as best she could. Since the acid had damaged her eyelids, however, she could still see through them unless she was in pitch darkness. Sleep was a mercy for her.

When they made it to the horror ledge, they shuddered every time sand or rubble skidded until their tires. They were barely breaking 5 MPH—and still it seemed like the ground would give way beneath them. Inside the other car, Cedric was trying to keep his mind busy. To that effect, he tried to remember the exact motions for the nerve pinch he'd learned online, that would render people incapable of speech. He had obtained it specifically to make his bandmates shut up—eventually they would have to submit to his decisions if they could not speak up against them. Focusing on that victory was enough to get him through anything, and soon, they were all on the other side.

Surrounding the property of the overgrown estate was a picket fence, which enclosed a lawn large enough to house both of the cars. As they pulled in, Nikola Shorter kept an eye on Cedric, to make sure he wasn't still raving. Perhaps the imposing sight of the house would finally quiet him—and Mother of Mercy, it did. Even though the morning was coming up, the shade of the trees near here seemed unnaturally dark, and in any case there was a tension in the thin air. The air shouldn't have been that thin at what was still essentially a low altitude, but perhaps their bodies had quickly learned to love the rich air of the valley. They were at loss for words as they observed the house, and saw that its windows were dark.

But at once, they still felt like they had to go inside. After all, the man had invited them, and had specified no time in particular. Alex told the crew to stay outside, and they did so wordlessly. They didn't seem keen on the grounds, and a few of them went back into the cars, though they didn't dare try to brave the pass again just yet. Cedric rubbed his back, as he stood hunched over, and Nik looked out over the town of Astaroth.

For the first time, she was struck with the feeling that coming here was a mistake. That was emphatically placed in her mind, like a brand on a wax seal or a tea brick. Though they had seen no one in the town, and though it was a beautiful if rundown place, she almost immediately felt like she was standing next to a seed of terrible wrongness, an eeriness that couldn't be placed.

She was certain she had heard stories of towns that provoked this wrongness. She just hoped this wouldn't turn out to be the sort of wrongness that precludes stumbling upon a Klan meeting.

The old, scraggly buildings below them were like broken and rotten teeth. Near the town square stood a dilapidated old church, and the bent spire rising from its hulk was straight of out of *Castlevania* or *Headhunter* or some other video game. There was a vampire in that church—there had to be. She could feel it, though she demonstrated no prior knowledge of being able to sense vampires before. And she never would again.

Tamaron could be a vampire. Anything was possible.

Suddenly, Alex was at the door, pushing it inward and stepping inside. Nik was the first to follow him, and Cedric was at once clearly loaded with cowardly humors. Were he in a better mood he'd gripe about he'd wish they'd let him keep his gun license, and how license fees were too expensive. If he had his way, and Tamaron had something up his sleeve, he'd just blast him into oblivion. That's just what was Jefferson would have wanted, after all. The enemies of the American Experiment would perish by the sword with which they sought to ravage the Daughter of Liberty. Now, he was worried about having his throat cut in the dark and cold of someone's old patio.

It was spooky within the house, but at once they saw it was not entirely dark, even though thick curtains were drawn over all the windows to stop the intrusion of the morning sun. But within this artificial black was another light—the tangerine flicker of candlelight. When they crossed over from this dark entrance hallway into this main chamber, they all had the impression that they had not been the first ones to do enter here who were outsiders, nor would they be the last. This was a room that had the stink of some significance to it—Nikola knew that was a poor way of articulating it, but it was immediately apparent to her that stepping into this room was a bad idea. But at the same time, it seemed like there was nothing else to be done.

And once they were inside, it turned out that the three of them hadn't been in alone in their passing through the entryway. There had been a man in robes, who closed off the room as soon as they were all within. Cedric started screaming, and this only intensified as he saw that every avenue of the room was blocked off by dark-robed men striding into view. Ahead was a passage descending down into a cellar, or perhaps a dungeon. Additionally, another corridor veered from the left-most end of room. When Cedric looked downward, his shrieks were so loud that he nearly collapsed. On the ground, painted in a crimson pigment, was a pentagram.

There were five black-robed persons in the room, now, before any of them could do anything about it. One of the men who emerged from the cellar stepped forward, and with a flourish he pulled his hood back. Underneath was a smooth and sleek face, a youthful face, lit with large but natural-seeming blue eyes, and a crop of short, combed, blond hair.

"Goddamn Babylonians," Cedric spat. His voice squeaked—screaming had broken it. Nikola considered him a pushover.

"I am Edward Tamaron," this magnetic man said. "And I have no idea what you're talking about."

CHAPTER III:

Tamaron realized he'd scared his guests, and so he immediately called for them to be brought tea. Knowingly, he added some whiskey to each cup, to their silent gratitude. The kitchen was a cozy place, with many large wooden cabinets, where the wood was so old it had turned gray like the surface of the moon.

"Thanks for letting us in, Mr. Tamaron," Alex was quick to say. "I assume you'll want us to do the performance tonight? We can spend today setting up and rehearsing, and play for you and your group once the sun goes down."

"I would like to discuss the terms of the performance you'll do for us, actually. You see, it is something of a complicated thing. For one, we've yet to discuss what, uh, *you*, want to get out of the deal. But perhaps it would be best to start with the basics. Why don't you introduce yourselves to me, Jagged Skull?"

Cedric and Alex lost their ability to speak at that time, though this time it was only from nervousness. Nikola said, "I'm Nikola Shorter. I'm Jagged Skull's bassist and vocalist."

"Your face...it is wonderful," Tamaron said.

"Thank you," she replied, earnestly.

"You remind me of the visions I've had of the Levantine king Belphegor, or the mummy-lord Tutankhapep."

"What are you talking about?" the singer asked, politely but with exhaustion in her voice.

"I will admit that the visions I had of those two was a lengthy meditation, bracketed by fasting and the consumption of Indian opium."

"Oh."

"Your name is Nikola, hm?" Tamaron said. "Any relative of Dr. Antonio Nikola? You may have heard about him in accounts of famous terror agents."

"What? No, I, uh. Look, don't tell anyone, but I'm the granddaughter of Nikola Tesla."

"Too bad. You rather resemble dear old Antonio in his later days."

"'Dear old'? Uh...didn't you just say he was a terrorist?"

"In a manner of speaking. There was a novelist, Guy something, who wrote about him. Exaggerations—and censorship, of course." Awkwardly, he then jerked away, and faced Cedric now. "Who are you?"

"Cedric J. Frost, sir."

"Please, there are no 'sirs' here. I see much of your inner self in your physical form, Cedric. I have no questions for you." His voice was an odd fusion of an East Coast sort of thing—perhaps a Boston accent, crossed with an upper-class or English RP voice. "And you are Alex Fischer-King?"

"I am, yes. We've corresponded."

"Yes, that's how I knew your name." His face didn't change—he still seemed to be going out of his way to be warm. "You are the drummer?"

"No, that's Cedric. I'm the guitarist."

"Your body is impressive. I imagine you play well."

"Uh...thank you!"

Nikola didn't know if she was supposed to be charmed that he directed the most energy to her. He seemed to view Alex and Cedric as objects, almost, if even that.

"So, then, moving on—what do you seek to gain? You must take me at my word when I say that when I feel gracious, there is little I can't find," said Tamaron.

Cedric had been zoning out, but he began to see his chance opening up.

"Well, sometime back, I had a chance to read the *Codex de Novem Milia Spectris Malum*, and..."

"Oh, yes, I'm quite fond of it," Tamaron interrupted. "Though I prefer the *Naturos Demondo* or *De Vermis Mysteriis*. Or, the one that I've stumbled across recently, *The Book of Ska*, which talks about that which I have kept in my cellar. Sealed within a block of solid stone is the Tomb of Ska, wherein the dark god screams to beat his wings...he is a fiction-demon, you see. He can physically enter the worlds of stories—so the stories say—and feed upon the beings that live there. The fiction-beings—the 'characters.' And they say that invocations to fiction, as a unified, living force, can bring him closer to freedom..." He cleared his throat. "But the *Codex*... that's the one with the Thunder Child, isn't it? Didn't you mention that creature in your letter, as well?"

"I-I didn't."

"Oh. Well, in any case, your face lit up when I mentioned it. It's a term of interest to you, isn't it?"

"...it is."

"Good." Alex at once had an impression that the same cloth from which Cedric was cut was also that of Tamaron, and yet it was obvious that Tamaron was smarter. There was something off about him, as if liking him was compulsory somehow. "Upon completing the performance, I will tell you about the Thunder Child. He is well-known to the Incomputare, and there are a great many out there with an interest in his legend. My own Master, Cyrus Sincodemius, enjoyed the tale, and had you access to them you would find notations of Thunder Children in the journals of Coppola, Hexen, and Purrlzig. I will teach you the Child's magic word, and you will have your dream of flying."

Just in that set of words, Nik's mind was lost in a sea of vaguely-defined rhythms, which called up images of eagles flying free on journeys through the dark. They hummed with Power and cut like runes. She was sold already, though she shared Alex's suspicions.

But then Cedric spoke up. "Actually," he said. "There's something even more important to us than that Thunder Child thing." And he took a long stride towards Tamaron, reaching out with both arms as he did so. His hands found the backs of his bandmates' necks, and with two pinches he knew they wouldn't be able to speak for a few minutes.

"And what is this other thing you desire, Mr. Frost?" Tamaron's tone seemed flatter now.

"Well, we've always believed that in order to obtain musical success, one needs to acquire a certain attribute," Cedric said. "The composer Franz Liszt supposedly induced a form of mental illness called Liszto..."

"...Lisztomania, yes. I'm familiar."

"And if you're familiar with it, you know how to induce it too, right?"

And at once, Tamaron glanced at Alex and Nik. They were now learning that they couldn't speak, and clutched their throats. Nik shook her head at Tamaron, trying to convey that Cedric wasn't someone worth listening too, but Tamaron merely raised one end of his mouth.

"I do know, Mr. Frost, but it is a grave secret. The fee for it will be very high."

"We'll be willing to pay any price."

"Ha! You're an entrepreneur, Mr. Frost, which is a fact that I thought unlikely."

The other two could feel their voices come back to them, but already Cedric's hand was in Tamaron's. "What are the terms, then?" Cedric said as he shook.

"Well, the performance is, as I have said, not exactly what one would call a typical performance," Tamaron replied. "It is greatly inspired by...dreams, or visions. With my financial compensation you will be going to three different locales and doing concerts at each. During this time you will acquire three items that I need. They are for my own personal experiments, and one of them will lead you to a fourth item will grant you both of your wishes. That is all the help I can give you. When I dream these things, they appear as images, rather than tangible, rational sequences; in any case, while there *are* some things I know about what's ahead which might help you, this knowledge is an advantage of mine, which I will use to keep you under my control, following the path I have foreseen. Please note that until the terms of the contract are settled—" and he now produced such a document from his sleeve "—you will be financially compensated only for as much as you need to perform and complete your missions." And he set his hand on Cedric's shoulder, pulling him away from the others as he handed him a pen. "Just sign here, Mr. Frost, and thank you." The others reached out for him, but it was too late. And he hadn't read a single line of it.

"That signature, incidentally, will be sufficient to my lawyer friends in my Order of Draco to stand for your whole group," Tamaron explained. And he chuckled to himself for a few moments. "Oh, and incidentally, since your music seems to endorse it," he said then. "You will use lethal force when necessary. And there is a significant chance that such necessity will arise."

"What?" Alex said. Finally, his voice had returned. He would have to cut off Cedric's hands so he couldn't do that again. He was quaking now, with fury. "I said that there may be times where you will have to kill people at your concerts. You are now bound to that by terms."

"What? No! No, we're not doing that. All the killing stuff—even the animals—it's just something we do for show. Those animals are rubber, in case you couldn't tell..."

Suddenly, the cabinets around them burst open. Their doors had obscured women and men who wore the same robes as Master Tamaron himself. In their hands were a variety of daggers, swords, and hatchets, and they closed in fast.

Tamaron didn't have to say a word.

"We won't be your—your assassins!" Nik shouted.

"Actually, being assassins won't be that bad," Cedric said quickly. "Remember, folks, that the word assassin is actually derived from *hashishin*, which is in turn derived from 'hashish.' The original assassins or hashishin were paid in hashish. So we're essentially just going to get baked."

"If that's what you want, as additional compensation, I'll be happy to amend the contract," Tamaron said. "Drugs are hard to find in this part of the state, but certainly hashish is not—"

"I'm not interested in getting paid in weed. I can't, or at least shouldn't, smoke," Nikola said.

"I'm not smoking near her for those reasons," Alex agreed.

"You guys are a bunch of pussies," Cedric said. "Being afraid of a few face-scars. Hash is good stuff, better than weed even, and I'll take it."

"It will be arranged." Tamaron looked over the contract that Cedric had put his scrawled John Hancock on. "You are evidently a fast reader, Mr. Frost, so surely you are aware of the fact that we cannot help you if you are attacked by the PMRC?"

"The PMRC?" Cedric asked.

"Precisely—you know just what I'm talking about. They will probably try to kill you, it's true, but..."

"This is stopping now," Alex said gruffly, and he turned to face the armed members of the Order.

"Mr. Fischer-King, perhaps you don't understand. I don't want to hurt you, because I do need your performances just as much as I need the objects you'll recover while giving them. Therefore, I'd like you to step outside so I can show you what I mean."

And Tamaron stepped past him to walk back to the entryway, and with his followers sweeping behind him, he took the band out onto his lawn. Here, the crew was assembled, still near the cars but some distance from the entrance to the house.

"What is this?" one of the men said.

"Don't worry," Alex tried to say, but soon Tamaron echoed those words.

"Yes, don't worry," the robed man pronounced. "You will all be taken care of in the coming days, when you help your band on their concert tour. All save one of you, who must serve as an example to the others."

Nikola couldn't help but compared the way he said that to the villain from some Italian Nazisploitation movie. "An eggzample to ze *UTTERS*." But this was no laughing matter (and it only normally was if the Nazis were the Nazisploitation kind), and at once Tamaron raised his hand, pointing at the crewman closest to him. Calvin, she thought his name was.

"Somewhere around here your killer is hiding. You will never see them coming. When I give the order, they will kill you...thus!"

And there no noise. Immediately, Calvin cried out, but only for a split second. He dropped to the ground, it was plain to see he wasn't breathing.

"What the...?" Cedric whispered.

"If an autopsy were to be performed on him—which it never will be—you would find a small needle, lodged in his foot," Tamaron said. "The poison will dissipate from his system in less than thirty minutes. The formula isn't from the In-computare, but from a Chinese Doctor whose name you would recognize if I could safely speak it. Long forgotten in this age, of course."

"You're a murderer—!" Nikola said.

"That could be inferred by the fact that I employ assassins," Tamaron mused. "And by the end of this business, you will be murderers too, but rest assured that your 'victims' will hardly be worthy of the term. They won't be the members of the PMRC, but they will be the thugs and goons hired by their more radical members to..."

"Hold up." Alex took the time to speak now. "Who are the PMRC?"

Tamaron only grinned. "You'd better head for Montpelier, Mr. Fisch-er-King, your concert starts soon. As for the PMRC—they are the most dreaded enemies of anyone who would play the sound called metal. They will be waiting for you, and I suspect their timing will be well-rehearsed."

CHAPTER IV:

Asking around that smaller franchised Brattleboro airport, one of the crewmen found something of interest. (Alex was sure he was called Reynolds.) "According to some people, 'PMRC' refers to the Parents Music Resource Center, apparently a music censorship board of some kind," he explained. "They formed three years ago during a Senate hearing on music obscenity. They forced an obscene lyrics rating on one of Frank Zappa's instrumental albums."

"I see," Alex said.

"A lady also told me that there's a cruise line by that name: Proper Musical Regulated Cruise. It grew out of an older company of a similar name, based in Duluth, that had some sort of scandal about twenty years ago. They provide cruises with 'sanitized' music only, with traditional ballroom dancing being the only thing allowed. This is usually Lawrence Welk fodder and the like. The thing is that this PMRC wants to impose its musical tastes on the rest of the world by any means necessary."

"They'll probably be the ones to look out for, then," the guitarist murmured. "Thanks, Reynolds."

"No problem, Captain Nemo."

"What was that?"

"Oh...uh...some of the guys call you Captain Nemo. Because you're sort of the Captain for stage stuff, and because there's 'No-one' in your life..."

"God, does that have to be a thing of ridicule with everybody? No more stupid nicknames. If Cedric brings them up to you, ignore them. Nik and I will pick the ones we actually use."

"Oh, we always ignore Cedric, sir."

"Thank God."

Alex leaned against the sterile wall of the airport waiting room. They had fifteen minutes before boarding, but already he was anxious to leave. Nikola was nearby, and she stood up now.

"I used to dream about being Captain Nemo," she admitted.

"Oh?" Reynolds asked then.

"It would be nice to live on a giant submarine, obscured completely by miles of water." She turned to face Alex. Her face was obscured by a widow's veil—her distinctive face would attract some of their fans, and perhaps stop them from reaching their flight. Such a thing had happened once, in Japan. To back it up she wore a ratty gray cloak with sleeves much long than her hands. "What's the first thing we're looking for, Alex? An ugly statue of a bird of prey?"

"No—and cut that out. In this first mission we're looking for...a Mirror. Apparently a rather large one. The size of these objects is supposed to continuously decrease, and the third artifact will be the hardest to locate. The Mirror we find should be a full-body one."

She simply nodded, but saw the stress in his eyes. "I'm here to listen if you need it," was all she said.

He sighed. "What would Maiden do?"

She laughed. "Are we making that a saying now?" she asked. "I think they'd be in the same way as us. Panicking. Any of them would be—Sabbath, Priest, Queen, Rush, Motörhead, Terrestrial Shackles, fuck, even Claws of Agthrunsthaaa."

"I dunno. I think Ozzy could fuck some people up."

"That's probably true. Anyway—take faith in knowing that we're reacting to this in a human way. I mean, they'll clearly kill us if we don't do what they..." With his hands, he urged her to lower her volume. "Sorry. But here's my plan. We need to find Tamaron's limitations, and so when we do this first concert we'll look to see if he has anyone keeping tabs on us—or doing anything else, for that matter. With the information we get from that, we figure out if we want to run, if we want to get the cops involved...or if we need to keep stringing them along."

"It's possible we may not learn anything in the first concert."

"Yeah. Still, we..."

"...have no choice. Yeah."

Alex opened his mouth, then, sucking air in to fuel words, but Nik shushed him, pointing. Cedric was coming up to them, holding a beer in his hand. They weren't under the impression the airport sold beer, but it didn't matter. They just hoped it didn't forbid beer, because then he would probably get rough with some-one before they were able to board.

Of course, he would probably get rough with someone on the plane, too. If there was one thing that Cedric loved more than metal, it was engaging in gratuitous violence. One of the other things he would say about himself was that he was the one who made metal violent. At first, they assumed it was an idle boast, one made by other bands roughly around their age. But the details he provided were always just a bit too far, in that they showed a hint of sincere regret.

Cedric, essentially, was just a ball of rumors, deceptions, and fictions. They knew more about him than he probably knew about himself, but all they knew was all the weird shit about him that had to be untrue.

Maybe that was why they kept him around. Someday, he'd do something really crazy, and there was no such thing as bad press.

At least Tamaron was covering things, financially. That would keep them out of debt for a while. He even said that he would provide a crew if their present one, though they sincerely hoped that wouldn't be the case. Tamaron's followers were also his muscle, and if they were close they'd likely muscle in. Both of them refused eye contact with everyone on the plane.

Montpelier and Astaroth were not too dissimilar from each other. They were both the epitome of a gentle New England town. Nikola leaned close to Alex as they were dropping in. "I doubt this place has a serious metal scene," she said.

"Are there serious metal scenes?" he replied. "I think part of the reason why I did this was because it was a little funny..."

"Just as long as we don't go into comedy territory like Cedric," she shuddered. "I'm sorry, the older I get, the more I just hate comedy. I start to get more and more interested in the darker aspects of metal, even if taking it *too* seriously makes it a comedy again, at your own expense. Maybe I think that's what we need to make it. After all, again, it's because the sell is on..." and she waved her hand in front of her veil.

"As long as we get to keep doing sunny shit," said Alex. "Just be careful. I, um. Hm."

And there was a pressure in the air for Nik then. She assumed it was because they were descending, but for the first time in a long while there seemed to be a heaviness to Alex. Maybe it was just stress getting to her but she had the sudden paranoid feeling that he was leaving something unsaid.

"What's up?" she asked genially.

"Do you remember New Year's?"

"Yes, I do," she said.

"You said you thought your burns were starting to rot—to rot *into* you. And at first, I thought you meant that you were having a medical issue with your burns, but you meant something more spiritual."

She remained calm. "Why are you mentioning this now?"

"Well—before every concert I feel like I'm gonna die. You can't beat an anxiety disorder, you can just put its fucking mouth underwater for a while. I've had it my whole life, and even though I've really lived to my dreams, I haven't gotten away from it. And since we *could* actually die in the course of this show, I wanted to get this off my chest. And I think it's something putting pressure on your chest, too."

She remained quiet for some time. "Just as long as Cedric never hears a word."

"Is that why you haven't brought it up? You were worried I'd tell him about it?"

"No, no. I didn't bring it up because I don't do so well mentally past 11:30. I couldn't remember if I'd really said it or not."

"Oh—I'm sorry if..."

"No, Alex, it's fine. It's good you mentioned it, and that I really said it. Now wonder I woke up so content the next morning, without being able to say why. It was probably the relief of letting that out..."

"Well, what did you mean by it?"

The plane was nearly landed now—it was just a half-hour flight—but the instruction of the pilot and dings and clangs of the various alerts were distant to them. "I meant that it *did* feel like I was having a medical issue with my burns. Like they were getting infected, and that infection was slowly worming its way to my mind and my heart. The way music beats worm through you. And I was thinking that maybe all the anger we throw in was getting to me, and its low beats were turning me into something with a heart that looks like my face—rotten to the core, animated solely by an agonized will."

The way her tone changed as she spoke would ordinarily be disconcerting or obnoxious to others, but to Alex it was a sign that she was healing by talking about this. Maybe this would be their next song, about a storyteller driven too deep into obsessions.

They'd already chosen their set list for the evening. The centerpiece was supposed to be "Splintered Light," which made them all happy. That one was decently solid, and so they hoped it would go over well. It would be tough for them to find the mirror if they weren't looked upon fondly by the locals.

The bar they were headed for was called Diana's Grove. Nikola had been the one to notice that this was probably a pagan name; when she pointed it out to Alex they looked it up together. Sure enough, this pub had been founded in 1961 by Calixta Caswell, who had converted to paganism upon hearing stories of her ancestors' encounters with a monstrous albino serpent of some kind. Calixta apparently had a lighthearted view on such things, and never involved herself with monsters outside of her patrons.

They told Cedric it was a Wonder Woman joke. He was fine with that, having never read the comics and learned which mythology informed Wonder Woman's own mythos.

At this point they had been inside so many bars that when the three of them at last entered the Grove, its physical appearance didn't strike their minds that prominently. It was a large place, big enough to accommodate them, and to have its own parking lot. In this lot were a variety of motorcycles, and at once, one of them caught Nikola's eye. She grabbed Alex's shoulder and pointed.

In the sidecar of one of these numerous iron horses, there was an out-of-place artifact. Particularly, a piece of furniture—a mirror. A full-body one, hugged in a gorgeous silver frame. Coiling around this frame were the pewter images of wide-mouthed snakes.

While jumping into the process of how obtaining the mirror would work, Alex idly remembered an uncle of his telling him about the Montpelier motorcycle gangs. The Hawk Cup Protectors, the Wild Desert Bikers, and the...

...and the Savage Templars.

The name was deceiving. These Templars—such as those who populated the bar in a six-person pack—were often known to be charitable, especially to vagabonds, lost souls, and artists. That included musicians. All one needed was the courage to walk up to one of them, hulking as they were, and strike up a friendly conversation. The more relevant the conversation was to the Templars' interests, the better.

He had a credit card from Tamaron. While Nik directed the crew and

Cedric met with the manager, he rolled up to the bar next to one of the guys and scanned for the right wine bottle. Excellent. "I'll have a glass of the 1782, please."

Then he glanced tellingly at the Templar on his left. Out of sight the bartender's eyes widened in surprise, reflecting in gratitude on how that was the last time his son would have to make a payment on his tuition loan.

"1782, huh?" this man barked suddenly. He was nearly seven feet tall, and a yard wide. His forearms were hams emerging from the boundaries of his sleeve, and his short graying hair was held back by a skull-crossed bandana. "'82 was a good year. A good year! You know why?"

"I do know why," Alex said. "That's why I asked for it."

"Oh yeah?"

"1782 was the year that the Knights Templar decided to reform into a horseman gang, which is sort of what it sounds like if you're thinking motorcycle gangs," said the guitarist. "This is, of course, accounting for the fact that the Templars *did* survive their apparent extinction on Friday the 13th, 1307—albeit only barely. The Inquisitors did their work well, and the surviving Templars disguised themselves as criminal gangs to keep on practicing their rituals in secret. But eventually their disguises became them, and they lived as a group of pickpockets for centuries in Venice, Paris, Rome, and almost everywhere else. Dick Turpin was among their number, and it was in his image that the '82 Templars rebuilt themselves, coming to America. The Savage part, surprisingly, wasn't meant as a slur against Native Americans, who could freely join in on the plunder. You guys ride bikes now and mostly do charity work, but sometimes that charity work involves trimming some of the upper crust..."

"Well, jeez! You take a big chunk out of your pocketbook and ramble like a professor for God knows how long just to get on the good side of a Templar? Alright: what are you selling?"

"I just wanted to make a good connection. I'm a musician, you see, a metal musician. And presently, I need..."

"Keep that talk down, pal. Most of the folks here won't know what metal is, but they won't take kindly to it. It's a matter of religion, sorry to say."

Alex blinked.   "...then the original suggestion I was gonna make is important," the musician said. "We need security. In the past, we've been attacked by people with violent conceptions of Christianity. See Nikola over there?"

"Oh my gosh. That's...horrible! Who...?"

"You probably heard about the case, friend," Alex said. "The guy had been following us for some time, focusing directly on Nik. He thought that her singing and bass playing, along with my guitar, were the tools of a demon that took the form of our band, incarnating in three different bodies. In order to expose the demon, he needed to get rid of Nik's flesh."

"Oh no..."

Alex couldn't help but be charmed by the concern of the big man. It was an entirely Platonic charm—he just enjoyed seeing compassion. "And so a bottle of acid it was, then." He sipped the wine. It was okay. "The guy who did it, the police say, was Jacques 'Dame' Paris III, the political 'satirist' with his comic strip."

"Good Lord. I'm glad that fucker died on the wrong end of a hypo," the biker replied. "I just wish it had been the street's needle, and not the state's. More painful that way." The two shook hands. "My name's Eberhardt Grant. The Savage Templars are at your service. Play hard and loud, and if anyone starts up some church-y mania, we'll stop 'em like the Angels at Altamont."

Alex choked hard on the wine. "Um..."

And Eberhardt laughed richly. "Don't worry, my friend, I'm just making fun of your clear knowledge of history."

Alex grinned, but privately he could feel the earliest traces of sweat form on his brow. Though they altered their speaking volume to suit the scene, some of their words had been heard by the teaming crowds that filled this place. Man, it was much bigger than he'd first thought. And people of all classes and customs were here. At the edge of the bar, mixed in with bar-flies, were foppish gentlemen with overripe martinis. Hockey dads and soccer moms, with ugly sweater and faded high school jackets, sat with fashionable teens, each with a leather jacket, something neon, or a walkman. He walked over to Nikola.

"Something weird is going on here," she said suddenly.

"Thank God, I'm not alone in seeing that," he whispered. "Well, if my uncle's lore is right, and I'm not a gullible idiot, we've got protection...and a quick path to the mirror."

"What's that about the mirror?" Cedric said suddenly. He was now standing between the two of them, flitting his head back and forth at them with his mouth wide open.

"We may be able to get it soon," Alex said succinctly. "Is everything set up?"

"Everything's on its way to getting set up. We'll be ready in twenty minutes. My beers from the airport wore off, I'm getting a scotch..."

"No, you fucking aren't," Nik hissed. And at once, there was a dart of motion at her elbow. Automatically she glanced at it, then looked away, then shot back at it. One of the fathers, clad in a sweater with a maple leaf on it, had begun staring at her. He didn't seem to take notice of her face, but nonetheless was filled with bad sentiment. He *seemed* hateful of her presence, not for her deformity, but because she'd said the word "fuck."

She ignored him, and the twenty minutes passed quickly as they continued to restrain Cedric from drinking. Eventually they got him behind the drums, and as the patrons figured out what was happening, the members of the Savage Templars, under Eberhardt's orders, surrounded the stage, taking powerful stances like they were their forebears around the Holy Grail.

Nikola was at the mike, and if she still had sweat glands in her face they'd be fully active. Still, there was one rule that Alex insisted must be obeyed at all times, which she agreed with 100%. *Don't fucking choke.* It would have to be a perfect sell, no matter what. And as long as she believed she could do that, sell perfectly she would.

"Hello, Montpelier! Are you ready to rock and roll?"

There were a few aged hippies who stood up with the handful of teenagers who bothered bearing excitement.

And, with a tongue planted firmly in her scarred cheek, she said, "We are Jagged Skull, and we are here to take you away from this world of ads and churches and nuclear Commies. We are here to take you back to pagan days—to the Unfolded World, where things were kinder and better. There was magic in those days, folks, until a civil war broke out, and everything fell apart. At least, we like to think that's how it happened."

And behind her, Cedric's hands clicked wood together four times.

Once in time we were sublime
We were the best as we could be
We thought nothing of it,
as we came to love it,
it was the powers of Gods we could see.

Immediately, all suspicion dropped from the crowd, and at once it seemed there was divine reasoning behind the myriad diversities of the crowd. On the Jagged Skull album tour they had seen it before, faintly—a group of disparate people suddenly fusing into a single unit under a good noise. The weight of the sound broke them apart and fused them back together stronger. Music was an experience, and experience was the word for things that killed the mind, and forced it to regenerate into something better.

We tamed the flowing wonder,
that dwells
in nature's breath.
We tried to topple existence's tower,
so we wouldn't have to face up to death.

It was getting faster, smoother, jazzier—the vocals were even, at least, being based more on rock singing or opera than the growls or screams used in something of the other subgenres. It could be for anybody, if they were willing to adjust. There was something compelling about myth: it was part of everyone's ancestry, after all. These oldest of stories were the dressing by which humanity first made contact with the divine. To connect it to music, which was as old as religion, was only natural. Most of the people here were white, and it had been long since they had been connected with myth's floral music. Nowadays, what they heard in the churches was commercial in some sense—hyper-material.

Without names, we tamed the light,
uncounted, the dark was ours.
But pride swelled in time,
and we were no more sublime
For war came and forged our cell bars.

To escape we'll have to break it
And I just hope we'll make it...

The notes hit, with meter that popped. It was still rough, and raw, but it was what they had, and before they'd started weaving all this stuff they hadn't really felt the same goodness.

In the background, Nikola's eyes briefly caught a glimpse of a man entering the establishment. He was wearing a long brown shirt that she at first mistook for robes. He had an aged and uncle-like face, with a graying bowl-cut for hair. His shirt seemed to have a crude hood sewn onto it, like a monk's habit, though on second glance that hood was just a hallucination.

Light
Splintered light
Smashed to rainbows and to doom
Light
We were bright
Now we're broken and we'll fall

Will we ever rise again?
Can we?
Can we?

The monk-like man was creeping through the crowd, striking up small conversations with various people. "Splintered light, hm? Don't you think that's a reference to something like, say, the failure of the Crucifixion?"

Once long ago we were made to flow,
There was brotherhood in us still
It was easiness itself
to put kindness on the shelf

and wizards did warlocks kill.

We broke the holy mountain,
the place
where Beauty thrived.
Over conflicts as feeble as manners,
It was in evil's name we did strive.

"Well, that's just out in the open now," said the sometimes-hooded man, as that last line hit. "Can't get more on the nose than that..."

Fists were clenched, but only because of the interruption. The newcomer grinned faintly. In a big city like this, people would be lost to impious ways. It was time for a more tangible demonstration.

Uncountable we ruled your world,
Incomputare our creed.
Now our kingdom is done,
raw chaos has won,
And a savior is what we need.

That was the last of it. The doors of the bar were kicked open once more, only barely audible over the sounds of the band. The eyes of the Templars widened. Here were men dressed like legitimate commandos—bullet-proof vests, belts thankfully armed only with nightsticks, slick black gas-masks. Across the imposing surface of their vests was an enormous ornate print of a Crucifix—the same design was on their helmets.

"The world already *had* a Savior, goddammit!" one of these uniformed individuals yelled. The band didn't stop—they couldn't. But they knew at once that this had be Proper Musical Regulated Cruise, the PMRC they'd been warned about. What they were doing in a landlocked city, God alone knew—unless they had gotten wind that there would be a concert of this variety here. "Stop this at once. This music is not properly regulated. It contains none of the word of Our Lord Jesus Christ!"

The music, as ever, was louder, but none of the three trapped on the stage could break their eyes away from the seriously-dressed intruders. If they did, it was only to shoot a pleading glance at the men who ringed them with their arms crossed.

To get out we'll have to burn it down
And you'll have to lose your king's crown...

Light
Splintered light
Smashed to rainbows and to doom
Light
We were bright
Now we're broken and we'll fall

The PMRC couldn't take it.

Simply put: they began to wreck the place. They were impatient, and in a few moments it was time for the Templars began to do their duty. Patrons were pitched from their chairs, and those chairs were hurled aimlessly at the stage. Photos held in time and glass cases fell cracked and battered as the walls rocked. Some of the chairs even punched through the walls, exposing hissing plumbing. The bartender cried out, but the music muted him, too. He ran into the back to call the cops. Once he was gone they got behind the bar, and wines far more valuable even than that which Alex had tried became their projectiles. Some of the troopers had taken out their nightsticks and brandished them haphazardly, wiping out the bottles in what was probably some worship of Prohibition. Desperately, one of them beat at the cash register, denting it enough to break the lock on the till drawer. He furiously stuffed dollar bills into the front of his pants, which were crossed with the pattern of forest camo.

Their audience lost faith—they couldn't have asked for more—and began to run for the exit. Some of them made it, others were grabbed and shoved back inside. The soldiers were gibbering, quietly murmuring some repetitious catchphrase, as they pointed condemning fingers at these innocent panicked bystanders.

Will we ever rise again?
Can we?
Can we?

Fists swung, mouths screamed, the Tusc Tube amp blared. There was a circle of people near to them who regarded the violence almost absentmindedly. Then, in a tradition that was now just dawning, they prepared their own sort of violence—a play-violence, which would free them from the compulsions that wracked the men who had decided to crash the show. By trapping viciousness in the land of fiction, and in this, the pit of moshing, they healed themselves of the beast heat that humanity is still laden with.

There was something geometric in the sounds they were making, some sort of math that began to impose an order on them, and not the sort of order the PMRC wanted. Oh, their eyes went wide when they saw this weird sort of dancing. But there was more mind in that mosh pit than there was testosterone or boneheadedness.

Now today it's not okay
Our potential's fully gone
It's the End of an Age,
so I think it'd be sage,
to rest this game anon.

Only now was security making any headway. At this point everything was a mess. The floor was a minefield of shattered glass and ceramic, slick with booze. The hardwood floor was irretrievably stained with dark wines, beers, and brandies, and tables had been flipped to scatter greasy fries and pulverized nut shells amidst the wet, sharp madness. To Alex and Nikola's mild joy, their volunteer helpers were seizing the guilty parties and gently carrying them outside, rather than living up to Eberhardt's words and unleashing lethal force. No one would die here today. And they figured a one-song set would be adequate. Tamaron hadn't specified how long a set had to be, after all...

The flowing wonder slumbers,
to wake
thrice again.
I've seen this all before now,
and it was sad,
but then...

With no end, the cycle turns,
Incomputare shall come back
for now it's the tomb
and the sheltering womb
as we perish under attack.

Though the bar was nearly empty, the monkish man was out there, but to Nikola he faded when her eyes fell on him. The soldiers were exiting hurriedly (they could hear police sirens that those onstage, and those moshing, couldn't), but one of them stayed. He was gesturing to the patrons who were hiding, terrified, underneath the tables. They had just wanted a bite to eat. But this man screamed out that catchphrase that people had previously just mumbled: "Those who don't join us are without virtue. Those without virtue are blind to the truth. They must be taught the truth, or they will be complicit with those sinners on that stage."

To get out we'll have to break it...

I know that we can make it.

Nikola barely got that line out, and not even because of its original context.

Light
Splintered light
The rainbow's gone, there's only gloom
Light
We were bright
Now we're divided and we'll fall

Will we ever rise again?
Can we?
Can we?
Can we?
Can we?
Can we?

And they would.

If anything because security had disposed of most of the dissidents. They were safe now, and how they'd kept their cool in the course of all that, they had no idea. In fact, they still hadn't gotten their cool. Alex was cotton-mouthed, Cedric was sure he'd shit his pants. Nikola's hands were shaking, but one of the Templars helped her down. At once, they were all struck with the impression they needed to get out of there. The issue of the mirror wasn't settled yet, but Eberhardt Grant was waving them outside.

Their stomachs soured when they saw the police waiting for them.

"This was certainly inevitable," Nikola hissed.

But Alex tried to be sunnier. "This may work to our advantage. We can tell them we're being held hostage. We may not have any proof, but..."

"Oh dear God," Cedric cut in. "I hope they don't test my piss...or do a cavity search. I-I've been to prison before, and they had me on the rocks. On the chain gang. They stopped using chain gangs in the '50s, officially, but there are some places out in the boondocks where they've never heard of modern laws." Though Nikola had hissed because she'd sung her lungs out, Cedric's voice was just as broken as hers, strained with desperation. "The things is, when I was out there for my six months, they never took the chains off of anyone—never. Even if the work had been too hard, or if you couldn't keep down the bread and water, or if you'd gotten an infection and it wasn't time for the gang to see the doctor. They wouldn't even come if by the time you got a doctor you were already dead—even then, even then, the chains never came off...”

Alex put his finger over Cedric's mouth. Grant and the other Templars were speaking loudly to the cops, now, while the cops shoved them back.

"Now, listen, here—we Templars are in the employ of this group, the Jagged Skull. We have sworn ourselves to them by our Code of Honor. We must render our services to those who understand the history of our order...”

"Now, listen, now, listen, we get it," one of the cops said. "We just want to know who's responsible. Who started this?"

"Everyone in that bar and their mother will tell you it was that damn PMRC," said Eberhardt Grant. "They...”

"They're a non-presence in this part of Montpelier, I can assure you," the officer replied.

Alex's eardrums were sanded by the notes bursting from of the amps, but he could hear what the cop behind this first one said: "Actually, sir, the PMRC has been active in this area for some time. They've been targeting this particular establishment for a few years due to its name.”

"It didn't help that you guys were playing that Satan music," the first officer said then. "Y'know, they say you Satanists control the Kindergartens that my kids go to. I hope you ain't doing anything gross over there...”

"We're not Satanists. I'm a Christian, actually, most of the time," Alex said.

"Whatever. We'll look at this PMRC business. But you'd better give us your contact information, in case we need to do some follow-up...”

And Alex stepped forward at once to announce that they were being held hostage, and needed protection. But the second cop tapped at his apparent superior's shoulder, sticking a thumb out back behind him. "There's no time for that now. We've gotta scramble."

"Why? What's up?"

"Orders just came down from headquarters. There are some oddly-dressed men on the other side of town. They have guns, and they...”

"Well, surely some of us can stay here and collect their information—”

"No! They've already killed four of our boys!"

And the first cop's face hit the ground. "Jesus fucking Christ. Let's go get those bastards."

"Wait!" Alex shouted. "Please, we're in danger—”

"Those guys on the other side of town may be some of those PMRC people. If we get them now, we'll be able to help you guys later. Okay? Okay. We'll be back—we'll find you.”

"No!"

But they were pulling away already, and as they stepped forward to try to catch up to the police to make them stay, there were too many pissed-off Templars in the way, who each wanted a piece of the cops for challenging their honor. Were it not for them, Alex was sure he could have stopped them.

"Great."

Alex turned back to look to Nikola for comfort, but found none. She was staring at the ground with her hands squeezed tight. He shared her feelings, and as such didn't bother looking at Cedric, bobbing in the background.

"Tough deal," one of the Templars said then. "I had an aunt once, she forced me to take one of those goddamn musically regulated cruises they do. I nearly went out of my mind—in fact, that's why I ended up on coke for a while, 'fore the Templars straightened me out. Having to spend two weeks at sea never knowing when you weren't being watched. They wanted to see if you were jerking off—so they could spring out and smack you with rulers."

"Sad to see the faith coming to that," Alex said. "But it's been like that since the Inquisition, and before that, even. Really, I've heard about these 'Christian' cults obsessed with order before. They're reincarnations of the Inquisition. They're just a bunch of bastards who like torturing people. Dragging those compassionate folk down."

Alex looked back at Nik, this time actually taking pains to move closer to her. In fact, he hugged her, and after that she seemed to relax. As he pulled away, he saw Eberhardt Grant come up behind. He set his hand on her shoulder, which aided her relaxation. "You guys can chill with us for a bit," he said. "It looks like you'll be needing it."

CHAPTER V:

They were in another bar, then, one that still had glass to keep its booze in. *Now* they were allowed to drink, and Cedric was doing so with relish. To be fair, the others weren't so far behind him, though Alex didn't like how alcohol tasted once he was drunk, and Nik wasn't thirsty.

But she was more amiable, now, especially since the ride up here in the cycle side-cars had given her a good look at the mirror. It had to be the thing they needed to get. She was sure there was a way to get it fairly.

"So what's your story?" she asked Grant.

"Me?" he asked in response.

"You, or...anyone else. Alex seems to know the history of you guys."

"Yeah, I'm sure he'll tell it all to you someday. Honestly, it's a little boring when told in its entirety. But I can tell you about our current cadre if you like."

"That sounds nice. It'll take my mind off things."

"Well, you see, it starts, as a lot of things do, in Vietnam. Not during the War, mind you, but close to it. Most of us was too young to get into the service in that time anyway. But I had an older brother, Donald, who had been in 'Nam, and he recalled a time when a group of Vietcong soldiers attempted to smuggle crates full of tons of gold out of an old Khmer temple, dating back to when the Khmer Empire had vassalized part of Vietnam. He killed the soldiers but lost all the gold in a bog. His orders made him and his buddies push onward but they vowed to come back when the War was done and become rich men.

"Of course, snipers got most of his buddies and in 1974, my brother was dying of what we'd today call the AIDS virus. Got it from a prostitute, a lady hook-er, I should say, 'cause it's not just homosexuals who get 'em. He told me and my own buddies 'bout that gold, and when he died he made me promise to get revenge on life by making myself a rich man when I got it back.

"The things we faced in that jungle I can't even begin to describe. There were four of us who made it out of that initial trip, and there should be a fifth here among us Templars. But one of them, Charlie—which is a bit of a sad name to have in 'Nam, really—"

"It's my fiancé's name, too."

"—we had to leave him behind."

"Oh."

"When that *fungus* was through with him, he was barely even recognizable as human. But he still followed us—for many miles.

"Then, of course, we found the Khmer city they stole the gold from. One of my friends, old Louque, had a grandpappy who knew the area, which was a re-mote patch of coastal forest near Warrior's Island. He'd left some old charts that we followed. We made a mistake of hiding from a storm in one of the temples there.

And here's where I want to interject a legend we Templars have. Back in '74 we hadn't heard of the Templars, but we joined 'em right after we made it home, those of us who did. There's a story, then, that some of the Templars who escaped execution in 1307 decided to put themselves in suspended animation, as living *mummies*. And if memory serves—can't guarantee it does—we learned the truth behind some of those old legends that some of these medieval Templars survived, having sailed to 'Nam, evidently. Further, some say—the tales tell that their ghost galleons have made it to a Caribbean island called Matul, or Santa Sebastian, which is said to have got a voodoo curse. Most of their number are said to lurk in rural chapels in Spain. Anyway...in those temples were mummies, or people dressed as mummies, at least, that tried to stalk us for...whatever reason. We were pretty sick at that point, from eating out of the jungle, and sick, too, from the smell of the leaves the locals called *tan'na*. We could've imagined it. But we went home, and decided to join the Templars, to find brotherhood. They offered us adventure, after all, and we desired it fully. It was nice being wild! We've loved great women, drank great beers, and dodged the cops successfully for fourteen years running. All innocent stuff, of course."

"Yeah, partying can be fun sometimes. You guys do good work, it seems like, if you offer security and everything," Nik said.

"Yeah, yeah, security's great. We do a lot of charity work, too. What do you like best about partying?"

Uh oh. Now it was sounded like he was hitting on her. Not like she minded. Still, there was Charlie waiting for her back home, poor boy. He would be getting anxious now, and though she worried about him thinking about him made her feel nice. She'd let this biker dude down gently.

"Well, I mean...making out with people is nice," she said, with a hint of genuine embarrassment. "Even just flirting's fine. But I drink sometimes, too. Don't do drugs a whole lot, but I'll admit, it moves the creative juices along when you're stuck on coming up with a tune."

"I can imagine."

His tone was odd, but she read it as best she could. "You the artistic type, then?" she asked.

"Sort of. Most of my creative stuff is, uh, philosophical, though."

"Oh! I wanna hear about it."

"Are you sure you do? It might be a little weird to you."

She laughed, and looked over her shoulder back at Cedric Frost. "Trust me, I've heard worse."

And he laughed too. "Well, first, I have some particular views on marriage. I think that people should be allowed to marry whoever they want, as long as everyone involved is an adult and they're okay with it."

"Right on. I stand up for the gays."

"But I also mean that people shouldn't be limited to one spouse."

"I know what you mean with that. A lot of people throw out polyamorous relationships as being 'harems,' or just people 'collecting' spouses. And while polyga-my can lead to that, it's not a guarantee."

"Right? Like, there are people like the PMRC who think that you need to keep all your love pent up, instead of letting it out. It's not like there's anything un-natural about having desires for more than one person or anything."

"Exactly! If you have an open relationship, cheating isn't a thing."

"Exactly." And he looked down and chuckled faintly.

"So really, your philosophy isn't that bad, from what I've heard so far," Nik said. "I like a guy who can fight back against the 'think of the children' mentality. Though admittedly that's always a two-edged sword."

"Hey, they say that it was outta the interest of kids that they killed Socrates. And in that same interest they put up the Comics Code Authority, which made all of the old '40s comics neutered into the stuff of Hanna-Barbera cartoons, which in my mind is meaningless. Plus think about the Hayes Code, all the shit it did to movies. It's just mass hysteria, y'know? The same that made all those Tanzanian schoolgirls laugh for sixteen days straight twenty-five, twenty-six years ago, or those people who thought there was a Halifax Slasher in 1938."

"Mass hysteria is fascinating! I love all of that stuff that just sticks out weirdly and eerily in our heads because of what we think is normal." And now she knew she was a little tipsy. "There was a mass hysteria outbreak in Mattoon, Illinois in the '40s, where people thought there was a guy running around gassing people. All throughout the Middle Ages, people would go into hysterics and dance them-selves to exhaustion, in what was choreomania or dancing plagues. And hysteria plays a role, too, in Jerusalem Syndrome, where people who go to Jerusalem, Mecca, or other holy sites have religious visions and delusions that sometimes alter their personalities..." She was grinning widely, and she turned to face another of the near-by conversations. "God! I...forgot how much I knew of this stuff. Alex, remember when you and I would discuss this for eternity?"

"I forgot you ever knew it, Nik," the guitarist said, looking away from the biker he was talking to. "You were the psych person, I was the myth person. And I've always wanted to be more obscure than you."

"Pig."

He only laughed at her, and had another drink.

"My Bachelor's is in history," she said. "At least, part of it, anyway. BA in music, minor in history. The minor ended up being more important since so much of the fine details of music slipped away from me. The history of music is usually easier on me—and playing this sort of metal, about all this fantasy stuff, having his-torical knowledge helps. But Alex, he really does specialize in the occult and mythic. He's the heart of the band, because of that." She sighed. "I mean, we all have a solid knowledge of some of the weird and wonderful things that our planet's been through. Cedric pushes it even further than Alex, though, and his history isn't even mythological. It's just wrong."

"Well, I dropped out 'fore I could finish up an Associate's," Eberhardt said. "But I *was* in for Psych. I wanted to understand why I was, uh, fixated on something."

"Fixated?"

"Don't worry, it's not like I was thinking about anything...anything *wrong* or improper. I just remember as a kid...well, did you see what I keep in the side-car for my bike out there?"

She inhaled sharply. "Oh, that mirror thing? I was a little curious about that."

"Let me tell you, when I was a kid, I always had a fixation on that mirror. It was an ol' family heirloom, y'see, but I always just thought it was so *beautiful* as a kid. And I always wanted to know why...so if you want to hear somethin' controversial, ask me about some of the things I've learned about psychology that I think are new discoveries. Those ones may shock you yet."

She rubbed her hands together, enjoying the boozy tingle. "Hit me."

"Well—have you ever read *The Manchurian Candidate*? Or heard about MKUltra?"

"I know the general facts. Those are probably ones Alex knows more about..."

"What matters is that you get the idea of a sleeper agent. Somehow who's been psychologically 'programmed' to 'wake up' when there's a trigger phrase used. Then, they will do the programmers bidding, no matter what."

"Pretty spooky."

"Yeah. Especially when the phrase is something common. Like, for example, 'What's your story?'"

She laughed. "Yeah, it would definitely suck if that was...the..."

She froze.

Then, her hand found its way to Alex's arm. He was talking hurriedly to the other Templars, probably about something related to the myths she'd just been referencing.

"What's up?" he asked. And he pointed at Eberhardt, and how he'd stopped blinking, and was instead now just showing off his glistening white teeth in an enormous shark-like smile. He didn't notice that the men he'd been addressing were making the same face.

"Shortly after returning from Vietnam in 1974, the PMRC caught up with us," Grant said. "And using methods they claimed to have gotten from the Soviets, they took away everything that made us sinners, and in return left...an implant. When the phrase is spoken we become *pure*, and I praise the Lord working through you to test my purity. I was testing you by revealing 'my' philosophy. When in truth everything I said could not be farther from the philosophy and the purity that now guides us...and your agreement with all of it exposed you for the sinner you are! Unlike you, *we* know how to stop ourselves from thinking about genitals, and to make ourselves go to Church each and every day, and to remember that men are the breadwinners. That women like you, you burnt-face pagan freak, stay in the god-damn kitchen!"

And he reached out to seize her arm, even as the other Templars grabbed Cedric and Alex.

"As for you two," Eberhardt barked. "You will be cleansed of your sins the hard way when we open you up to the gelding iron."

"But I'm not a sexual person!" Alex protested. "Like, seriously! Sexual attraction just isn't something I experience! I like friendship, and I like kissing and cuddling..."

"Those things are still signs of licentiousness!"

Nikola Shorter swung a punch into his face. It was a rough hit, and whether he was a sleeper agent or not, he was a biker in his truest form, and so he knew how to take punches. It took one or two of Nik's others to really bring him down.

But there were many other Templars, who were now suddenly dedicated to the same virtues that had taken over their sprawled and groaning leader. Alex was too slight to be a fighter, but Cedric had some muscle to him.

"What are you waiting for, you Skynyrd-loving sack of shit?" Nik yelled at the drummer. "*Hit* them!"

"I-I can't bring myself to hit a-a fellow Christian."

"These guys *aren't* Christians, though! Maybe they would be if what they'd said to Nik was sincere, but it wasn't! They're really more akin to the pagans you hate. If we're indulging the stereotypes...just pretend they're *Gnostics*."

"Gnostics? Those bootleggers *stole* Christianity, and perverted it! They'll pay for that. Gnosticism is the religion of cowards!"

But before he could go into unleashing blows of his own, the Templars flinched. On the ground, the battered Eberhardt Grant screamed. Not even Cedric wanted to assault these folks while they were screaming. The other patrons of the dark and shabby quarters were staring at them, but offered no assistance. Some of them were folks from Diana's Grove, tired that the band was carrying their problems with them.

"Now you've done it." Grant's voice was dimmer now. "That run-in with the PMRC in '74—that wasn't the last taste we had of the Comrade Boznik-Koronovich."

"Comrade...who?" Alex asked. He was in the dark twice over, having not entirely heard the story he'd told the first time of their run-in.

"Boznik-Koronovich was the man who perfected the Soviet method of creating sleeper agents, used on special occasions by the KGB." That helped Alex a little, but he still wondered why Eberhardt's voice seemed to be gaining hints of a Russian accent. "We didn't know it was he who gave the PMRC their methods, but he explained it to us in 1980, when he captured us personally. He had a little bit of a French voice to him, and we never found out why. But he was our sincere Comrade—we learned that when he applied his mental scalpel to us—and he opened a light to us that even the God of the PMRC couldn't match. So we turned our backs on this savage Christianity, with a code-phrase 'Gnosticism is the religion of cowards.'"

Nikola immediately saw a chance to steady the situation. "So the two sets of sleeper agent programming in you contradict each other?"

"Yeah. Under the Boznik-Koronovich method, personalities must never become what he called 'hybridized.'"

"B-but we don't have anything to *really* worry about, because those code-words are so rare that you must be agents for a special mission!" Cedric blustered.

"Say, that's...that's a good point, actually," Alex said. "The PMRC would want a common phrase so that you serve their cause intermittently but often. Presumably when it wears off, that allays you of any suspicion because an interrogation wouldn't reveal that you have the same beliefs as the people who run this renegade church-cum-cruise-line."

"But Comrade Boznik-Koronovich recognizes that the Communism of today is not the Communism that his forefathers served—the Communism of Stalin." At last, it wasn't just Grant doing the talking. One of the men behind Alex, leaning heavily into the guitarist with his ability to blink still absent, was delivering this new information. "Stalin recognized the importance of totalitarianism in the world he made, and totalitarianism, Boznik-Koronovich said, 'is the ultimate crime.' He was more concerned with the impact of *crime* on the world than the spread of Communism but he wanted to experiment with how crime would work under Communism...consider what it would be like for the mobs to seize the means of production. We're crooks in our own way—we're a biker gang, after all. There would have to be a pecking order, sure, but as long as we get our cut, we'd dedicate our full faculties to provide for the masses. I mean, crooks have controlled the garbage before—the water—and crooks today try to control the air, though they aren't mobsters anymore. They are *capitalists*. And so we wouldn't take that away from you. Why would we? No profit for us. And that pecking order—*that's* what Stalin understood. People are too evil to properly get Communism. So you need someone at the top who's willing to make deals. To be a businessman."

"Where is this all going, exactly?" Alex said. He couldn't stop thinking about the man's vocabulary churned and shifted under him. Like several personalities rubbing against each other.

"We are here on behalf of the KGB to spread crime, and with crime, social disillusionment." A third Templar was speaking. "We are to murder and rob as many Americans as possible, in the name of the Soviet Union to destabilize the Cold War and once more open the possibility of American conquest by the Soviets."

"Boznik-Koronovich is willing to settle on seeing the effects of intensifying nationwide crime in capitalist societies as well as Communist ones," said Grant, still grinning, even with a broken nose.

"Dear God, intensifying it *nationwide*? How many of you are there?" Cedric bellowed.

"Only the Templars serve Boznik-Koronovich," Grant said. "For now. We will recruit others, and Boznik-Koronovich is very liberal with allowing people to use his method..."

Once more, the bikers reached out to seize the three musicians. Nik saw only the briefest twitch of panic in Cedric's face, and Pavlov-style, he'd conditioned himself to try to intervene whenever he saw such a twitch. But he was too late, and the drummer shouted out hurriedly: "What's your story? Gnosticism is the religion of cowards!"

Nikola realized then that he would only know the first code-phrase if he was listening in on her conversation with Grant. She was fine with Alex eavesdropping but not Cedric. That didn't matter now. At once, pain wracked their assailants again, though when they clenched their bodies from the mental assault it meant they only tightened the vices of their hands. Nik wasted no time in once again hitting her attackers, even when eyes locked on them as they screamed. Her eyes flashed panicked from the crowd to the bikers, only to see that *still,* the bikers were not blinking, and even in agony they were smiling. There was no reason for them to have that expression, save for this "Boznik-Koronovich" being some sort of weird sadistic fuck.

And then Grant was bellowing, in the same way that Cedric had a tendency to do: "KGB make you disappear for Christ!" Now that hinted Russian accent was out in full, a relict piece of programming from Boznik-Koronovich, whoever he was. Alex, in a moment that surprised him, thought of this absent mind-bender as a fisherman trolling for suckers—an odd term for this case, he thought. They were the suckers, truly, for believing that their luck would let up. Of course there was a Russian puppet-master playing nonsensical practical jokes on them.

"Perhaps we nail you to cross in Gulag, da?"

"What is even happening?" Nikola finally screamed, before at long last her punches brought the long-suffering Eberhardt into unconsciousness. The other bikers released the musicians to run to their leader's side.

"Protect your fellow proletariat!" they shouted as they knelt, and there was nothing left to do. As the band exited hurriedly, the crew not far behind, Alex stayed to hold the door. He also gave directions to the crew as they left, concerning the side-cars of one of the motorcycles.

The ordinary bar patrons had reacted reasonably, beyond the notice of the parties of focus. The police were called, and their sirens were rising again—naturally, when they would arrive, they would be in opposition to Jagged Skull. After all, they were guilty of inciting a riot, and now, with a quick trip to Grant's bike, theft, too.

CHAPTER VI:

They found their way back to the cars. When people stopped them, seeing them carrying such an expensive-looking mirror in such a hurry, Nik improvised that they were "mirror-movers." Some of the people who stopped them said, "We are all mere movers under the Lord." When they didn't reply, these folk looked disgusted, but otherwise let them go.

"Uh...is Montpelier normally like this?" Alex asked quietly.

"Not from what I know, no," Nik replied. "It must just be that the PMRC is a bigger threat than people know."

"Careful with that talk. People will think we mean a bunch of relatively harmless music censors, who ought to peter out of significance in a few years or so. This is a group of Christian *terrorists!* They kill people."

"Maybe it's better to die than to be bow—bowdlerized, right?" Nik asked.

"I think that's it."

"Shit, I'm still tipsy from the bar. This is all going by so fast, Alex."

"I know. We've just been going since Astaroth, haven't we...?" The sirens were louder now. They were extremely close.

"It's okay. We're almost there. There are the cars...and it will all be over soon..."

"Oh, no, Mr. Fischer-King. I'm afraid this is all just the beginning."

One of the car doors was already open, and the speaker within was courteous enough to avoid leaving his identity a secret. He was dressed in robes, plainly those of the Order of Draco. They thought they recognized him from the house in Astaroth, standing near to Tamaron. He seemed to be the inverse of Tamaron— while the Master of Draco conveyed a weird old age, in a body that looked like a college freshman, this man had the physique of a twenty-something but the scars and creases of many mortal lifetimes. He had absolutely no hair, not even eyebrows or eyelashes. His eyes bulged out not from strain or effort, but because all the flesh that makes the eye an oval was gone, and it was just a circle instead, ringed with scarlet muscle.

"I am Keegan Salazari. I am the Great Lieutenant of the Order of Draco."

"I see Tamaron doesn't like getting his hands dirty himself?" Cedric asked.

"The Master is conducting some very important rituals at the moment. It's the Great Lieutenant's duty to stand in his place when he is unavailable. Now. I see you have the mirror."

"We do," Alex said, once more striding to the leader role. "What does Tamaron want with it?"

"That's his business. But let's inspect it together. I have to assure that it's the right object—and you may have a clue to what you need to achieve the goals my Master's offered you."

"What about the police?"

At once, Salazari's face lit up with a smile, one that was much more intelligent than those possessed by the KGB/PMRC victims. It seemed at once to be a curious echo of Tamaron's own. "You have a point, Fischer-King. Let's take this into this nearby alley."

They nodded, though they also wondered why they couldn't just take it into the car, drive off, and figure things out later. It was dark and dank in the alley, but they hardly noticed. The crew scrambled anxiously into the cars.

At once, the weird eyes of the man called Salazari went to the back of the mirror, looking eagerly at the connection between the body of the mirror and one of its elegant silver legs. Nik's eyes picked it out first—a tiny metal box, same hue as the rest of the mirror-frame. With leather-gloved hands Salazari took this box.

"A radio transmitter. Soviet make, I believe," he said.

"H-how long do you think that's been attached to the mirror?" Nikola asked.

"Not long. This is a recent model, and..." And the Lieutenant broke it open. "It's meant to transmit at a specific volume. It's...too quiet for people to commonly hear. But relax for a second—what's the song in your head?"

They waited a moment. Their eardrums were still worn out, and they had their own music in their head, though that always saved in their minds unevenly, never as good as the stuff that inspired them.

"I-is that the fucking USSR State Anthem?" Cedric asked.

"It is. For a few months now, this has been all that's played in the heads of the people around this mirror. Evidently Boznik-Koronovich isn't happy that there's another faction in the Templars' minds, and found a way to subliminally sustain his influence." And he started chuckling then.

"How do you know about Boznik-Koronovich?" Alex asked quickly.

"That doesn't matter. We have the mirror, and you have another concert to perform. We'll take you to a nearby town, and you may have six hours sleep. Then, you need to go to New York. There's a small town near Massena, called Castiglione. There you will play another song, another part..."

"Another part?" Nikola and Alex asked this as one, very quietly.

"I have accomplished my duties as Tamaron's representative," Salazari said. "I will find my own exit. I..." And he stopped. "Hush. Hide. We cannot be discovered together." He gestured to a nearby dumpster, and they ducked behind it. They felt each other's' fear, and for once, they all felt a sense of togetherness. They hadn't even felt that on stage, even on their older tour, before the crowd.

It was a brief moment. There was a policeman who came down the alley. It was the first one they'd encountered, when they'd come out of Diana's Grove. He didn't get a chance to say anything except, "Hey! You're..."

And then from his robe, Salazari produced a glinting dagger. With the casual grace of embracing an old friend, he approached the officer and cut his throat.

The three of them almost screamed out, but for each other's benefit they stopped themselves. Nikola Shorter clenched her fists, and was about to step out, probably to kill the Draco cultist. The other two couldn't stop her, but with a final flashed grin, Salazari walked backwards away from them, and ducked around the corner.

By the time they stepped back to the streets, he was gone.

"Figures," Nik murmured.

One of the crewmen poked his head out—Reynolds again. "C'mon, guys, let's get the fuck out of here. Jesus fucking Christ. He—he could that to us at any time, couldn't..."

"Shut up. You're right, we need to move." Alex's voice was harsh, and when he set himself down in backseat his face was in his hands. Reynolds wasn't offended. He was too busy hyperventilating.

They drove off, with the driver saying that Salazari had given him directions to a town of 9,000-odd called Barre, twenty minutes away from Montpelier. There was a small inn there, and a nice diner. No one remembered what they ordered. The sense of togetherness was fractured the instant the occultist had slit the policeman's throat. They were all complicit in his murder and there was never true unity between murderers.

But Nikola and Alex were still friends, of course, and they wanted to be there for their crew. They were too hard on them. At least now there was money to cover their fees, for the time being. They deserved more than they asked for.

There were three beds a room but that meant the beds were small. They didn't care—they were beds, safe from the world. This place wasn't likely to turn over credit card records to anyone, and if they did they'd be traced back to Tamaron, not Jagged Skull.

The trio said nothing. It was implicit enough that they were not going to bother sustaining consciousness.

Nikola made sure to close the shutters on the windows, lock the doors, and hide the keys. One of the crewmen had a key to their room but he would promise to keep it hidden.

"G'night, guys," Cedric said. And he laughed, but in a self-centered way— he didn't want the others to share his joy. "Thanks for not being Babylonians."

"Jesus fucking Christ." Alex was exhausted, but curiosity got the better of him. "Why are so..."

"I hate the Babylonians because of their concept of good and evil," Cedric said. "They were the original society to believe in the idea of philanthropy to the point of poverty." He was bizarrely solemn, but the truth of this emotion was up in the air. "It's a sin against the philosophers I follow to embrace such altruism. That leads to Communism."

"Why do you hate Communism, Cedric?" Nikola asked.

"I-I don't know. I can't comprehend it. I just know it's gotten a lot of people killed..."

"Stalin wasn't a real Communist, he was just a bully. Just like Mao or Pol Pot. Or that fucking Boznik-Koronovich guy."
"I know that. But those people were Babylonians!"

A beat passed.

"G'night, Cedric."

"G'night, Nikola."

"G'night, Cedric."

"G'night, Alex."

"G'night—"

"Shut up, Alex."

CHAPTER VII:

When they were next shaken awake, it was by Keegan Salazari. Each of them screamed when they saw his wizened but strangely vigorous form.

"How the hell did you get in here?" Nik yelled.

"I've always been in here," he replied, though they were positive he was lying. "I told you. Six hours. No more, no less. I will be in one of the crew vehicles escorting you to your next location."

"That, uh, that really won't be necessary," said the struggling Alex, but he felt the Lieutenant's bony finger at his lips.

"At this point, it is logical for you to want to escape. There are police even here in Barre, capable ones. And not everything is ready."

He grinned tauntingly.

The drive from Barre to Castiglione appeared differently to everyone else.

To Cedric Frost, born Flatow, the drive was stiff and harsh. The trees around him were solid and imprisoning—the fields bleak and empty, or else vibrant with insects and stinging things. The towns were decrepit and if they weren't, they would be soon. Time would sand them down, as it had sanded him down. Time was physics, and nothing could escape physics. He couldn't jump off the Earth any more than he could live forever, or maybe vice versa. Faced with this hardness he tried to slip into fantasies, his usual ones, like pretending that leaves on trees were dollar bills, all meant for him.

From Alex's perspective, there were no trees, no fields, no bushes or skies. There was only TV static, white noise, bursting around him like dying stars. Sometimes in this noise there was an interesting sound, but all too often it was consumed by something uncanny and evil, lacking even metal's melody. And sometimes, in the visual noise, he saw faces that stared at him, but he didn't know why.

Nikola's tunnel was not as bright as the snow of a television. In fact, to her, it was a dark place, almost psychedelic but toned down. There were great fluid globules of multi-colored paint, but the colors were smudged with feces brown to make them duller and fainter. These oozing pustules of rainbows in the dark had a sharp smell to them, which admittedly was the last thing she'd ever smelled. The dark that housed the smells was made of thick fog, and they traveled not on a road but on a shining bridge...

They made up for lost sleep in the car, but it wasn't enough. Once more they were shaken awake, by the same man. "So lazy," he croaked to them.

They were in a parking lot, now, of what appeared to be another bar. The exterior was a product of the '60s, and it was generally identical to the worn-down cream-colored boxes with the pied glass windows of the other two bars they'd so recently seen.

"What's this place called, then?" Nikola asked wearily.

"Fester's Forge, I believe," replied Salazari. "At least, that's what it opened up. Up until a few months ago, there was a second owner, a man with the surname of Hedge. Hedge-Fester's Forge was the name I encountered it under while help-ing the Master organize all of this. I suppose Mr. Hedge must have died or been disowned, as it's just Fester's now..." Then he looked away from them, his sleek bald head resemble that of a bird. "I believe we have made our schedule. Which means that the owner is ready for you and your crew." And he cleared his throat somewhat. "By the way, Mr. Fischer-King, it would perhaps be better if you initially refer to yourself as one 'Cactus Cloud.' Your Midwestern accent should be a benefit to you. Now, I must go again. You will still be observed."

And with long strides, he got away again.

"I'm going to fucking kill him," Cedric said. But he only whispered it, and only when Salazari was a thumbnail-dot on the horizon.

"Get in line," Nikola replied.

They had no choice. They went inside the bar, and the absolute generic impression of "a bar" was once more forced upon them. Dark lights and dark walls; pool tables, dart boards, feeble arcade machines; cigarette smoke; leather. The stage looks cramped, ready to collapse, and unused—it creaked under its own dust. At once, there was a man upon them, with a tight suit, black string tie, strong military hair, and thick tinted glasses.

"Well, hello there," he said, in an accent that was straining to not be from New York. "I take it you're all is Cactus Cloud and His Cloud-Busters. I'm Klayton Welsh III. Been owner of the place since Hal Fester left it to me in his will, after that duel he had with Morg Hedge what killed both of 'em."

"'You're all is...'?" Nikola whispered, trying to determine if this man had even heard a Southern accent in movies.

"I take it you're all here to play us some good old-fashioned tunes, right? Nice and prim?"

"Uh, shore thing," Alex said. "Prim's the word."

"Well, swell, partner. You pilgrims just get on over there and get set up. I'll be watching you all."

And he stepped away approximately three yards to a nearby table, and drew himself up a seat. He was the only one in the bar cognizant of them.

The crew took to their work with relish, if anything because relishing usu-ally implied enthusiasm, and enthusiasm made things go faster, even when forced. They wanted to get out of this place with its weird sideways cowboys.

The band couldn't do anything before they were ready to test but knit their eyebrows in worry. Except Nikola lack such things, and Cedric suddenly lapsed to his old persona as craftiness ebbed from his eyes. It was Nik who caught another set of eyes locked on them.

A man and a woman sat at a table: both of them were older, probably being in their late forties or early fifties. The man was wearing a dark coat that sometimes had a crimson shimmer to it—it had maybe been red velvet at some point, but any dye in it had faded from years of overexposure to the sun. He had a crown of silver hair at the top of his head, covered mostly by a dark violet fedora. His face was lit by two moons of bulging eyes, which were somehow even wider than Keegan Salazari's seemingly-injured sockets. His mouth darted back and forth between an inquisitive "O" and a somehow-uncanny toothy grin.

The woman had a baby-face, probably the babiest of all faces Nikola had seen. It was lined now, with time, but her blonde bob-cut gave her a flapper-like youth. Once that hair had been lengthy and free, and yet still there was an almost presidential authority about her. She wore a long dress, white, which was lined with thin black horizontal stripes (a pattern that had always made Nik go wild, for some reason).

These faces were strangely familiar, and yet...

"Your face reminds me of someone," the man said. His voice was very deep, in a way that almost made it sound like he had a distortion pedal on his vocal cords. "It's very beautiful, as long as it doesn't represent the spirit within."

"I don't like to think it does. Unless you think far-right Christian fundamentalist cartoonists are on the side of good," she replied.

"Oh, no, we're not like that," the woman said. "The universe is much more complicated than any of your faiths. No offense."

"None taken. Are you guys Bohemians?"

"Well, we're not from Bohemia, if that's what you mean," the deep-voiced man said with that eerie grin. "We do like traveling. Oh, I'm sorry. I'm afraid I haven't any sweets to offer you at present."

"I didn't expect any," the bassist said. "Who are you?"

"Now that's the question. I'm called Nebogipfel, or the Dreamer, or Nebogipfel the Dreamer. You can call me Moses—actually, no, don't, please. Ansyne or Merlin work better for me, these days. This is Fredrich 'Fred' Whatzit, braver of tesseracts and Dark Things." He gestured to the blonde woman, who waved politely.

"Are you guys...acid casualties? You look the right age for that."

"Does it make things easier to understand?" the one called Fred asked.

"Kinda."

"Then go for it," Nebogipfel said.

"Well, what are you guys doing in this town?"

"We enjoy small towns. Only two hundred-odd people in this one, they say." He tapped the side of his nose.

"Are you musicians?"

"I've been told I'm good at some wind instruments, and the spoons. Fred, what about you?"

"No dice. I like knitting."

"Ah, yes, of course." The weirdly-named man leaned back. "We're undercover, my dear. We popped in from the next story over. We're looking for a monk who likes being a trickster and interfering in things. Has a detestably round style of hair, sometimes looks like he's wearing a habit. Have you seen him?"

Nikola looked at the ground. Faint description, but it did sound familiar... "I, uh..."

"Hey, Nik!"

For once, it was Alex interrupting, and not Cedric. They were all set up— she'd heard the riffs and drum-beats as they'd been talking, but they hadn't reached her. He had to take her place at the mike. "Break a leg!" She looked back, and the shockingly cute face of Fred was beaming at her.

What she didn't catch was Nebogipfel, behind her: "Do you think we should've told her this town is controlled by that extremist cruise company?"

Nik was once again in charge of intros. She didn't want to reuse anything. "Good afternoon, Castiglione!" she called out. "We've been told we're expected!"

The people here expected Jagged Skull as much as the bar patrons in Montpelier had. Frustration waxed in Nik, and she decided to pull a punk trick, and fuck with the crowd. "What's wrong? Is the 'g' silent in Castiglione?"

Nothing. It didn't matter, though—the sell. The sell.

"Right, well, clearly you're waiting with bated breath. We are Jagged Skull, and this is...'The First of the Great Demons'!"

Drumsticks clacked. It was time to begin.

I sat in the chamber where the dead mourn
I rose in the room where the werewolves are born
I opened my third eye in spite of my scorn,
and I saw the shapes
of
the
Great Demons.

I stood in the space where the Bloated Things squat,
I stole all the secrets and I never was caught.
But in the course of my studies I never once thought,
that there was something
to
the
Great Demons.

There was a notably heavier feeling to the song, and with it, there was a low gloom that came over the room. Not like it was a particularly great atmosphere to begin with. There was a poison in the air, something that chased out the curiosity that drew them to making these songs happen. Nikola couldn't tell what it was at first, but when she felt it her guts twisted into a spaghettoid configuration.

Nonetheless, the song would go to its conclusion—they always saw to that, no matter the crowd. The lines ticked by, with a heartbeat drum and floor-scrubbing guitar work. She let herself drop to a growl this time, but it wasn't long before they sped up. Her pitch shifted up sharply, as she let out a long baying cry. Soon they launched themselves into infinity, to catch photons.

> *Burning fire*
> *Freezing snow*
> *To Hell's Gate*
> *We all must go*
>
> *Three there are*
> *The Enemies*
> *The Universe*
> *a toy to these*
>
> *True names must be veiled*
> *in mystery*
> *for it's not the right time*
> *in history*
>
> *But their tales*
> *you cannot guess*
> *so we'll sing of the First*
> *though not the best*

There were a few glimmers of amusement from the crowd, but the amusement of Southerners and those who imitate them can be a disguise for its opposite. Deconstruction in action, two opposites canceling each other out. A smile concealing blood lust.

They cut to get in some melody in a higher pitch. Another spike of energy, which went nowhere, but still mattered. This place was a black hole for music but it could still sometimes light their way.

> *Sorcerer this man is called*
> *Servitor of Ba'al*
> *It's his title, and his curse*
> *We'll see his life, preserved in verse*
> *Succeeded by the King of Time*

The subject of another rhyme
Emperor is called the Third
His name's a blight; it can't be heard
The First, our subject, he is hard
To look upon, and for the bard;
He was born in the previous century
Destined for the penitentiary
The Sorcerer was a killer true
He slew his parents with blood of blue
The Devil who called him was a Master;
Ensuring the warlock's life's disaster
"Sincodemius," the legends sing
When this Master's name must ring

It has been clear enough that music was a screwdriver that loosened the minds of the trio called Jagged Skull—and in this half-drunk state, Alex wondered where exactly he'd gotten these lyrics from. He'd written them, obviously, but the story was odd. Three Enemies—three terrible men or creatures destined to destroy reality. It seemed like a nice concept to base a song or album on. Of course, there were three of them in the band, but they weren't these Three Enemies. The name "King of Time" meant nothing to him, even though his last name had the word "king" in it. No, he'd had a vision of the subject of this particular song, The Sorcerer, the First Enemy. And now, like how he'd seen the phrase "Thunder Child" before he found its true meaning, The Sorcerer stood out now in the light as Edward Tamaron.

The crowd wasn't aware of the lore about the song. They just heard "Ba'al," "curse," "Devil," "Master," and "Sincodemius." Ba'al was an awful name. It was in his name that the Heresy of Peor, from the Book of Numbers, had been committed, a total betrayal of God—his name on Mount Peor, Ba'al-Peor, became Belphegor, another name for the Devil. And Sincodemius...he was a warlock like the ones they burned at Salem, who promoted devil-worship and baby-killing. Just like there was music that promoted those things.

The First
He will claim
The dominion of God
He will break all that's right
And will
rule
us
The First
will show us

calamity great
He will split right from wrong
And will
fuel
us

A man entered into the room.

It was not the first time Nikola saw him enter a room. It was hard to mistake the wizened but childish face, not blessed with the innocence and curiosity of childhood like Nebogipfel's. This was the childish face of an idiot or a brat. Indeed, it was only an idiot or a brat who would wear that half-sphere of salt-and-pepper fluff. How had he followed them from the last show...?

He had to be one of Tamaron's servants, or at least a friend of his. And yet now Nebogipfel and Fred were looking urgently at him as well, with recognition. The intruder seemed unaware of the two of them, and crept amongst the crowd. Nik became aware that he was whispering to them, and despite the lighting and the weakness in her eyes she struggled to read his lips.

"The singer has the Mark of Cain on her face."

"The guitarist has a profane lack of attraction to people."

"The drummer's sins are without measure."

The hardness of the music and the ice in her blood were one. If she was reading correctly, he was trying to make these people kill them. And that, in turn, made her want to kill him. She was tired of this, tired of being persecuted and pursued like an animal. At the same time, a lighter spirit flickered within her. She tried to hang onto her compassion, even as her vocals became sharper and meaner, along the thoughts that guided them.

They say he's claimed a thousand lives
And every face is his
And all that hasn't happened yet
It is foretold in this;
These lines will warn you where to look
and in the guise he schemes
But we don't know what happens yet
For we learned this in dreams

Again, the story-contexts were cut off from the mob before them. It was like there were battle-lines drawn, behind which there were two sets of mutual foes. Each totally hateful of the others' ideologies, on principle, for all it meant. The creed of one side said it was damnation to throw a stone first, but they were getting stones ready all the same.

We know his second face will be
A man who dreams of stars
But when he learns to love his fans
This form will be his bars
Under UFOs he'll bind
some poor unlucky souls
But when they want to Heaven reach
Rockets roast them to coals
The third body will hate a man
A wretched Prince of Space
Humanity will see learn to rue and fear
His unrelenting face
But into aether we will go
To stop his mad conquest
Prince of Space will die in vain
But the Sorcerer he'll best

These were side-stories, sub-stories, that Alex didn't really have fine details for. Lore was his favorite thing. When he made his own up he liked to keep it vague sometimes, as Tolkien and Lovecraft did. But sometimes he knew he took it all far too seriously.

A few more whispers. The crowd trusted this monk, because, well, he was dressed like a monk. At least sometimes he was. His words were dragon teeth from which sprouted the skeletons of a riot. There was a serious malice in this group. There had been confusion and fear in the faces of the previous audience, who were the victims of the PMRC—and the PMRC agents themselves were more like a swarm of gnats, albeit ones who caused tremendous property damage and tried to assault innocents. These people here, however, were closer to the men and women who surrounded Tamaron. They were extensions of a will, a message. An evil message—evil, partially, in that it was a good one turned wrong.

None of it's good
All of it's cruel
But we can fight back
We have all the tools

Unity, brotherhood,
this is the way.
With all of us equals
the wizard will pay.

The surging crowd had its own unity. They represented the one true band or clan, and this town was their home. The Protectors of this place had their ways, and they had agreed to live here because they agreed with those ways.

Castiglione was a utopia they engineered. The Protectors told them of how, long ago, there had been a similar to what they tried here—a Christian palace-city on the island of Caphar Salama. It had been infected by former servants of the Church, who were supposed to have been exterminated, but came back in hideous decrepit forms. Caphar Salama had been claimed by the sea at the end of the 17th Century, but here they would stake their claim once more. The monk rallied their pride, and their training did the rest. They weren't like the bikers—they weren't programmed, artificially. This was just their world.

The crew was forced to come to terms with the fact that there was no security. They were the security. And none of them wanted to die. But then, Nebogipfel and Fred were there.

The fault of threatening all of space
Is self-defense is a wicked pace
Heroes bold and villains true
Might be hateful and jealous of you
The Multiverse is full of life
The First should beware mortality's knife
For all the magicks in all the realms
Doesn't negate someone else at the helm

The Dreamer and Fred were still listening to the song, politely, and found the lyrics in it were almost Christian. It didn't matter. This was a simple power struggle, the same as what they'd righted before. They were old, now, but they'd been old before.
     In front of the wide eyes of Jagged Skull, the two of them stepped forward and began to route the shrieking, charging crowd. Fred stayed largely in the background but nonetheless displayed a certain skill at a particularly alien-looking form of martial arts. Nebogipfel the Dreamer did the same until cornered, at which point he produced a lengthy faded ribbon of violet fabric, which he swung about like a whip. It was incredible to see such energy in a man his age—the crowd had to run from it.

That was good. The song was breaking up. Alex had wanted to touch on this "Sorcerer" character for a while now, but he could never get it right. This was a rocky song, trying too hard to be something it wasn't. And now it was drowned in some shit memories, to boot. In fact, in what transpired, they may have skipped some pieces of it.

A dozen cultists piled onto the old man and his companion. For a cliffhanger second it looked like they were lost. But somehow the musicians knew they weren't.

The First
He will think
He's the God of our kind
He will break all that's right
But we'll
displace
him
The First
He believes
He's the Lord of Magic
We will split right from wrong
And we'll
erase
him

That was it. They finished it. Contract obligation fulfilled in full.

Mr. Welsh was curiously absent in the brawl that happened. In the back, in a private room he'd made, where he scattered the necessary bones and fetishes into the correct configurations prescribed by Regulatory Cruise. He had to make sure everything was in position before he called the Protectors. (*Never* "the police." "Police" was too soft a word for a man of the Lord.) Before he picked up the phone, he made an apology to God for being in the same room as a woman. It was always important he stayed back here, away from the fair sex, and their lustful, throbbing bodies. That was why he usually had others man the bar.

The musicians began packing up their equipment, but it was clear that the crew was not with them in this decision. Alex Fischer-King looked painfully at his trademark Gibson Flying V. It had cost him an arm and a leg, and it had been with him for years even before they formed Jagged Skull. It did not matter; his life was worth more than his art, though it hurt to remember that. Like a battle-ax it came down on one lady who was trying to bite at his Achilles tendon. He didn't expect to break it, because if he did it would break her skull. But the chances of this thing surviving a full-scale tavern brawl were decently tiny.

Nikola caught the briefest glimpse of Cedric barreling over the crowd, before he got to the door. "Hey—!"

"It seems your friend doesn't care much for sticking up for his comrades." The warm voice of Fred Whatzit had changed to a sharp tone, which nonetheless carried a degree of comfort to it. It was clear she wasn't a woman interested in cowardice as well as violence. "No matter. We'll be out of this soon, right, Dreamer?"

The Dreamer wasn't answering. His scarf-like rag dashed out again and again, catching legs and arms, and throwing them around with aplomb and chaos. "Blasted disagreeable philosophy," he could have murmured. "No manners at all." (Spoken as "a tall.")

"The secret with the Dreamer is knowing when to run!" Fred barked then, and she could have been addressing their foes just as easily as she did the vocalist. Nik and Alex nodded at this cue, and once the towering man dressed in crimson made a path for them, they all ran; some of the crew privately noted that not all of them made it out, though they didn't recall who was lost. They would admit amongst each other from time to time that life was foggy for them, as if their identities were perpetually clouded, even from themselves. Did they all have names? Did they have families...?

To the band, or at least to Alex and Nik, these men and women were more than what they defined themselves as, but at the same time they now were just another source of sensory assault, as they were a chorus of screams when they saw what was coming towards them down the street as they exited the bar. At first glance they appeared to be police, and wore the white-and-blue uniforms convincingly. But around their heads were the gas masks that PMRC "commandos" in Montpelier had donned. They didn't have guns, but there were metal orbs in their hands—no, they weren't metal, they were glass, and swirling within them was a yellow fog. Alex was running as he saw them hurl these weapons, but Fred was bolder, and she walked towards the arc of one of these spheres. Soon it was between her palms, and she knew she couldn't throw them at the masked legions. Instead, she took a glance of only a moment in through of the bar windows, and tossed the sphere in there instead. She aimed where there weren't people gathered, to give them a fair chance, and in the interest of protecting and serving, the lockstep-marching officers broke ranks to defend the townsfolk instead.

They didn't stop until they were outside of the town. Previously they had not paid close enough attention to the décor of the streets of Castiglione. They should have noticed the stiff green letters that spelled out the initials of the PMRC—it was entirely possible that the green was meant to be the opposite of the red of the Soviet Union. Or maybe it was the green of a Christmas ostensibly under siege. In any case, the letters poked out like the angular silhouettes of a prison. None of them bothered reading the slogans that accompanied this omnipresent logo, only catching words like "faith," "order," and "obey."

When at last the village was behind them, at least for the present, Alex had to stop. His neurons were still blazing from running his fingers over the strings.

In his sweaty hand was the Flying V, only slightly damaged—its value had faded from his mind as he made sure Nik got away, and yes, that Cedric escaped too. He thought of how, when he'd gone to church as a kid, it had drawn him in not necessarily through the community, or through all but the most crucial of lessons, but because of what it did to people. Not in how they celebrated it, and formed friendships through it, at least not in total. It was that sometimes, as all Christians did, he doubted his faith, and it really did feel like a grand play rather than an institution of great importance. And that didn't give him scorn against faith—rather, it strengthened what faith he had. The human brain reached out into the universe, helpless against its pull, and it *made* things, things it thought it *found*, to bring order to that pull. And that ability, that compulsion, was so mysterious to Alex that it had to be sacred.

This wasn't mysterious. This wasn't compelling. This was materialism, and obsession and exhaustion in the material world. He couldn't remember the particular passage, but he was sure Jesus said something about how those who took the most public pride in their faith were the ones who lacked it most severely.

"Well, nice news that's over," came the rich voice of the aging vagabond. "Ms. Shorter, are you alright?"

"I am. We...all are...maybe."

"Maybe's better than not. Now, as much as I hate to say it, because you and your friends are all very lovely people, but our target has eluded us, and we need to follow him."

"You meant that abbot-like guy, didn't you? I *remember* him now. What did he do?" Nik asked.

"He's *interfering*," Fred said, with irritation. "Those riots had to happen for a reason. Maybe someone is using them for something..."

"I was wondering if he was linked up in the guy who's been giving us trouble. I didn't get a chance to tell you, did I?"

"No, you didn't," cooed Nebogipfel. "Who's giving you trouble?"

"We've been pressganged into working for an occultist called Edward Tamaron."

"Tamaron? Now, say. That *is* trouble, isn't it? Now I really do wish we could stay." And a pained look shot across his face, as he surveyed the panting persons surrounding him. "Look out for cruel-looking princes, wizards, or aliens with prominent beards—a fellow like *that* is *not* the one we're looking for, but they're equally tedious. And ohh...good luck, my dears!"

And he turned to go. Fred, leaning close with that wondrous face, shook Nik's hand. "It was lovely meeting you." And they grinned at each other.

Then they were gone.

"What was that all about?" Cedric asked.

"Just some wandering good guys," Nik replied. As she said that, she realized there was a newfound weight in her hand. The handshake had pressed something into it. When she looked down, she saw a shining white knife in her hand—elegantly crafted, probably decently expensive. Coiled around the handle was a silver snake.

"Is that what we came for?" Alex asked. "God, I nearly forgot we were supposed to pick something up. Wonder where she got that..."

"It doesn't matter. We have it now," Cedric said. "Christ, let's get the fuck out of here."

"Yes, let's."

The voice they heard was gentle, like Nebogipfel's, but it was much higher in pitch, while still displaying a cool charisma. "Certainly you have forgotten that you were being..."

"Yes, Salazari, we remembered you were watching us," Nik said.

"Good," said the hooded old man, as he descended down one of the wooded inclines surrounding the road. "This dagger is precisely what we have sought. You are doing well, Jagged Skull. Let it be known that the Order appreciates your services. It's almost over, now—and ideally, your next show will be a briefer and quieter affair."

"Why did you keep sending us to the PMRC's doorsteps?" asked the singer. "Why are you deliberately causing these riots?"

"You should already know at this point that answering your questions is not in the contract. Now, we should get to work on the third concert at once. And for that, we'll need to transport you to a locale in Canada that you won't be able to report on."

The Great Lieutenant raised a single gloved finger, and crooked it back into the woods. Nik spotted the man in the black robes too late—he had one of the yellowish spheres in his hand. Salazari pointed at the group, and the ball was hurled. The last thing they heard was the sound of shattering glass.

CHAPTER VIII:

And the next thing they heard was the sound of helicopter blades.

The first thing Nikola noticed besides that was that this sound bounced back to them. Having lost 10% of her hearing to those amps, she knew how sound waves felt. If those were chopper blades, that bouncing meant the chopper was close to the ground. Indeed, she saw green grass spread out before her in a great carpet. Breaking the carpet was the lip of a stage, stacked high with equipment. The amps, mike, and light array had cords leading to a system of heavy portable generators. Resonating in her ear was the cold, hard floor of the chopper—it wiggled and wormed under her as she struggled to push herself up. A hand met hers, and when it pulled her up she was surprised to see it was a stoic-looking Cedric.

Soon Alex was up, too, though it was only then that they took notice of the men in robes crowding behind them. They shooed them with their hands until they dislodged. One of these robed men gestured to a trunk, and upon opening it, Alex found it contained their instruments. There was also a note taped to the inside of the lid—as he extracted it, he saw that the helicopters were leaving. There was a veritable fleet of them, probably necessary to move all the equipment and men. They were in another valley, and this valley was in another forest, this one much thicker than before. The valley within the forest seemed perfectly round, and the stage was in the perfect center of it. There was a decent amount of space surrounding this stage.

"Jesus," Nik whispered. "What's that say, Alex?"

"One sec, my brain's—my brain's still catching up."

"Let me read it," Cedric said. "I'm the Brains of the Beast, after all."

They didn't object even though he was wrong. He took the stationery and read. "'To my dear performers—please continue your excellent work. The third treasure will be the hardest to locate, because it is well-guarded. You must be on your best performance, and give the show of your lives, if you are to please the audience. They are what you may call "tough customers." Commence playing as soon as you are ready. Your audience in this place, the Valley of Nyx, is comprised of some particularly shy individuals. Do not be discouraged by their apparent lack of attendance. Best wishes, Edward Tamaron.'"

He set the note down. "Well, he's got one thing right. I don't see even a hint of an audience. Do you think we should go into the woods to look for them?"

"No, that's probably not the best thing to do," Alex said. "Tamaron wrote of them like they were his friends. I don't want to know any more of his friends."

"Besides, those woods give me a bad feeling. There's kind of a bad smell coming off of them, don't you think?" Nik asked.

No one replied. Nik narrowed her eyes and blinked as she struggled to determine what the smell exactly was.

It took them awhile to set up the equipment. Though Salazari had mentioned Canada, they felt like they had traveled south, not north. It was humid here, even though the sun was setting rapidly. They would need those lights, and it seemed like there was a long license on how much time the Order of Draco expected the show to take up—one of the men discovered another crate, full of tents and sleeping bags. Another was full of cheap, high-protein rations, like gas station energy bars.

As they worked, their senses began to expand. Normally, sensory expansion is associated with tampering with illegal drugs, but isolation provokes a similar response as well. And so they fixed a hyper-focus on the trees that ringed them in that curiously-round circle. Sometimes they heard animals rustling, and they lost track of their ears' ability to regulate volume, so occasionally this sound was almost preternaturally loud, and they jumped. They tried to ignore it at first, diverting their attention to the wind around them, or the crispness of leaves in the breeze. But they didn't talk. For some reason there was nothing to talk about.

But they couldn't ignore it forever. Nik was alone, helping a crewman with the amp, when she heard and felt a breath in her ear. Just a sharp "hahh." And she couldn't stop herself was letting out a yelp.

The crewman hadn't heard anything but he set his hand on her shoulder compassionately, before glancing over his own shoulder, a worried expression clouding his face. Alex and Cedric responded to the yelp and stepped over.

"We just have to pretend nothing's out there." Alex's words were to the point. "Tamaron's insanity culminates out here. We play to nothing, and we wait for them to come pick us up."

"You're right," Cedric said. "But I *do* still sometimes, y'know, hear things out there. Um, is anyone else—is anyone else noticing the...fucking sound?"

"The fucking sound? Like... the sound of..."

"The sound of flesh smacking on flesh. Like...like someone beating off."

Alex allowed himself a smirk. "Are you suggesting we're surrounded by a group of perverts who like watching people set up sound equipment?"

"No. I'm just saying that that's what it sounds...akin to."

Nik nodded, to mean that she'd heard it too. At first it seemed like she was going to lapse back into that uneasy silence. But it wasn't to last.

Like the trumpet at Jericho: "What the fuck do you want with us?"

"Nik!" Alex cried. "Calm down."

"No. Get out here, you bastards! I want to see whites of your goddamn eyes!"

"No one sounds good when screaming angry threats, Nik! Trust me, I know!" Cedric said.

Her voice was lower now, in volume and pitch. "I want to cut their goddamn balls off."

"In my experience, they may not have balls," Cedric hissed.

"Then I will mutilate their ovaries."

"I'm saying they may not have those either."

Nikola never trusted Cedric when he had fear in his eyes, but now, there was a sincerity to it which shook her.

"I'm a pacifist, Cedric," she said. "Or I was, and I can't be again. I-I can't go on carrying this terror..."

"What terror?" Alex replied. "I haven't seen a note of it."

"I've seen a few notes," Cedric said. "But Alex has got a point, Nik. You haven't seemed scared so far at all."

"I've basically been shitting myself this whole time. Like. Not literally. But."

"...but you haven't shown it, Nik," Alex affirmed. "And I've been the same way. Cedric..."

"I've shit my pants, Nik," Cedric said. "I know that's awful to hear about, but it's true."

"Y-you did a good job of hiding that," she said. "You're really not lying?"

"I can't bring myself to, right now."

"Even though I want to kill people? Even though I want to find Tamaron, and flay his face so it's like mine? It's not right. Tamaron is a blackmailer and a gang leader, and probably a Satanist to boot, but he's still a human being. Look, it's okay to be afraid of someone, but the second you take away their humanity, that passes into cowardice."

"Nik, the fact that you're thinking this stuff over means you're braving through it. You're concerned about doing the right thing even when someone has done something bad to you." Alex hoped he was saying the right thing.

"I still want to carve my name into that wizard's chest."

"I do, too, my friend. Even if I know it's wrong. This is a time where I think it's okay to separate thoughts and actions, don't you? It's okay to want to kill someone who's a bastard even if you don't do it—and only if the bastard's as big of one as Tamaron."

"I still want to cut his fucking genitals off."

"If he even has any."

"I'm not going to be the same after this."

For a moment Alex had felt like a Saturday morning cartoon, but he would never achieve the role fully in a place like this. At this point the sensation in the air caused by the faint noises in the silence mutated like a flu, and the anxiety induced hopelessness. Suddenly, Nik's words resonated for him, and the prospect of change slugged him hard. The band hadn't been doing great before this, but they'd been surviving. But here, there was no survival.

They needed a song to inspire hope. And they all knew the one to fit the bill.

It was dusk when they took the stage. The crew sat on mounds of sleeping bags—some of them began pitching the tents, but other than them, the field was empty. The feedback whine of the mike that echoed through the trees finally hushed the faint things they could hear out in the dark.

"O-okay, here we are!" Nik yelled out to nothing. "The Valley of Nyx! Kinduva hole in the ground, yeah?" And she struggled to avoid coughing. Her legs shook. "Now, listen, let's just get started! Rock 'n' roll! This is one of our classics—we call it 'Realms Bearing Closer.'"

Four clicks to doomsday. Then they jammed.

There's another world tucked away from here,
there's a place where there's
shining light.
But in this light there's the darkest gloom,
the shadows of the night.
And in between there's all shades of pale,
and colors and hues still unknown.
There's a temple for nightmares and your dreams,
carved from steel, wood, and bone.

And this brave new world's not
a single world;
it possesses many parts.
It can't be touched, or seen
or felt;
it only lives in hearts.

They froze, and the air froze with them. The moon was coming up on them fast. The chill, though, was painful to them, even though they were the ones who created it. It was like the music was wrestling with them, like an entrée struggling back up a throat. The woods had to grow accustomed to the melody, and it was spitting back at them as it drank in the potion they were pouring.

It's the world of witches
A world of beasts
Shimmering oceans
Hero's feasts
The legends are here!
The gods are too,
All for charming
me and you.

It all began when we lived in caves

We ran from thunderous skies
"Surely it's the gods," we said,
"that makes my children die."
And lives we lived as beings do
we knew the gods must have lives too.
We dreamed these lives and missing points,
"These visions are how God anoints.
I must obey these dreams," we said.
And religions spawned within our heads.

Then from there it was so simple,
the virus spread its germs.
And mythos grew as dragons came;
the creatures known as wyrms.
Gilgamesh and Enkidu
They did the things that brothers do,
And in this world of things divine
these man-like creatures made out just fine.
As we hailed these tales with bated breath,
their lines could shield our homes from death.

They broke again, but immediately rolled into a salvo of heavy drums, before breaking out into an unfettered guitar solo. The arcs and amplitudes rose up to the clouds. The music was a dance, and history was the dancer.

Out in the trees, the barriers gibbered and flickered; they performed their own imitation of dance, shimmering like razors through the soft gel of the space around them.

Ulysses!
He traveled the sea
Nightmares
Were what were waiting for he
In noble men like him we saw
A shade of ourselves
Until one day our former thoughts
Were put on the shelves
More than ever they call to us,
these worlds of bard and skald.
Some of us were trapped forever,
we could never be recalled.

Be-ulf!
With the sword in his hand
Grendel
Was the scourge of his land
As knights filled genre we all thought
And our thoughts grew strong
These ideas became "characters" and
To plunder them was wrong
In times close now the copyright
became the standard tool.
Protection is important,
if it don't breed packs of fools.
But let's not get ahead of things;
the history goes on.
As a certain saying goes,
it's just a stupid song.

As the words spilled out of her, Nik clutched her gut. It hurt her diaphragm to do repeat shows, but this was different—it was higher up, and lower, too, in both her lungs and her guts. It was like food-poisoning, and the smell in the air fit that. Whenever she got food poisoning smells overwhelmed her, and anything that reminded her of that which made her sick only doubled the pain. This was something wet, like trash or mushrooms after a rain. But it was salty, too, like the coarse winds of the sea—or rather, the warm salt within the sea, which scrubs at the skin of drowning people.

And she was drowning. In low notes. In dark chords. In twisted feedback—in the wavebands at the bottom, that carried rhythms only the paranoid could hear. A sunny girl was there until the black acid washed her pretty face off because she liked sound, and then the black split with the teeth of a grinning blond man.

Regain an older rhythm. Draw strength from the past. Then throw something new into at the end.

Then came the world of dandies,
The world of fops,
Cavaliers,
And Ms. Malaprop.
Victorians
would set the scene
as Shelley called in
Fron-ken-steen

Sci-fi grew from that girl's pen
Martians of Wells, and Burroughs, came then
As cowboys faded
The Queen she died
Old manners got jaded
And Tarzan thrived

The pulps, now,
were the world of men
Two decades after
Nineteen-ten
And superhero teams
were formed
Shaking up
our conscious norms
Suddenly we saw the story
A single fiction
In all its glory

But the time arrived,
and then, they say,
much of these characters
were sealed away.
Past Bradbury, Rohmer,
and Derrida,
the saying became
"You must pay the law."
And writers all should earn their bread;
were it not for them, we'd all be dead.
Keep them and their children safe,
free as a people, not as waifs.
But in the name of sanity
Community's not profanity.

Nik vaguely thought that it was merciful that Alex stopped there. Another punk leaning, this one a bit too far—*politics* were leeching in. But a lot of musicians their age always pumped in politics; hell, this journey had had many other self-righteous moments. Alex wanted the story—*the* story, as they said—to be holistic. That meant including the stuff outside *the* story (*the* story). And that meant the desire to remix the story just like music was remixed.

But she could only *vaguely* think. She was ill, so very ill. She could feel that Alex and

Cedric felt it too. Alex was a slave to his fingers, hoping that the sparks of endorphins that always mixed with the pain of the rubbing strings would go on to his fill his whole body, as they always did. Behind them both, Cedric was crying, doused in his own pain. Every nameless fear they felt was out there in those woods, but if they didn't play a song to those fears they would be murdered.

> *Once the armor came it grew more complex,*
> *But we began to grow an Eye.*
> *This orb would see the patterned hex,*
> *the web we can't defy.*
> *Holmes could joust now with Lupin,*
> *or solve cases with Dupin.*
> *Sword and sorcery, and the knights,*
> *could bring mad scientists to their fights.*
> *The tropes of present, past, and future;*
> *there's no wound they cannot suture.*
> *This work's a toolbox, a melange,*
> *promising une vie étrange.*

Drool slipped down her chin. The drool was like a jelly, like a flesh-jelly, shaking a trembling with anticipation just out of where it couldn't be seen, in the shadows of leaves, behind the crooked arms of vines.

Trumpets were meant to burst here, like celebrations over a king coming home. But they didn't have the trumpets live. They felt them anyway.

> *And soon the tapestry's unveiled,*
> *the truth's exposed, the vision's failed!*
> *It's from the Word the World we make;*
> *all that's not Fiction is the fake.*

> *Come down now, curtain, spell it out!*
> *We'll explore what all this means next*
> *If you don't like truth, you better pout*
> *for through postmodern lens we're vexed.*

Nikola choked, nearly vomited. Those weren't the last lines, but they came out okay. What was she talking about...? She saw the Monk again, the Abbot—a beautiful woman in the crowd staring at her, admiring her...they were a blurred and rushing orchestra in her mind. At once she found her mind unable to shake the sense of *Tamaron* being in her head, forcing those words out.

In the images she saw his basement, which they hadn't seen but which he'd alluded to. It was less of a basement than a musty cave, humming with a low chill. At the far end of this chamber was an enormous black coffin, which was too small to contain anything but a child. But there was something *in* there…something vast and winged, breathing heavily. He had said something earlier about a…fiction-demon, hadn't he? Something called Ska, spoken with greater emphasis than the music genre of that name usually was, that would not be free for another decade-and-a-half…

The vision passed, and night and silence reigned over them.

What happened from there can't be easily said, but they slept after tearing down, having no other choice. On tour they could loop *Jagged Skull* twice and probably in some covers, too, if the setting allowed it. Suddenly, on each of these shows, a single song was enough to take away all of their energy.

It was good they were exhausted. To be conscious in the Valley of Nyx during the nighttime was said, by those in the know, to be an unforgettable experience. Only one person opened their eyes during the night. It was Cedric, and he wasn't even entirely asleep anyway. More than anyone, he was struck with the impression of being watched.

He was being watched, and upon awakening the next morning he couldn't remember if he finally saw the eyes, and if he did, what they looked like. Only distantly could he recall the ferns brushing and buckling under him, sticks snapping under his decades-old brown shoes. There was a place he was headed to, and which he found, in those woods, but what happened there would almost certainly be an eternal mystery to him.

All they knew in the morning that came was that they had the last treasure. Alex felt it rolling under his pillow, and he could have easily missed it before the helicopters returned. When he pulled it out from underneath the pillow, he felt that it was round, warm, and sticky. He wondered if maybe it was some sort of mucus-covered egg, but instead, it was a gem. It seemed to be an opal, since it was a pale yellow, and cut into its surface were dozens of facets. Trailing from it was a thin thread, which formed a loop—meaning it was meant to be worn as a pendant. Turning it over, Alex found that one of the facets was filled with a painted pupil. That made the entire thing a staring black eye.

The operative word was "staring," and after showing it to his band-mates, Alex quickly swathed the eye in a blanket. Even as he did so, they began to feel a chill wind passing, followed by an ominous, deep resonance. They looked up, and already, the helicopters were blocking out the sun. Alex's arms reached out for those of Nik and Cedric, and they locked arms together as the hooded head of Keegan Salazari gazed down on them with a smile, his head bobbing and weaving like an owl ready to devour a mouse.

CHAPTER IX:

The only things they took with them were their instruments and the Eye, which Salazari had referenced with a minute degree of apprehension. The way he said it made them sure it was supposed to be spelled with a capital letter. He didn't say what this Eye was, or why it was warm.

"The three treasures have been assembled," he said proudly, though the pride wasn't directed towards the band. "You will soon have access to the powers of the Thunder Child."

"Oh, God, I'd nearly forgotten," Nik admitted. "We were *looking* for that. Now that everything's done, care to start on that explanation? I think we'd like our payment sooner rather than later."

"Only the Master can describe the process—and we are en route to see him. We'll be going to New York City, this time, to an office we took from the old Lekokinov spy ring, which you and the rest of history would probably better know as the Rosenberg ring. There, the contract will be completed when you play the final show."

The three of them were too weary to protest, and none of them could remember the number of shows Tamaron said they'd have to do. Maybe that contract said they had to do as many shows as he pleased.

The thought of suicide entered Nik's mind. It appeared frankly and with a burning twist in her stomach. Deep down, she knew she could fight it, but for how long, she didn't know. The woods had been the last of it. She was ground down now, to her core, to her base, and the black flames were licking at that core.

She was like her comrades, in that she didn't notice the length of the flight, or the appearance of the city around them. There were just long hours, a jolt from a helicopter to a car, and finally poking and prodding up a staircase in an old brownstone. Tamaron probably owned this entire building, for, once again, black robes adorned the members of the Order of Draco, even in public.

Behind a shabby door was a shabbier room, with aging gray planks wheezing under heavy, ancient furniture. They were sure there wasn't this much dust in Egyptian tombs, and upon entering, the thick coughs they gave brought them back to life. The cold disconnection of the trip here was gone, and yet the sight that greeted them was Tamaron's joyous smile.

"Good to see you again," he said coolly.

"You fucking putz," Cedric said suddenly. "I've got a score to settle with you, and with that fucking Lieutenant of yours, Salazari."

"Ah, yes, Salazari. Poor Salazari. You didn't notice that he left you upon landing, did you?"

"N-no. I didn't." But now that he thought back, Tamaron was right. Salazari had left the helicopter and from there, it had just been the Order goons who had escorted them. He also realized that only a single car had arrived—none of the crew members came with them from wherever it was they'd landed at.

Before he could say anything, however, Tamaron spoke again. "I'm afraid Salazari doesn't quite exist. He was an alter ego of mine. That phrase, alter ego, is derived from the spell-word *Altosagha*, the origin of which I do not know."

"Alter ego? What are you talking about? We saw him. He was clearly someone different."

Tamaron turned, and clapped his hands. A folding chair was brought into the room, and at first glance the Great Lieutenant was sitting in it. But he was too light—the ones carrying the chair weren't putting any effort into it. They could see then that the patient form, with his hands across his lap, was only an empty robe, with flesh-like gloves and a mask imitating skin.

"B-but that's..." Alex whispered. "That's..."

He couldn't finish.

"Now, my friends, I will explain to you the secret of the Thunder Child. Your crew is now occupied in setting up tonight's concert, the show that will launch you to fame and fortune. The Thunder Child will be with you, or rather, in you. One of you."

"What is the Thunder Child, Tamaron?" Nik asked.

"To explain, I will show you one of the assets we gained when you recovered the Mirror in your first mission," Tamaron replied. "The Soviet transmitter affecting those poor bikers was receiving broadcasts on a secret frequency, which we were able to hone in on using equipment in this apartment that the Soviet spies left behind. This led to a Soviet warehouse a few miles outside of the city, which was a cache of valuable supplies—most significantly money. I consider it compensation for what I've spent on assigning you to this ritual. After all, you are the sole beneficiaries of tonight's ticket sales. Don't worry, I've had the promotions ready for some time..."

"What we did was a ritual?" Nik asked. Had he called it that before...?

"Oh, yes. Actually, in regards to the transmitter I mean to be talking about—the Mirror, which it was placed on, as well as the Dagger and the Eye, have bathed in the energies you released by giving those excellent performances. Music is essentially just auditory magic, after all—it has meter and flow, like the words of an incantation. You knew that, didn't you? You'll be pleased to know it's quite true. Now I'm torn between using these newly-enchanted items immediately, or hiding them for use in the future. I dedicated them to Serpentis—a very powerful demon. You should be honored to have your energies used for his purposes."

"You were talking about the transmitter?" she said, ignoring most of his words.

"I was," he replied. "In this warehouse, you see, there was the arsenal of a secret Soviet operation intended to be tested here in New York. Before American projects like MKUltra got around to it, the Soviets wanted to learn what illegal or experimental drugs could do to people. Not necessarily for use on Americans—Stalin would have probably wanted to know what these drugs could do to control the Soviet population.

"In any case, we were fortunate that they had gathered these drugs, because one of them is the secret to the Thunder Child. It is capable of inducing what Mr. Frost has called Lisztomania."

Cedric paled. He had nearly forgotten his unique desires. The word left him spellbound.

"Have any of you ever heard of what the native people of Brazil call *yage*, or *ayahuasca*?" Tamaron asked.

And even more color drained from the drummer's face. "Oh, no," he whispered.

"You have heard the tale, Mr. Frost?"

"What are you planning to do with that drug, Tamaron? Are you giving it to the audience? Or..."

"I'm giving it to one of you. At least, I already have. I've given it to you, specifically, Cedric. You just didn't notice."

"No. No, no, no, no..."

"What is it? What have you done to him?" Nik shouted. She'd kept her voice level so far, but she couldn't keep it up now.

"*Ayahuasca* is a brew made from certain vines in the Brazilian rainforest," Cedric murmured. "Oh, my vision's getting blurry already...it's used in spiritual rituals. People who consume the brew often have encounters with their deity, or deities. And that's because it's the king of psychedelics. B-but it's not really a spiritual substance...the active ingredient is DMT. And th-that's a *chemical*."

"Drugs are chemicals, yes," Tamaron said wearily.

"It's not *natural*, and therefore it's *wrong*," Cedric insisted. "Listen, guys, I already know what *I'd* find out there, if I took the drug. You know, too. I'd find the whispering demons of Babylon..." He trailed off, and they could see rich torrents of sweat begin to pour down his face. He seemed to be grinding his teeth.

"DMT is a necessary catalyst for the Thunder Child process. Evidently the writers of your grimoire, Mr. Fischer-King, knew about the drug," Tamaron said, after a few moments of silence. "A Thunder Child is a human being who channels external magical energies through the use of something that induces a spiritual state. There are Thunder Children out there who can access their abilities with the use of a magic word. Yes, just like your Captain Marvel and his magic thunderbolt, Mr. Fischer-King. 'Shazam' was not the first magic word—consider 'abracadabra.' It has..."

"...it's been tied to the Great God Abraxas, the great serpent with cock's feet, who was worshiped by the Gnostics," Alex interrupted. He paid no mind to the fact that he hadn't talked about the comic book stuff in front of Tamaron. "In addition to worshiping Abraxas, the Gnostics also declared the Old Testament God to be a manifestation of the Demiurge, or Devil, whom they called Yaldabaoth. This explained His lack of benevolence; the Flood and the Plagues and all that. And to Crowley 'abrahadabra' was the Word of the Aeon, which..."

"No, what was that you said?" Cedric was the one to cut in now. "About... about God the Great Beast?" Alex gasped when he looked at him. His pupils were distended, and he seemed to have difficulty standing up straight.

The drummer's drugged eyes locked on Tamaron. "This Beast-God...his name is Deus Mega Therion, isn't it? That's what that means?"

And Tamaron froze for a second, before he leaned forward, his smile becoming quieter. "What leads you to that pattern of words, Mr. Frost?"

"I-I see the words in front of me, made of geometry," he whispered. "I see 'Mega Therion' besides Alzubador, Mocata, and Jadran...and a few others."

"Excellent," the wizard hissed. "It's working—you are becoming a Thunder Child, Mr. Frost. The words you see are my thoughts and memories. Those are some of the other names I've had over the years. I took 'To Mega Therion,' or 'the Great Beast,' from Crowley, after I...displaced him. Deus Mega Therion does indeed mean 'God the Great Beast,' like Yaldabaoth, the Satanic God of Gnosticism."

As soon as Tamaron said that, Cedric found another turning point in his trip. They were distinctly "turning points"—his psychic self was lost in a grand ballet in a formless place, which was specifically the color mauve, though sometimes it would shift to a crackling witch-green. Sometimes below him there would be orange-and-yellow platforms, made of fused and melted candy corn. Dancing on these platforms were what the heroes of lore called "machine-elves": the geometry-daemons of DMT's spirit-void. They were flickering lights, surrounded by B&W photograph-flashes of pipes, rods, cones, and cubes. Every so often, however (whenever the sea turned green), they would become instead ruddy-haired crinkly midgets dressed in potato sacks, gawking with bulging rictus eyes or brooding with empty recesses left in the place of such. Now these elves or goblins, along with their platforms, were moving aside, as a snake swam through these mind-waters, with the head of a horned lion. Cedric may have had his faults but he had sanity enough to look away from this deity. This was the dread one Yaldabaoth.

"I refuse to believe this," Alex said then. "Telepathy doesn't exist, Tamaron. Cedric can't see your thoughts."

"If he can't, he is no Thunder Child. But he is probably the only one of you three who can become one. You two do not have the right minds for the DMT to affect it properly. Franz Liszt was fortunate—he had what was probably the best brain for the job, by a miraculous fluke of genetics. And he was an adventurous youth, which would pay him dividends as well. He had a Brazilian contact who would bring him yage, and he would use it before his shows to enhance his performances. Unbeknownst to him, his mind stretched out under the drug's power, and he made his audiences fall madly in love with him. He became the first pop star, and Listzomania was born."

"And I—I will have that power?" Suddenly, it was as if the fear faded from Cedric's voice, replaced instead by the greed of being able to control a teeming crowd.

"It's the least I can do for you," Tamaron said. "You have given me power—power to enchant those treasures, of course, but also something more. I believe you, Ms. Shorter, will particularly remember my associate Abbot Margong. He has been guiding me on how to use the excess energies of your concert to prepare for a battle I have in my future. I've been thinking for a long time now of finally following an old foe of mine to Greece...and..."

"What are you even talking about now?!" Nik bellowed. "How many different rituals did we perform? What are all the things you were trying to do?"

"I'm a busy man, and therefore I needed every iota of energy I drew from your performances. But empowering the treasures, and enhancing myself for my clash with this female detective, were all I intended to do with that power."

He stood up, robes trailing behind him, and clapped his hands. "Come! Time is of the essence. Mr. Frost must take the stage before the drug wears off to ensure your victory."

Cedric showed an eagerness to leave, as Order escorts came down to guide them. "Hey, guys, I know what we need to do," he said. "We need to do 'The Great Power Switch Is On,' but we'll rewrite it a little bit..."

And his voice cracked with a weird, alien giggle. "Opening track is gonna be 'Deus Mega Therion.'"

CHAPTER X:

They didn't catch the name of the place they were playing at. They just knew it was huge.

Seeing the golden expanse before them brought something back to the Crispy Mistress. Indeed, the concert chamber seemed to be made of gold. It was the size of an opera house, and the angular Art Deco walls were lined with ochre paint. There was a colossal crystal chandelier balancing high above the decadent scarlet seats. This place could hold a thousand people, easy, and when they stepped out, almost all the seats were full. Tamaron had mentioned promotions but he must have gone overboard, not only to land this place but to get the crowd to fill it, too. Surely not everyone here could have heard of them previously.

The Ice-Cold Man was surveying the backdrop they were going to roll out partway through their now-rewritten opening song. "The Great Power Switch Is On" was supposed to be on *Thunder Child*, but it clearly needed some work, being originally a vague anthem for some sort of cosmic force that would re-energize imagination. Flimsy, even for a first draft. But now the pigs were flying—Cedric had actually managed to come up with a good song. "Deus Mega Therion" flowed better than what they originally had. The Fissure Man felt the old song come back, as he looked over this poster Tamaron had made for them. The words "Deus Mega Therion" printed high over their logo was healing energy to him.

The Thinker, or the Brains of the Beast, was lost in his visions. He kept drifting back to Tamaron, as he desperately tried to use the drug to see if he was for sure a member of the group he hated above all others. As showtime approached, he calibrated his thoughts to instead focus on Franz Liszt, and how the name Cedric Frost would soon be spoken in the same breath as that arrogant German bastard.

The tests were done. The gates were closed. They had a packed house, and they were scared for the first time in their careers that they couldn't be heard over the audience, if the murmurings were any indication. And yet to command those deafening murmurs to silence, and turn them to bated breath as they unleashed their sound—this was it. This was finality, the conclusion to everything they'd done since they started it. The Big Break.

Time was standing still for them, leaving a vacuum for them to step into. Tamaron was right on one thing: music was power. *Metal* was power. They didn't just *play* metal. They *were* metal. They called on the Thunder, as Nik moved her burnt lips to the microphone.

"Good evening, New York City!" Her scream was a wave of antimatter, erasing all sound it touched. "*We. Are. Jagged Skull.*"

And the moment still hung.
Her voice bounced off of gold and crystal.
Everyone stared.

"*...booooo!*"

"Oh, fucking Christ," Alex said.

They stood from their chairs, and without being able to help herself Nik pulled the mike in close. "What's wrong? What's wrong?"

And collectively, all of them together began a synchronized chant—one that chilled them to the bone. "We want Liszt! We want Liszt! We want Liszt!"

"No, Cedric! You're not supposed to actually give them Liszto..." Alex began to shriek. But it was far too late, and his voice stuck.

They began to come at the stage, like they were the PMRC all over again. The crew truly abandoned them; no payment was worth this. For the rest of their days these crewmen would tend to each other like brothers, never forgetting the suffering they wandered through together.

Nik had to pull Cedric away from the drums. She had her bass 'round her neck, just as Alex had the Flying V, and even with the burden they wouldn't leave them behind. Cedric and his drums lacked the bond they had for the things they played. They dove under the DMT poster as the mob surged up to the electrical equipment backstage. They knocked aside the few who remained, who worked at this theatre, and they began to tear apart the controls and cables. Sparks flew everywhere—the lower corners of the poster caught flame...

"I really am the Phantom of the Opera, now," Nik said, once they had a door behind them. (They didn't stop running, of course. Once that crowd was done with everything back stage they would keep hunting for a sign of their beloved Liszt.) And she laughed. "Tunnels and everything!"

"Let's hope we've got a Spirit of Music on our side," Alex replied. Cedric weakly groaned.

"Hang in there, buddy," Nik said to the drummer. "There's a turn up ahead; we can loop around to the entrance and escape down the street. We're running from Tamaron, now, too."

"We won't get far without money..." the drugged man muttered. "We should try to get our cut from the office before we go."

"Are you nuts?" she shouted, but Alex raised a finger as he ran.

"He has a point. We are officially without a cent. And tonight, at ten bucks a head, we've probably got close to ten grand. We'll have to keep working, but..."

"But we were gonna do that anyway," Cedric said.

They didn't speak from there on out, until they turned again, and saw another door. They'd passed through one on the way backstage, when crossing through one of the theatre's public corridors. The door ahead of them was one of the elegant crimson-and-gold double-enders that led out into the theatre proper. Probably the lobby.

They could hear the screams of the riots in the main chamber, when their suspicions about the door were confirmed. The lobby was nearly empty—only a few drifters lingered here and there, who seemed oblivious to their presence. They saw the box office. They would have to be quick, because even if they were entitled to their payment, skipping the step of check-cutting was probably still illegal. Even if they weren't already in trouble for being the accomplices of a cult of murderers.

But the ticket master in the booth was in a unique sort of trouble. There was another man in there with him, and he had removed his belt—not for any perverse purpose, aside from wrapping it around the ticket master's throat, and crushing his trachea with it.

"If your establishment will insist on *hiding* the genius of the Great Liszt," the man grunted, "then all who labor under its roof will be eradicated..."

He stopped as the man turned blue, and Nik couldn't tell if he was breathing or not. He'd cut himself off because he had noticed the three musicians approaching—now, he stared at them with twitching eyes. "You are the ones who are hiding him. I don't want to listen to the damn *opening act*, I want the real thing...I'll flay you alive, and *nail* your empty skins to the ceiling, so we can listen to the maestro's rhapsodies while we dance in your blood!"

He was going to lunge for them, but a shot rang out through the tremendous lobby, and the wild-eyed man dropped dead in an instant. In the distance were two of the members of the Order of Draco.

They didn't get a chance to run. One of the cultists had a gas-orb from Castiglione—he was probably the same man lurking in the trees of the town, who'd gotten them after the second show. There was the brief chime of shattering glass, and with a final glance at each other, Jagged Skull hit the floor.

When Alex and Nik woke up, they were together and safe. They spent hours combing the beach they woke on for Cedric, but they never saw him again. As the sun set upon them, they collapsed in the sand, without heed to where they were or whatever had happened to the drummer.

For endless hours they listened to the rush of the water.

The golden sunlight reigned in both of them. They had touched the sun, and survived the fall. Now, that was all that mattered—it brought grins to both of them. The next morning they would begin the long process of returning from the island they'd found themselves on. They would learn it was called Philiahenosis—and that it was in the Aegean.

Back in the United States, there was a dark room. In this dark room was a bound and gagged man, who had vomited from what DMT users call "The Purge." Experiencing a spiritual high like that always came with a price, and so *ayahuasca* made Cedric Frost puke his guts out. His eyes were still vibrating with the fractal visions of another world, a faerie-world. The sense of enlightenment was gone, and this was due in no small part to the fact that he was in a kneeling position at the boots of Edward Tamaron.

"Please make your peace with your current identity, Mr. Frost," he said. "I have plans for you."

Cedric could hardly summon words to his mouth. "W-whuh..."

"You recall the Savage Templars? The biker gang descended from those heretics who made themselves into mummies?"

"Y-you mean those...those traitors...? Those Commie bastards?"

"I expected you to come in contact with Boznik-Koronovich's remnants. After all, it was the KGB that taught me my methods of making sleeper agents to begin with, so I know his way of things," Tamaron said. "I can easily alter memories, through chemical and psychological means. I don't have to waste any legitimate *magic* on making you, Mr. Frost, into my subject..."

"Y-you're gonna make me into a Ruskie Manchurian Candidate?"

"Yes," he replied, his eyes lighting up suddenly with disdain. "Yes, I am absolutely going to waste my time making you into an enemy of America, possessed with a hatred of democracy and a desire to burn or blow your nose on the Constitution. Of course. No, you utter idiot. Unlike those bikers, you are a personal opponent of mine, and therefore I am going to make you into my assassin, and in doing so I must erase all of your memories and personality. Eyes on me, Mr. Frost..."

Some people make dumb mistakes. It was a legitimate lapse in judgment that Cedric Frost looked up Tamaron's face.

And as Tamaron focused his gaze, he knew he had enough skill to bifurcate his mind, and he could hold idle thoughts, early celebrations, even as he focused his will onto Cedric's, which slowly shrunk in him until he was merely a vessel, like a jar or a bowl. He considered speaking aloud, telling Cedric, as he withered away, that he had even *greater* control than that. He wanted to tell him that PMRC, too, was in his hands, though they didn't know it. Of course they rioted—they'd heard metal music before, and had been *conditioned* to hate it on the first note. Now there was focus on those riots, and those shining that focus would twist and mold it for their own ends, just as he twisted and molded everyone for his. It would be easy to say the music was responsible. These leather-clad, makeup-donning bards of blood and death. They would take the focus away from his Order, and once more he and they would live in the shadows.

In those days, The Sorcerer was young, and there was still mercy in him. The sun shined on him, even as it shone on the people he allowed to live. Doing this awful thing to only one of them was fair, he felt. Merciful. He knew that time, as it always did, would take the sun away from them, and they would waste away and grow old, and die in pain. He always refused the fact that one day it would do the same to him, but not before it also took from him that capacity for mercy.

www.ingramcontent.com/pod-product-compliance
Lightning Source LLC
Chambersburg PA
CBHW020134180626
46810CB00004B/1557

The Divine Mrs. E
Or, The Adventure of the Textual Lacuna
~~~~~

CHAPTER I:

Dark old eyes of vast intelligence washed over the pages hungrily. There was a fire in them that threatened to burn out any errors, any lapses of judgment or continuity, any excess of hyperbole. For this sort of literature, the truth was most important. She could not tell the entire truth, of course, but she could tell her version of it. Occasionally she would scratch across words out on the typed pages, with a force that disguised the fact that earlier, her use of a pencil had been gentle as she painted those smart and sharp eyes. She did all her own makeup, as ever. Today's shoot had been no different.

She was glad the shoot was over now. This book was driving her today—really pushing her. Perhaps it was old age catching up with her, though that was silly. She was only thirty-eight. 1988 was a cold year—and she *was* born in the early '50s, right? It didn't matter, even if this movie was one of *her* movies. That gave it that a special dimension.

She pushed herself back into the book. So far the details matched up. She would have difficulty working the inevitable bullshit into the mix, but she would find a way. It was bullshit that *happened,* after all.

At least, in some manner of speaking it did. It seemed long ago now. Life went by fast for her, even as the decades dragged on—adventure after adventure after adventure. Now, there was finally a halt to that, and she was doing her swan song, putting her biography on the printed page along as well as on film. This film series had been going since 1969, and it seemed like whenever they filmed something, something new cropped up, even weirder and more intense than what had come before. Someday it would end, and she would get a fine retirement.

But now there was a silhouette outside her tent, and her eyes snapped up. "Mrs. E?" a gruff male voice came. "Come and change into Costume 25-B. Your next scene is on soon. The assass..."

"The assassination, I know," she called to him. "Give me just a second." And then, under her breath: "Fool." But then she smiled.

She already had Costume 25-B on. It wasn't really what an ordinary movie would call a costume, but this wasn't an ordinary movie. The expansive whole of her dark, sleek skin was only covered by some scarlet threads and a red stripe which thinly covered her privates. She was considered well-proportioned and she had aged well. She tried to recall again, however, the reason as to why anyone would be dressed like this while assassinating someone.

But then, the Emperor Commodus was killed in the bath, wasn't he? And this certainly looked like a swimsuit of a kind. She remembered faintly that the script called for something along the lines of her seducing him in the bath...she would figure it out when she got in there. There was no way of her knowing if this was how it really happened, and she *should* have known, because it was her movie

and as such it was a fragment of her life. So long ago now; poor Commodus. He had opened the floodgates for the decline of the Roman Empire—they had said he sent it from gold to iron to rust. His death was a significant marker for the fact that the world would never be the same again.

Making her way across the camp and to the bath, she crossed the threshold. She briefly stood on the lip that divided the worlds.

Lying in the bath was the Emperor Commodus. Surrounding him were the trappings of a murkily-remembered Rome.

And yet beyond the threshold were the whirring cameras of eighteen centuries hence, a crew dressed not in togas but in t-shirts.

She was already formulating the lines in her head. (She didn't care if they were the ones in the script or not.) And before she knew it, those thoughts were coming forth from her mouth, regardless of whether they were unrefined and awkward, or poetic and thoughtful. She had this.

"Mrs. E in *the Days of Commodus*, Scene 25-B, Take One. Cameras. Action."

Her words went something like this: "Your theories are correct, my Caesar. Your visions of death and darkness will come true. You assumed that you could carry out your plans eternally, and never be punished. But now, you will be the ultimate victim. Hold me, Caesar—not for my sake, but for yours. You will be given final pleasure, because I am merciful."

Commodus couldn't resist. He pulled in close and soon the thong was merely a distant memory. They buckled around each other, lost in passionate glory.

Of course, they weren't actually doing anything—he wasn't even hard. She made it look good, though. This was the end of the movie, after all. The special effects guys would take care of making the murder part look good—her stunt double did most of the physical work these days. By now, after doing approximately fifty of these movies, she didn't want to do stuff that was too strenuous. In any case, again: she didn't remember being the one to kill Commodus. She couldn't have, because she lived in the 20th Century. She grinned again.

The scene was wrapped up in a hurry—many more were up ahead. They never actually filmed the ending last. It made no sense to film a movie in chronological order. That was fine by her. She was in this one so little because of the prestige old age had given her. Now she just had a chance to get the continuity of her films straight. The Mrs. E films.

In one of her cheekier personas, she would have said, "Someone has to be married to Mystery, don't they?" But she was more into the cool, reserved, serious thing now. Or something to that effect. In any case, "Mrs. E" was a trademark name. In 1959, a woman named E. A**** published a book about her sexual escapades called Mrs. E, and starting in 1969, they started making movies out of them with *A Man for Mrs. E*. A long history erupted, and it was that history that she was recording in her book, back at the tent. (Time was moving like in a dream. She was watching her stunt double now, standing back with the crew.) There had been several

fictional incarnations of Mrs. E beyond the real one, the original writer. From there, things became...complicated. Because the films were based on reality. There were real women, playing themselves in the movies, reenacting adventures they once had. They were Mrs. E.

And this current Mrs. E was one such woman. Being in a unique position as she was, she always desired to journey into herself. All the sex she had, on film and in life, was just one mechanism by which she made that journey.

The scene was wrapping up, and her eyes watched as sweat dripped down the back of her twin, who rose from her Lilithine position atop the Emperor. This sweat mixed with the red paint oozing from his body—the deed was done, and it was done quick. (And cheap.)

Mrs. E turned as they called it for the day. As she stepped away from the scene, her thoughts swirling fretfully in her head, she began to feel the world melt away, and become a dream. An old idea nudged at her, suggesting that this wasn't a dream, but she was...

And suddenly, there was a scream.

The crew was calling out, and heads were turning, including those previously turned by her. Even the director, Mr. Jimmy Mathews, was looking, as was his cohort and lieutenant, the writer Clyde Anderson. A scream broke through the cries now, and it was a deathly scream. She'd heard it many times before—she'd elicited it in many men before. Someone had died.

And it wasn't just Commodus.

CHAPTER II:

The details of the murder were properly defined in a matter of moments. Provided, no one involved was an expert on crime, except for Mrs. E. And no one specifically requested her help—Mathews and Anderson knew her past, or at least some good parts of it. She had broken up gangs before, and been to prison. They figured that if she wanted to help, she would.

What they didn't tell her, she overheard, and she withheld a reaction for the moment. Waiting and assessing was a detective's first and most important tool; people could betray falsehoods, show tells, or reveal relationships if all they got from the expert was silence.

The victim was an American cameraman by the name of Gabe Caruso. He had been killed away from this particular set, being slain instead inside the walls of another of their recording studios. An extra, Raine Salt, was the first to notice his body—she had been the one to scream. To Mrs. E, that fostered the chance that Salt and Caruso had a personal history, if they were spending time together while they weren't working. He had a knife in his back. It was one of the prop daggers, ostensibly, but if it was truly a prop it shouldn't have been sharp enough to kill him. It was identical to the dagger her stunt double had used to "kill" Commodus. That implicated someone in props. And finally, a spotlight was turned perfectly on the body. That meant the spotlight should be inspected for fingerprints and the like, and that the killer was seemingly fine with their crime being discovered.

She was sure there were countless other details that would prove to have importance, but she wanted to focus on those three veins, and assume that many of the necessary things to know would float to the surface later.

Mr. Anderson approached her as she stood blankly staring at the body. (Another detail: there was something of significance about this room.) He was wringing his hands, which was uncharacteristic of him. "Mr. Mathews is wondering if we should call the police."

She surveyed the landscape, and the myriad fluttering tents, and considered it. But it didn't take long for her to answer. "Remember, Clyde, that we're in the middle of nowhere. Isolated in the middle of Greece. The closest things are the ruins we saw driving in."

"That is true. We'd hail the police on the radio, anyway, but they would have to travel for a few days—or get a helicopter. Nothing but hick towns out there, so they'd have nowhere to stay if they went by car."

There was a moment of silence between them, but evidently such a thing was overwhelming for Anderson. He was shaking now.

"What are you going to do, E?"

He was looking for reassurance. She had none to give. She sighed. "I'm going to go work on my book."

He nodded. He trusted her, as Mr. Mathews did.

She tried to zoom in on the place where Caruso died, and why it struck a chord for her. All of this Roman rubbish was part of the leftover set from Igor Horwess's *New Story of the Emperor Commodus*, a movie from six years ago. Old Igor had made many of her movies, many more than the Mathews-Anderson alliance, though Mathews had had her host of a pair of those disgusting Mondo movies back in '77: *Mondo sexualis* and *Mrs. E and the Sexual Evenings*. She knew that in order to find the significance of his '82 *Commodus* film she had to study the genre in general...

Oh, there were so many of them. In 1979, they had started the chain of events with the release of, well, Commodus. Sponsored by *Condo* magazine, written by some famous novelist or playwright—the most expensive adult film ever. It was so profitable that dozens of those movies appeared all throughout. Igor's film. *Commodus and Marcia*, by Mr. Mathews. *Commodus II: Marcia, Marcia*, by Frank B. Corlish. *Commodus Reborn as Attila* and *Commodus Reborn as Stalin*. Everyone wanted a crack at telling the story of Commodus, a Roman Emperor who was fond of forcing people to watch him murder animals, who destroyed the Imperial economy, and who was self-centered to the point of denying the divinity of the Caesars who came before him. *Condo* had insisted on making their *Commodus* sexually violent and deviant, with necrophilia and bestiality and the like being in evidence, and most of the movies followed suit—some making it even worse than the original. Now, for better or worse, Mrs. E was getting the chance to travel back in time and join in his legendary orgies for herself. And that was exactly what she did.

Or was to do. The scenes hadn't been shot yet. Almost idly, she considered that she had a month—the remaining shooting schedule—in which to solve this murder. This was realized almost pointlessly. She knew it wouldn't take that long, somehow. She had a bad feeling, as if the climax to the murder was already rushing up on her before she was ready...

The book. For now, she had to satisfy her cravings to work on the book. Her brain wouldn't let her move forward with her work until she reviewed the lines she wrote. She had finished editing just the first two pages of the intro.

"...four of them, ultimately. Four of them, at least, who have repeat appearances in some form or another. At best I have been able to compress the total list down to sixteen characters, and half of those are not actually named 'Mrs. E' in the real film. The addition of the name Mrs. E to the titles of these ersatz films was an issue of the foreign re-releases that sought to cash in on the 1974 classic. Some of these were based off of Mrs. A****'s novel, and predated the release of the 1974 film adaptation of the 1959 novel. The most populously-appearing Mrs. E is the original herself, whom we will call Mrs. A**** or Mrs. A, played by Sylvestra Blot. Next is the 'Black Mrs. E,' or Mae, as she was called in her first movie, played by Laurette Tinti. The 'White Mrs. E,' or Moira, was played in three films by Annemarie Billard. Mrs. A was also Caucasian, but apparently a distinction was necessary between she and Moira; less charming is the choice to name Amy, the last recurring Mrs. E, 'Yellow Mrs. E,' based on her Asian heritage. Amy was played

by several actresses, including Taguchi Kumi.

In each of the chapters that follow we will be examining the lives of these various women named E, assembling chronologies from their films, with some liberal allowances. This experimentation is based in part on Mr. Philip Farmer's concept of 'creative mythography,' which was the basis for his works Tarzan Alive *and* Doc Savage: His Apocalyptic Life, *wherein he proposed his Wold Newton Family concept of crossover fiction. The Wold Newton Family is a clan of heroes and villains, ranging from Sherlock Holmes to Fu Manchu, who are descended from several persons mutated by a meteor strike in Wold Newton, England.*

Following Farmer's example, all dates given in the timelines are placed as though they were real events—if the real events inspired the films, it is likely it would take around two years to create an adaptation. So the original 1974 film would theoretically 'take place' in 1972..."

That was some awful shit. Boring, crude, and crass. The stories, she felt, paid off, but the intro was the most important part. She needed some sort of setup. On the first page she'd explained the boom in "bootleg" Mrs. E movies after the success of the first one, to the point where they numbered in the dozens, with sometimes two dozen or more appearing per year in the mid-'70s. Now *that* had taken a lot of her. Staying so desirable was tough, even if everything was just reenactment.

"Just reenactment." She wanted to get to the heart of that statement *now*, but she knew she needed to build the foundation first. To apply an obscure literary theory to an obscure film series to the origins of an obscure actress, or series of obscure actresses, meant that this was project would be a tough sell.

She ignored the faults in the intro. She sucked in her breath deep, and sat down. She prepared to type Chapter One, about the fictional incarnation of A****, aka "Mrs. A." She had all the films up till this year memorized, and it was just a matter of joining them together. Actually, she already had the outline. So it was just a matter of prose.

Her fingers trembled. To put a timeline of one's life on paper was like draining one's blood. She expected nothing less than a spiritual experience.

But again, there was a shadow at her tent. The frame was a little stockier now, and radiated one of the strongest auras of seriousness she had ever felt. "Mrs. E, it's Mathews," came the voice. "Let me in. I've thought it over and I think we'd better fix this whole killing thing before we continue filming."

"The studio will recall you before you finish if you do that, Jimmy," she called to him.

"Not if you help us."

"You mean do all the work." She went to the flap and unzipped it. His hairy bespectacled face looked out at her.

"I don't mean that," he said. "I'll help where I can. And...don't you always

boast about your friends? In 'high places,' I believe you're fond of saying?"

"It will take time for my friends to get out here," she said. "But it is a possibility."

She went quiet, but exited the tent entirely. "Let me have a meal first. I didn't take my meal break when I was scheduled. Once I do that, I'll take another look at the crime scene."

"Thank you, E. I knew I could count on you."

She said nothing, but merely smiled, and were it not for the practice behind his seriousness, he would have melted into her smile as everyone else did.

CHAPTER III:

In the luxurious silken tapestries of the warm and humid depths of the set, Mrs. E ate in the nude. At one of her sides was a salad oozing with dressing, covered with fruits of every degree of juiciness. On her other was a plate topped with hot meat, which she tugged at meekly between her pearly teeth. The fruit she ran up her body, up her neck, and onto her curious and probing tongue.

She had to stay in practice—it was an old habit. Mathews and Horwess used eating as a go-to cheap porn gimmick. A lot of men enjoyed watching women eat, imagining that instead of roast chicken or pheasant, it was their phalluses that they were taking between their teeth. So desperate was this drive, she reflected, that they were apparently okay with the idea of their genitals being bitten and eaten.

Whatever. When she had lovers, she had lovers. They gave her affection and she had a lot to give in return. Which was funny, because Mrs. A had been encouraged by her teacher, a man named Luigi, to dissociate the erotic and the romantic to properly enjoy sex. Mrs. A had been a good friend, but Mae (Mrs. E) knew that it had been this dissociation that had probably encouraged Mrs. A's vanity. There had been the surgery, and in their last correspondence she had talked about the idea of transferring oneself into a younger body. Certainly, Mrs. E, in any form she took, had a reputation to uphold in the world of sexuality, but Mae had accepted that one day her time would pass. Now she was nearly forty, and there were still many men and women who were interested in her. Many of the lovers in her past had told her that she would still be sleeping around into her sixties, and she knew it.

She was nearly forty, but she wasn't actually nearly forty.

There was a murder to solve. And while it had been seven years since she'd had to solve a murder, she knew her skills weren't rusty. She'd been in this business for a long time. She considered herself, in totality, to be something of a sexual detective—a sleuth who used sexual skill to gain an advantage in solving a crime. The phrase stuck in her head for some reason. It was sort of like that "Satanist Detective" she had met and fucked in Minneapolis back in '67. There were just some word combinations that inspired positive feelings in her; she was a pulp fan at heart.

She remembered her first clue: Raine Salt, and the victim Caruso, were spending time together on their breaks. Salt had been the first to find the body at the very least. She would likely be in her tent, either dealing with the trauma of the murder or pretending to do so to allay suspicions.

Mrs. E had taken the precaution of memorizing the tents of each of her fellow cast members, even what few extras they had. Soon her knuckles were at the entrance flap—it felt weird to knock on canvas, which she only realized afterward. After just a moment, the tent opened, and the brown-haired shorter woman emerged. "Oh! C-can I help you, Mrs. E?"

"You can, I think. And please, call me Mae."

"I thought you called yourself Laurette?"

She took a long stride into the actress's quarters. "If you find that name more appealing, you may use it," she said.

Raine Salt seemed to shrink a little, but it certainly wasn't from fear. Mrs. E grinned.

"You were the first to find Gabe's body," she said gently.

"Y-yes, that's true."

Without blinking, she asked: "Did you kill him?"

Salt seemed to shrink further, and this time it was a response to fear. "I-I didn't."

"How were you two involved? Were you dating?"

"No, not at all!"

"It's hardly a forbidden thing to do. Love is a good thing." And she paused, running her hand down the outer side of her leg. "Did you hate him, then?"

"That's black and white thinking."

"But did you hate him?"

She looked at the ground. "...yes."

Mrs. E kept smiling. "Just because you hated him doesn't necessitate your killing him. I don't think you are the killer," she said.

"You don't?"

"Not yet, anyway. Why did you hate him?"

She let her take her time in answering. "He was making fun of my career," Salt said. "Just seven years ago, I was in South America—I was making *Ferocious Cannibals*. It certainly wasn't any *Cannibal Harrowing* but it was something. And do you remember about five or six years ago, when we did those women in prison movies together...?"

"Good Lord! You're right! Mr. Mathews was there for that. *Mrs. E Goes to Prison...*"

"...or *Harmful Circumstances in a Women's Prison...*"

"...and I was Mrs. E in another one..."

"...*Mass Killing in a Women's Prison.*"

Suddenly Salt seemed annoyed. Mae had entirely forgotten about their working together—and they had been main characters together in those films. Mrs. E let her body admit her shame, and carried on with a sympathetic look.

"So Gabe, he—he made fun of you for being an extra in this film?"

"*Just* an extra."

"There's no such thing as just an extra. Think of how flat this movie would be without your character there to bring this world to life. Are you powerful?"

"Am I...?"

"Are you powerful, Raine?"

"I-I am. I think I am."

"Good. Your character plays a part—occupying the screen—and you think

you're powerful. You have purpose and confidence. That's all one needs."

That seemed to cheer her up, and in that cheer, she saw innocence. Or so it seemed.

"Do you know anything else about him? Do you know anyone who wanted to kill him?"

"Lots of people, genuinely, Mae. He was a...gadfly, you could say. You liked trouble, and he was *extremely* hammy for a cameraman. I know that he stepped on the toes of Pietro, the, uh...the guy from props."

"Props?" Interesting. She had suspected that there had been a "mix-up" with the knives. She would check that out next. For now, she was getting tired.

"You've been very helpful, Ms. Salt, thank you. Um. I seem to be a little weak on my legs—is it okay if I rest in your bed for a little while?" And she stepped towards the bed, sprawling herself out on it with no resistance from Salt. "Just a few minutes."

Salt zipped the tent behind her behind her.

CHAPTER IV:

Once Mrs. E was entirely rejuvenated, she returned to her room. More editing awaited her—her rejuvenation process, after all, always inspired her, whether it was in writing or in planning a new vacation to go on. She was familiar with writing—she was usually a reporter, after all. It was just that she kept getting stuck, and that was probably the fault of the gaps between her films. She hardly traveled in those seven years, and had particularly...domestic affairs. She even got married again, a few times, though it never lasted. Marriage was her dating at this point.

Here was another fragment, another chunk of her clunky introduction. Beginnings were always the hardest. But still, they were always necessary, in all their ugliness.

Just the facts, then.

"In 1978, American director George Romero released his genre-changing movie Dawn of the Dead, *which swiftly opened itself up to all sorts of imitation. In Italy, the film was released under the title of* Zombi, *and in response, a sequel to 'Zombi' was made in 1978 by director Lucio Fulci.* Zombi 2, *also just called* Zombi, *became the nom du crime of many European zombie films that hitched themselves onto* Zombi 2 *in an attempt to appear to be sequels to* Dawn of the Dead. *Movies that are connected by this giant web of phony sequel cash-ins number in the dozens, if not hundreds.*

The history of the Mrs. E 'series,' the subject of this book, is nearly as complicated as the vast web of films linked together under the ever-persisting alternate title of 'Zombi.' While films containing the character of Mrs. E date back to 1969, the first big burst was the 1974 adaptation of the 1959 erotic novel Mrs. E..."

Mae could see now that she had restarted the intro several times. She could probably fuse these fragments and cut out redundancies. Still, that was the gist of it. There were *hundreds* of these films, and so many of them were twisted to be about her. Or she twisted to make them about her. Something like that. *Swap Meet at the Love Shack* became *Mrs. E Meets the Spouse Traders*—*Erotic Diary of a Lady from Thailand* became *Mrs. E 3*—and weirdly, something called *Ninja in the Claws of the CIA* was released as *Kung Fu Mrs. E*. An agonizing and baffling array of crossovers and cinematic spillage. It was probably poisonous, she reasoned.

But she had tracked every last one of those films, and she compiled her list of sixteen Mrs. Es. She began where it all started—in 1972, when it "happened in real life," with her, with the first...

"The first Mrs. E was Mrs. A, the fictional incarnation of E. A****, played most famously by Sylv Blot, and played by a dozen other actresses in films from 1969 to the present. She is also

sometimes known as Diana.

Determining the appearances of Mrs. A in films is based largely on the fact that there are many characters who are based on Blot's Mrs. E, who are simply named Mrs. E. The name is given no elaboration, and it is implied with a certain carefree confidence to be the same character from the novel and film. I have decided to take the filmmakers' words for it, and so if they are actually named Mrs. E in the film, and they are not clearly other, pre-established individuals using the name, they are the original.

*The first Mrs. E was born in 1942 in France, and when she was just seventeen years old, she fell in love with one of her teachers, Dr. Muller, with whom she had a sexual obsession. (*A Man for Mrs. E*) Dr. Muller was a libertine who would later form a sexual utopia, where he encountered a pseudo-Mrs. E[1] named Isabelle (*The Erotic Daughters of Mrs. E*)—he faked his death to get away from Isabelle, a trick he first demonstrated to elude Mrs. E. (His utopia may have been based on that of the Divine One, in South America.) When Mrs. E was 25 she learned of his "death" and was heartbroken. In 1972, however, she married a man named Johann, who would in some form or another awaken her sexual desires by encouraging her to have affairs, both for his own pleasure and so she could rid herself of the memories of Dr. Muller—and she succeeded, with the aid of a teacher named Luigi. (*Mrs. E*) This encouragement was hugely successful. Everything about their marriage created ripple-patterns of sexuality; the two were separated once, and in an attempt to reunite, Mrs. E had several affairs. (*Mrs. E 2*) However, they separated in 1975 (*Farewell Mrs. E*), and she married a man named Franco two years later (*Mrs. E at the* Tropic of Capricorn*), only to leave him in the same year (*Mrs. E and Carolyn*), and remarry Johann in 1980. (*Mrs. E Exposed*) She must have left Johann at some point after this, however, for she was married to a man named Michael in 1987 whom she left to instead pursue a romance with a lesbian writer named Leona. (*Mrs. E the Lady*) In this time before she underwent plastic surgery to restore her superficial youth, she had several adventures, including avenging her sister Francoise, who was abused by her lover Carlo, in 1973 (*Mrs. E's Revenge*), posing as a French streetwalker named Diana in 1974 (*Mrs. E in 1976*), having sexual adventures with a woman named Lolita in southeast Asia in 1976 (*Mrs. E and Lolita*), becoming a stripper in an attempt to star in a movie that was part of a ploy to sweep the Academy Awards in 1978 (*Mrs. E* Goes to the Oscars*), and, in what was probably a related incident, blackmailing a director in London's Soho in 1979. (*Mrs. E in Soho*) In 1982 she underwent plastic surgery to make her forty-year-old body resemble that of a woman half her age. (*Mrs. E 4*) She actually went to the Academy Awards in 1985, where her fans stripped her naked; thereafter she was nearly captured by a banana republic dictator. (*Mrs. E 5*) In 1986, she went to South America, where she was captured by a drug cartel—possibly related to the criminals whom her friend Mae, 'Black Mrs. E,' kept having run-ins with. (*Mrs. E 6*)"*

Yes, that was basically the sum of it. Not much left to add; now she tensed up. <u>The next section</u> was the one about her.

1   A pseudo-Mrs. E is a Mrs. E-like character who appears in a film with the title *Mrs. E* who is never referred to as such in the film proper. (Mrs. E's footnote)

'Mae Jordan, sometimes known as 'Black Mrs. E,' Janice, Haylee, Dr. Celeste Amsleni, Mrs. Brandish, the Divine One, Shirley, and Jo, was the second Mrs. E. She took the name in homage of her friend Mrs. A.

Jordan was born in 1950 of southeast Asian descent. She may have had Chinese relatives whose descendants included Amy Wong, aka 'Yellow Mrs. E.' Her name was almost certainly Anglicized but it is not known what from. She appears to have lived on an island in the Mediterranean with a brother with whom she had an incestuous relationship. Occasionally men would wash up on the island and she would have affairs with them. This happened once with a young engineer (The Real Mrs. E), and with a heroin addict who killed her father. He left her to the hands of her brother but she evidently escaped the island. Perhaps she killed her brother. (Mrs. E on Forbidden Isle) In 1973, when she was twenty-three, she met Mrs. A and the two became friends. A, as a writer, helped Mae get a job as a reporter. Later that year, under the alias 'Mrs. E,' she ruined a marriage in Africa. (Black Mrs. E) This was her first adventure and it inspired in her a thirst for similar extravagances. She later went to Bangkok, where she met the ritualistic Prince Satiin, who had ties to a mysterious order of Tibetan monks said to have the secret of eternal youth. (Mrs. E in Bangkok) In between assignments, Mae had a fatal affair with a man named Judas, who was killed out of jealousy by his brother Julius—Mae killed Julius, perhaps committing the second murder of her life, and far from the last. (Mrs. E Goes to Tokyo) In 1974, she had an affair with Moira Larssen, who had her own series of sexual adventures. (Black E and White E) A year later, she had her first run-in with the criminal element—which would rub off on her in time, and lead her into desperate straits. As part of a journalist assignment, she broke up a harem and a snuff film racket. (Mrs. E in the U.S.) She also stopped a human trafficking ring (Mrs. E Around the World), and traveled to South America, where she encountered a tribe of cannibals, the Mara, who Moira Larssen had also encountered. (Mrs. E and the Penultimate Cannibals) As a result of the strain of her career, she decided to experiment with religion, and became a nun. But the experience seemed to unhinge her, and she became more sexually deviant than ever, and was eventually forced to leave the convent, after she faced down an escaped serial killer. (Mrs. E the Wicked Nun) Upon leaving the convent, crime again caught up with her as she stopped another human trafficking ring, perhaps one related to that which she broke up earlier. (Mrs. E and the Slavers)

In 1976, she tried to go on vacation, and, having become somewhat infamous, traveled to a small Italian village under the name 'Dr. Celeste Amsleni.' Here she used her sexuality to control a political scandal. (Mrs. E in the Village) It then seemed like she was willing to settle down. She found a lover and enjoyed a relationship with him for two years. (Black Mrs. E – The Hot Woman) However, he left her, and she latched onto a wealthy man instead, taking on the name 'Mrs. Brandish.' He abused her, and after a life of running in with violence and abuse, she hired a hitman to kill him, having attained political contacts from one of the gangs she busted. However, this hitman blackmailed her and assaulted her stepdaughter, Leeta. Leeta eventually escaped her abuse (Mrs. E: Empress of the Termagants), and Jordan fled to South America to escape the

criminals chasing her. Perhaps she hoped to assimilate with the cannibal tribe she found. Instead, she again encountered Prince Satiin, who was running a cult with an ideology similar to a fusion of hippie ideology and the monastic order that trained him. This cult he ran was called the Devourers of Life. He offered her the position of the Devourers' Divine One to Mrs. E (as he had deposed the previous Divine One), and she accepted. Leadership went to her head, and she was temporarily maddened by the experience by what she claimed was "the revelation of her divinity." After suffering many abuses upon her servants, followers of the previous Divine One returned to reclaim control of the Devourers. The interference of this woman, Hexen, splintered the group, leaving two warring factions: one which continued calling itself the Devourers of Life, and one which was subsumed into another organization, the Order of the Madonna. Both orders denounced Mrs. E and both claimed to have butchered her. (Mrs. E the Divine)

She escaped, however. She spent the next year recovering, and again with the aid of Mrs. A, she regained a reporting position. In 1980 she was sent to do a report on a supposedly corrupt prison on behalf of Amnesty International. (Harmful Circumstances in a Women's Prison) *She took a vacation but learned that her old friend Moira Larssen had been raped and murdered by a group of mercenaries. She trapped and seduced these mercenaries, killing them out of vengeance.* (Mrs. E, Regent of the Sands) *Strangely, these killings were not known when false charges were drummed up against her in 1981, which resulted in her becoming a true inmate at a prison. A group of male inmates broke into the women's prison and attacked the inmates, but Jordan survived and disproved her charges.* (Mass Killing in a Women's Prison)"

It was true.

All of those films. And she'd managed to get it out, in the order it happened.

Oh, she'd had other adventures. She wouldn't have started on the book if she didn't have the experiences necessary to fill 60,000-odd words. And these were mostly outlines, for now.

She feared writing more than just the outlines. To bring all those memories was horrible. Moira's fate, all those criminals, enslaving all those women. Seeing a man get eaten alive, and hearing the screams from such a thing. And when she incarnated here, she had to deal with that business with her brother before she left...

At once, the cascade of emotions that rushed over her, pulling her writing away from her—she felt guilty. She was being...sentimental. Overly so. And that was the peril of people her age. The past was a trap for them.

She was needed elsewhere. In particular, she owed a visit to Pietro of the props department. He was on the other side of the set, over in the camp, and she wanted to feel the heat of the sun on her skin. So she only wore a sheer black thing that draped around from a ring around her throat, and underneath she wore underwear also sheer black. The two sheers on top of each other censored her body—in the right light. Indeed, she wore it casually, not expecting to have any sort of interactions with Pietro. If she remembered correctly—and she probably did—Pietro was

one of those "dedicated woman-haters," who were apparently populous enough to get a title of their own. All the same, he would bow to her wishes.

As the Divine One and the Madonna, she had used force to get her way. All that crime had unhinged her, she figured. After what happened to Leeta—the tortures she went through—she wasn't in the best of spirits. Now, she would only use light force, usually in the form of slaps. But if threatened, she wasn't afraid to kill again.

And here, on the set of an Italian exploitation film, there was no law. Mr. Mathews and Mr. Anderson certainly would not interfere. After all, they were reliant on her talent.

She knew Pietro's tent as well, and once more, she knocked. This time she was weaker, as her blood was still drying on the page.

The stout man came to the front. His face was weary, and there were bags low below his eyes, from stress, age, exhaustion, and alcohol. He appeared to be in his thirties but his wispy hair was fading out already.

"Can I help you...?" he said.

"Yes. Why did you kill Gabe Caruso?"

At once, the haggard eyes widened. At first, he tried to close the tent, but she pushed herself inside. Then, as panic displaced reason in his mind, he shoved himself out and tried to push past her. But she seized his arm, and twisted it backwards, pushing him gently to his knees.

"I do not wish to bring pain to this world," she said. "You have just revealed your own guilt. That's what this has to mean, right? Your choice to run, that is?"

"N-no, Mrs. E! I swear! Please don't kill me."

"I won't kill you, but if you are a killer I will at least break your arm. What was your involvement with Caruso? Did you switch the knives around?"

"What knives?"

This time, his voice broke, and she felt his pulse jump. "You're lying," she said. "How did you know Caruso?"

He didn't speak for some time. "I was paid to switch the knives, so that a real knife could be accessible. Mr. Anderson was the one that did it—kept knives away from everyone, that is. He had everyone's personal blades confiscated, and he had someone lock up all the kitchenware in a trunk after dinner."

"And why did you make this knife accessible?"

"I was paid to."

She jerked his arm back even further—now it was dislocated. "By who?"

"I don't know his real name, he uses an intermediary. And the intermediary keeps his name hush-hush, too, but he calls himself the Serpent, like he's a pulp villain or something."

Mrs. E had had enough experience with those. "What does he look like?"

"Well, as long as he doesn't find this out—I took a photo of him, once,

covering the flash on the camera. I keep it on me so that people can find out who he was in case he was the one who killed me."

"Smart man. Give me that photo."

He took it out, and handed it to her; at once, her dark eyes swept over it, and faint concern filled them. It was obvious that the man in the photo was significantly older than he appeared, and was using a king's ransom in makeup and latex to conceal it. He wore an atrocious wig to disguise his lack of real hair, then wore a wig-cap over that wig to put a disguising wig over that. But his face was pinched tight, like a skull, and the cheekbones in particular were jagged. He was ghastly pale, as if he was a living dead man...or if he was doped heavy on something.

"You'll have to face justice when we get back to civilization, Pietro, but thanks for your help. Keep your work up on the movie like nothing happened."

And she popped his arm back into its proper socket, and as he cried out something flashed in her mind. The man in this photo—a servant of the man who hired Pietro, who must surely be some sort of crime boss—was not a member of the cast or crew of this movie.

Someone was paying for the petrol to get a car out here and back again, and the driver was professional enough to evade detection. And evading her notice. It was entirely possible this someone was aware of her, and acting accordingly. He could have studied up on some of her past transgressions, and on what she'd done to people back in South America.

She left Pietro behind her, his pain fading already, his heart thudding.

CHAPTER V:

Night had fallen, and she dressed in something closer to her body, and more suited to the colors she'd been losing herself in. She was hiding in the darkness outside the camp, and thus her outfit was black. It was a catsuit, like the women wore on that British series, *The Avengers*. That show had amused Mrs. E greatly—and intrigued her, because there was nothing better for her than women who adventured. She hadn't told Pietro she was spying on him, but sure enough, she knew that he was an impatient little specimen. He wanted to be quick in removing himself from his burdens, and therefore would waste no time in getting in touch with his man. Depending on how he arrived, she would disable him, kill him, or pursue him back to his point of origin.

She had managed to get in touch with some of her contacts, and based on her radio description of the photo they had made a guess at the identity of the Serpent. His initials were C.J.F., and he was an American musician. A few months ago he had vanished, and in those months he had proven himself to be an accomplished killer, something which he previously had a notable lack of aptitude for—apparently. Mrs. E thanked Iris, and knew that whatever was happening now had its root in the United States. She hoped she wouldn't have to go there to stop the perpetrators of this Grecian mystery.

If this was an American crime cartel job, why use Caruso? He was a cameraman, and this was probably one of the few really scandalous movies he had worked on. And even then, they weren't even killing animals in this one.

She wouldn't have to wait long to find out. With its headlights off, but still stirring up great pillars of shifting sand, there came a jeep. The hunched figure of the sickly Pietro waited hungrily just outside the camp. He thought he was invisible under the shadow of the set wall, but he wasn't.

Mrs. E had excellent hearing—Prince Satiin had taught her how to meditate into a state wherein her senses were enhanced. Of course, this was facilitated by the opium he had offered her when they had first met. Nowadays she stayed clean and yet still had these abilities. Once the jeep parked, the driver took his time in emerging, as if he was making absolutely sure they weren't being watched. Mrs. E could have the comfort Pietro unjustifiably possessed—he would see nothing.

When he decided to come out, Mrs. E stifled a gasp. There was a reason he was called the Serpent. Her analysis of the photo had been correct, and now, in the eleventh hour, Mr. C.J.F. decided to forego his disguise. At long last, everything nightmarish about his soul was revealed, in a raw and pure form. The lines that creased the leathery face were like scales, and there was no hair on that head. So decrepit was the form that in the white light of the moon he had a strange greenish pallor to him. Behind his head was a hood, like that of a cobra, and in a shape imitating the snake's curves.

His voice, too, was perfect for the role, being a hushed hiss. Even Mae's trained ears had difficulty making it out, but she strained as hard as she could.

"We are here only on our good gracessss," the interloper was saying. It was clear that he was being a *little* deliberate with his stresses(ssss), indicating that he maybe still had a will of his own. "You did well in assissssting us in dispatching Carusssso. But you have to continue to be ussseful to usss."

"I will be. In fact, that's why I called you here," Pietro replied. "That actress, Mrs. E, she—she knows what you look like!"

"How does she know what I look like when I have never exposssed thisss to you, my true appearancsssse?"

"I-I gave her a photo of you."

"You *what*?"

And the collar seemed to puff now, and his aged head weaved back and forth to the rhythm of an invisible song. At once the air was full of menace, even to Mrs. E, sitting a few hundred feet away.

"How did you get a photo of ussss?"

"I-I took it s-secretly. In case you...you..."

"In case I killed you?"

And suddenly, the mouth snapped open, revealing a full-on glimpse of the teeth within. The Serpent's teeth had been mutilated—cut and ground to become fangs. If this was painful for him he didn't show it. Pietro began screaming as the fanged mouth went for his throat.

Mrs. E couldn't stand back anymore. She sprinted forward, heedless of the fact that she didn't have a weapon. She yelled as loud as she could, hoping that that along with Pietro's scream would wake the camp and cause the Serpent to flee. In any case, her old estimate seemed confirmed, and this man was nearly ninety. Amidst the hissing, there was an elderly tone. Drugs, or hypnotism, or both, had crushed his cadence flat into monotone, but he still had a soul. And he was still old. She could break him like a fucking twig. But she didn't want to. Not yet.

Sure enough, the set lights were switching on now, highlighting and blurring every feature of the old man's face. He screamed and covered his ravaged yellow eyes with his bony fingers, even as she tackled him. He whimpered, but with an uncanny strength shrugged her off. He scrambled over the sand and returned to the jeep, but he seemed frantic and unfocused. And if she was right about him being drugged, he would hardly be cognizant if she reached the jeep before him, and crouched behind it.

As soon as she heard the car start, she climbed onto the back of the jeep and kept herself folded in the middle, so her head couldn't be seen in the rear-view mirror. The exhaust was hot near her ankle, but she clung on. She didn't know how long she could maintain the grip but if he had learned anything in the midst of all these adventures, it was that Lady Luck was on her side.

She looked behind her as the camp vanished into the distance. Pietro had a

starburst at his throat, which was leaking crimson slowly but surely, burning bright under the solar white of the lamps.

She swallowed and tried not to think of the cannibals. She had to learn to let go of their memory.

They traveled for about thirty minutes, and Mrs. E continued to weaken. However, at no point did the Serpent indicate he knew he had a secret passenger. And Lady Luck shined through again. Forty-five minutes in, a new sound joined the wind and engine noises—there was babbling as the waters of an oasis struck shallow rock. The vehicle slowed, and as it did, Mrs. E released her grip. Her fingers were bruised red now, but that wouldn't impede her. Her ankle was nearly burnt, too, but only nearly. When the car lurched to a halt, she watched as the Serpent climbed out hurriedly, and looked around, sweeping his ugly head back and forth. There was a moment where it seemed like he had noticed her, and that was why he stopped. But instead, he wandered to the rocky shore of the oasis they'd pulled into, which consisted of the pool of fresh water, and a single fruitless tree. It was hardly a forgiving place, but the Serpent knelt and drank only a few long sips of water before rising. He stood and took quite a long time in moving; namely, he froze, and looked up at the moon, and he didn't look away for what Mrs. E calculated to be about ten minutes. She took this time to climb under the car seat, of course, but it was alarming to see him refuse to do anything but stare for minute upon minute. Upon further inspection, his lips were moving somewhat.

When he returned to the car her skills were put to the test. She was underneath the front passenger seat, and when the Serpent took the driver's seat, she was lightly jostled, but he did not hesitate. The car started and started moving. From there, she was undisturbed and even a little comfortable for the remaining hour and a half. The Serpent seemed to be driving leisurely, perhaps to navigate this road-less terrain. Mrs. E couldn't see where they were headed but she heard a handful of voices speaking in Greek. The car parked close to a massive black tent—she could see that much. And as she craned her neck around, with her head emerging from below the seat, she could see that this tent had a window right next to the car. There was no light visible within this window.

The Serpent left, and his wizened voice also spoke Greek. It was a language she was quite fond of, and she spoke it herself, so their words were no secret to her.

"Give us your report," an unfamiliar voice said.

Robotically, the Serpent replied: "I went to the director Mathews' camp, but was confronted by a woman."

"A woman? Milos, certainly she is not *the* woman?"

"It's possible, Baltsaros. We will bring him to the Master, and he will determine what to make of these words. Only he knows the ways of their cult."

A cult? Which one?

And the prospect of "the woman" being here: it was enough for them to limit their questioning of the Serpent to one query.

Even on sand, she heard the footsteps of the retreating men. She waited until they were out of earshot—she thought she heard the muffled sounds of entering a far-off tent. She was in the clear and had her chance. She crawled out from the seat. She stood up—

The tent window burst open and a pair of fur-shrouded muscular arms emerged. A low Neanderthal grunt came with these arms, and she screamed. There was the air-splitting noise of fabric tearing, as the bearer of those arms came all the way through his tent. She couldn't twist her head to look at him. She just smelled the foul breath, which was full of the scent of sausage and vodka. He hadn't bathed in a while too, probably.

The grunts continued, but were broken by a howl of pain as Mrs. E's elbow drove back into his stomach. When the arms forcibly relaxed she rolled out of his grip, and when she whirled around to face him she saw his hairiness was a global trait—and his lower jaw stuck out, with the canines rising up so high and thick that they were more like tusks. His eyes were cloudy and animalistic, and his nose squashed. He was shirtless, and no skin was visible beneath the thick hair.

In jerking away, Mrs. E had sprained her shoulder. She was tired of using violence, anyway. She raised her hands in surrender.

For a time, it was clear enough that the ape-man (as she couldn't help but call him) was not aware of what her gesture meant. She slowly backed away from him, refusing to give into forceful actions. She mentally prepared herself for whatever sort of death awaited her.

At once, however, a voice came out of the darkness. It was a warm voice, and soft, like melted honey, and yet it had the chill of command to it. "Leave her alone!"

The encroaching creature merely slowed down, refusing to halt entirely. "*Leave her.*"

Now the brute-man stopped. Mrs. E breathed a sigh of relief.

She turned towards the source of the voice, and at once her eyes lit up with horror. There was a man standing in front of her, and he was just one man. But in him was a legion of men, the menace of a legion. At least one of her girls, her incarnations, had run into him, and he filled her with the fear of death. She hoped he didn't recognize her in this body. His blue eyes were piercing, and perhaps "piercing" was too accurate a word. The short blond hair sat atop a head barely aged, hardly even looking twenty, when he had been around for much longer than that. He was the reverse of the Serpent. The robes they wore fluttered in the desert wind. Behind him were several Greeks with rifles, but they weren't aimed at her.

"You have come a long way," the gentle, youthful voice said. "Who are you?"

She couldn't speak for a while. She blinked, and to her mind that act of blinking lasted a lifetime. When it passed she had conferred with her friends, and one of them had agreed to lend her her name. "My name is Helene Senechal," she

said. Then she waited to see if he would bite.

He stared at her. "Welcome, Helene. Come to my tent. You will be given food and shelter."

She merely nodded, and it was entirely possible she fooled him.

But she knew Edward Tamaron better than that, and there was a strong chance he was two steps ahead of her.

CHAPTER VI:

He took her back to one of the tents, the largest of all those present. Inside there was a metal card-table folded out, with several antique armchairs around it. Each of the chairs, of which there were four, were in different styles, from different eras and different countries. Also in the tent was an exquisite-looking four-poster bed (an advantage to her, if she played her cards right) and a large desk, as well as several chests.

"Please be seated," Tamaron said. Three of the chairs faced one, and he gestured to the one. He took the centermost one opposite hers.

"Now, let's get right to business," he said then. "You are an actress from the film they're making nearby, aren't you?"

"I am."

"What's your name? Your real name. If you're an 'Helene,' then I am an Australian aborigine."

She played along. "Helene Senechal is my theatrical name, it's true. My real name is Amy Wong."

"Wong, yes. As I said: you look Asian, without a trace of the French 'Senechal' in you. But you're darker-skinned—closer to the equator, it looks like. Chinese father, Melanesian mother?"

"Close. Indonesian, both sides."

"Interesting."

Neither spoke for a while, but they maintained eye contact. She knew she had to, even if that meant he could use his hypnosis on her, or perhaps look through into her soul. If she lost focus, he could kill her in an instant. In spite of that, she decided it would be best—or easiest—to take the same direct approach she'd used on the man who'd led her to this fate. "Why did you kill Gabe Caruso?"

He laughed, and it was a laugh with two beats. "That accusation is ridiculous. I presume that you think I'm some sort of occultist supervillain, with these robes, like Mocata or Father Rayner, by that tiresome British thriller author? Or maybe you don't care for the fact that my employees are Greeks...? Not an uncommon sentiment even today."

She laughed right back at him. "No, a great-uncle of mine was Greek. As for thriller novels, I'm afraid I have no idea what you're talking about. I don't think you're an occultist at all. I just know that you hired that man—" and she pointed at the Serpent "—to work with one of our props people to help in his killing one of our cameramen."

"I find that unlikely."

He was trying to get under her skin, and he was succeeding. "Just tell me why you're here."

"Perhaps I am looking for wise souls with whom to debate philosophy."

"Not in 1988."

"I'm deeply interested with the idea of the nature of the soul. Namely, its ability to be transferred between..."

"That's enough."

And he stood now, in such a way that she immediately sensed she was in trouble. It was probably linked to the fact that he was still smiling. "I'll say when it's enough," he said. "It's reasonable that you cut me at that particular subject. After all, if the stories are true, you have known many forms."

She was old enough to know when she'd been caught. She was getting tired of playing games with him. "If the stories are true. And that's a big if."

"What should I call you now? Astaroth? Godiva, Penthesilea? Medusa? Ayesha, Antinea, Omphale, or Sumuro? Is it Sal'lah of the Sky Brigade, or V...?"

"You take me back, Tamaron. Now, it's a different letter: you can call me E."

"Ah, yes. You spent so much of your time and energy appearing in women named E. Your desire to become a movie star is odd to me, especially since, while you are usually charismatic, you've generated little interest and revenue."

"It makes me happy."

"A shame. We were supposed to hold honors and sacrifices to you, and you go off in pursuit of 'fun'?"

"This is all based on the idea that all those stories are true. Look at me. I'm in my late thirties. People say weird things about me, but I'm an ordinary woman."

"A coping mechanism, in all likelihood, to deal with immortality. I will likely face it myself someday. Perhaps I'll do something just as ludicrous as becoming an actor, or retiring to be a schoolteacher or something."

She ignored him. "Was Caruso a sacrifice?"

"Nothing so crude."

"Tamaron. Why did you...?"

"Why did I kill him? I don't know yet."

She paused. She was the vulnerable one now, as she was now emotionally compromised. Physical exhaustion was catching up to her, too—and if the stories were true it was likely Tamaron's mind exerting influence on hers. If for nothing else than the dedication in the eyes of his guards, he was bombastically and finally powerful.

"Why would you arrange a murder if you don't know the reason? Are you just a lunatic now?"

"Our clashes in years past should show you that I'm not mad. Madness is seizures and sobbing and short-term memory loss. I have been riding life's high curve for many years now. I killed him because I had the intuition that it would be important," he said. "And the best way for me to demonstrate would be to show you the source of my inspiration."

"I'm not interested in traveling with you, if that's what you mean."

"We won't be gone for more than a day—give or take a few. Additionally, I should mention," and he cleared his throat, "that you have no choice in the matter."

And at once, his bodyguards raised and cocked their guns.

Her face immediately dropped into a frown. Though she could not fight, her face would promise to him that she would get revenge for this. Behind her, she heard the intrusions of guards, and her arms were seized and bound with handcuffs. It had been awhile since steel had brushed her wrists, and it *almost* turned her on. She would hang onto that arousal in case she needed it later, and she knew she would.

They led her away, into the night of the desert. Idling now was another car, but it was a truck, not a jeep. It seemed to be an old American model, abandoned or sold here at some point or another. Before she could prepare for it, they threw her in the shadowed chamber of the truck's back.

CHAPTER VII:

It turned out quickly that she wasn't alone back there. There was a faint light coming in from the cabin via a small slit through which she presumed they would watch her. There was no way of knowing where they were headed, but the glimmer of eyes and smiling teeth in the dark was enough to make her uncaring of such a thing.

They were men, six of them. One of them was taking a liking to a switchblade, which he ran up and down the length of his tongue.

"Stand back, all of you, or I'll break your necks," Mrs. E hissed.

"No worries, dearie." It was an American accent but a fusion of several Northern and Southern states. "We're prisoners just like the rest of you."

"Then why aren't you handcuffed, and why do you have a knife?" she asked.

"Pull hard on your handcuffs, and you'll see."

She did so, having decided not to previously. They easily broke apart; they were just cheap plastic.

"That bastard Tamaron," she whispered. But she had only her pride to curse now.

"Is that his name?" This American seemed to be the chosen speaker of the group. "I don't suppose you know why he's kidnapped us."

"No. He told me he'd be bringing me to the place where he was inspired..."

"He's killed members of our families." This voice now had a Central American accent to it—he seemed to be from Honduras, if she was right. "He said that the reason for their deaths was here in Greece."

"Then it is true—Tamaron is just a lunatic. A shame. He did have quite the intellect, but now it's lost, in a sea of pointless murders..."

And she made a point of speaking this loudly, while also banging on the separation between the cabin and the chamber with her knuckles.

"What are you doing?" the American asked.

"You'll see." And then, louder: "I hope that Tamaron's death comes soon, so that he's free of his idiotic lapses of judgment."

The truck hadn't started moving yet, and she could hear men speaking hurriedly behind her. The prisoners cringed before all sight of them vanished—they closed the viewer into where they were being held. But there was new light as the back of the holding-area opened. There was a man, a white man, and Mrs. E predicted arbitrarily he would turn out to be English. She was correct when he opened his mouth.

"I have a shotgun!" he cried. "And I will not hesitate to blow your fucking brains out the first fucking second I get." He bounded aboard, and waved the object mentioned with a bit of drool leaking down his chin. "The reason why we let you keep weapons and break your handcuffs is...we *want* you to try something. We want

to see you be heroes just so we can kill you. The Master *loves* seeing heroes get killed. But I bet all of you are too fucking yellow to try anything."

Then he sealed them in again. "Good to go!" he called to the front, and the truck took off.

From his belt he produced an electric lantern, and lit the holding area up. In the eerie light Mrs. E had a good glance at each of her fellow prisoners, as well as her captor. The latter was a blond with a jaw akin to the lantern he wielded. His uniform was standard desert camo and seemed to be pilfered from the U.S. Military. The shotgun could have been an Army hand-me-down too.

"How long are we going to have to put up with you?" Mrs. E asked.

"The ride's two hours. And trust me, in that time, I'm going to teach you a new definition of pain. When we deliver you to our destination you're only gonna be shells of your old selves."

"I've been tortured before," she said. "What's your worst?"

"My worst? You think I can rank it? Well, fortunately, I have: there are usually six stages of dealing with me. The first is anxiety. I'll let you stew a little bit, wonder what's coming. Two: I actually start. I'll grab one of you and humiliate you in front of the others. You all have to watch. If one of you blinks, or looks away when I'm torturing him—I shoot you in the head. One chance is way too friendly.

"Three: you all get a little bit. A little whipping, or punching. That sets you up for four, where you turn on each other. You do it to the others or you get it yourself. Fight against doing it long enough and it's a bullet. And then five is what I call the Trust-Ripping Stage. You start questioning *everything*—I know how to make you do that. And finally, stage six is the Religious Stage, where you start worshiping the Gods. *My* Gods. And they're the same gods that the Abbot keeps in his Abbey. There are seams and cracks in our worlds, through which slippery things can be seen, and..."

"*Stop*," Mrs. E said then. "There are many things I refuse to accept. Let us speak of more rational things. For example, does your boss...compensate you for your work?"

And she took two meaningful strides towards him. The flick of her hips made most of the men turn away. They evidently felt it was inappropriate to observe the implicit happenings here.

"He compensates me in letting me indulge my thirst without consequences," he replied. "Ever since I was fifteen, when I fried a bully with a car battery...I couldn't stop. I couldn't focus on anything else. I dropped out of school because I hated every subject that didn't involve violence. So trust me...my desire to get my 'compensation' will..."

"No, I mean, I want to know if you ever get sexual compensation."

He froze, and that was good. She found a weakness. An old weakness—an easy weakness. But she would take it if it would save these men's lives.

"Well, I...uh..."

"Or is violence the only way you express those urges? Have you truly lost your ability to let yourself be loved?" And he ran one finger down his rough and ugly lips. "Loved in the physical sense, that is."

"I-I..."

"You have a wall between sex and violence. You're not truly into pain and suffering. And even if you were, you're not doing it right."

The men were impressed. That had scarcely taken any effort from her at all.

Soon she was on his lap, kissing him with the semblance of passion. At once, he was aroused below her, and she wasted no time in exposing her torso and upper body—from her sleek shoulders down to her soft, smooth belly. Eventually she would go even farther, and apply the same action to him, and they would be coupling.

It would be an uncomfortable twenty minutes for the rest of the prisoners as they were forced to watch the bouncing flesh, hear the clumsy grunts and moans, and smell the stink of sweat and musk. But when the deed was done, their captor was woozy. Before he could properly assess just how woozy he was, Mrs. E pointed to him, despite her nudity.

"We've got him," she said. "Do what you will with him."

The naked guard didn't get a chance to scream, as the prisoners hands closed over his mouth. Mrs. E was prepared for them to do anything. It didn't take long before one of the men, who hadn't spoken thus far, burst forward. He seized the man's head, and twisted it around so the neck crunched like a bag of chips. The limp body thankfully fell forward, so that only its posterior faced the air.

The man had features that reminded Mrs. E of the last time she was in Serbia. His accent confirmed this recognition: "That was the pig who burned my home to the ground—with my wife and her sister inside."

She merely nodded at him. "We have to start formulating our escape plan," she said curtly.

The man whom she previously identified as Honduran stepped forward. "We can take his shotgun," he said. "If we can break the lock holding the door closed we can jump out of the car. We're going through the desert so the sand would cushion our fall..."

"It's a long run to safety from there, but it's the best chance we've got," Mrs. E said. "Did everyone here that? Let's get ready to run. Who wants to shoot?"

No one said anything, but she took the silence as a vote. She took the shotgun from the corpse. She checked the ammo and cocked it. Then, she took aim at the base of the back of the space they were trapped in.

She fired. They would hear the shot, of course, and while they would assume it was their agent making good on his boasts, they couldn't take the chance that they wouldn't investigate. The first man to make the frantic leap out immediately faltered, maybe having broken his ankle or something. He was the American, and the second man to get out stopped to help him. The third tried to get him to leave

the American, and the fourth grabbed the two of them and started running. The fifth grabbed the first, and the sixth, the Honduran, helped him. Mrs. E helped the Honduran, and then, the chase was on.

It didn't take long for their captors to notice them in the mirrors—that was another thing she should've accounted for. They stopped, but only for a moment, before the driver floored the gas and took them around. Mrs. E took a glance back, wanting to see what tires they had. She'd never seen such a large vehicle display such grace over sand like this. But curiosity wasn't worth it, not now. She had to keep running, and she had to keep these men safe.

The men up front had guns and were firing at the prisoners. Mrs. E led by example, zigging one way and zagging the other. If she was fast enough, that weaving would keep her safe. By following her they saved their own lives. By the rate of fire they were clearly using machine guns of some kind, and this wasn't a movie. A single shot through the right area of the leg or ankle, or something else of seemingly insignificance, could be enough to kill. It was shocking how fragile humans were, and it made sense to her that they made themselves superhuman on film.

The truck was coming up on them, predictably, and she sensed that this was a fool's chase. It had been noble to try to get freedom, but out here, with no cover, there was no chance. The harmless sounds of the rounds striking the sound were cut with the sound of the shots smacking against meat. The man whom the Honduran had been assisting hit the ground, with the only sound being his last breath assimilating out into the atmosphere. Mrs. E knelt beside him, as did the Honduran, but it was too late. He had been dead before he hit the ground. Her hands shook, and she couldn't hold back a scream when there was another burst of bullets. The truck rolled up alongside them, and up ahead, they watched the American claw at the air as he fell dying.

"Stop!"

It was the voice of Tamaron, and he exited the truck now, black robes and blond hair blowing in the wind.

"The Abbot says that returning guests can never return in the same party, and the party must have a minimum of six members," he said.

"The Abbot?" Mrs. E asked, angrily. She looked down—her palm was red. She rubbed it against the sand.

He was ignoring her. "If you'd killed just one more, we couldn't enter the Abbey," he said to his men. "You were with me last time—you won't all be able to join us."

"Who is this Abbot?"

"His Abbey, Mrs. E, is a beautiful place, you will find. If we can survive our adventure there, we will gain enlightenment. The Abbot is not a Buddhist, nor is he from Tibet, or any other area of mainland Asia, but he has a Tibetan theme to his quarters. He is a very strange sort of person, as this rule regarding visiting parties implies, though he has a wonderfully intellectual interest in history as well as philos-

ophy." He smiled. "Since I am willing to give him the secrets of the Incomputare, he enjoys my visits greatly, though he cannot bend the rules for me."

"To leak the secrets of the Incomputare goes against their deepest—!"

"I am aware, Mrs. E. But these days, the Incomputare have given me so much trouble that I care little for their centuries of secrecy. They trained me, certainly, but today my loyalties are to my Order of Draco, for as long as they serve me." And he reached towards her to help her up. The sand had stuck to the blood in clumps, and he didn't care. "Indeed, I'm very good to the people who are loyal to me. And if you remaining five maintain that loyalty this will go a lot easier for you. The Abbot is rigorous..."

At first, it seemed like he planned to say more. But he didn't. Instead, they were returned to the truck, and wordlessly, Tamaron returned to Mrs. E her clothes.

CHAPTER VIII:

The Honduran was close to Mrs. E now—she appreciated that he had stopped beside her when she had stopped for the dead man. He appreciated that she was standing by them. If she understood Tamaron correctly, he had killed their families nearly as an afterthought, only needing to kidnap them so that they could access this "Abbey." Those circumstances implied that the kidnappings were incidental as well. She set her hand on his hand. "What's your name?" she asked.

"Hector," he replied. "What's your—real name? I mean, what's the 'E' short for...?"

She told him.

"That's beautiful," he confessed.

"Thank you," she replied.

"What do you propose we do to get out of here?" His voice was quieter now.

"We have no choice but to see what awaits us at the Abbey," she whispered. "If it's another cult, or an expansion of the one Tamaron runs, it's nothing I haven't seen before. I've...met a few."

"I have to admit that I'm scared. I'm a Christian, and it's safe to say that I've lived a sheltered life...if there's...perverse sexuality, or animal sacrifices, I'm worried I'll go out of my mind."

"Many of the cults I've encountered have been based around hedonism. Torture is used for both traditional and sexual purposes, and drugs are used..."

"Oh no. I've never even gotten drunk before. What sorts of drugs?"

"The common recreational ones, like opium, hashish, cocaine, or LSD. But sometimes hard ones, like PCP or rohypnol—they use those to wring out information from the confusion..."

"...oh no."

His forehead was clammy with sweat, but she squeezed his hand, and he grinned at her. "Thank you for your honesty," he said.

"In any case, I may be there with you. I've helped people through bad trips before, and while I can't say good things about rohypnol or PCP, some of the others you can enjoy. Don't worry about your faith, I don't think it's a sin to like those things."

"I can believe it. I scarcely believe that erotic feelings are a sin."

There was a moment of silence, but it was hardly an awkward one. Her face lit up with honest surprise, and a quick glance downward revealed that she had found herself a new traveling companion. She grinned and kissed him on the cheek. They couldn't afford to do anything else.

The trip continued for about two more hours. Though she didn't know which direction they were traveling in, Mrs. E figured they were still within the

Greek border. Even as she wondered how large a desert in Greece of all places could be, she was really starting to consider what sort of Abbey they were coming up on. Tamaron said it had a "Tibetan theme" which was another tedious white person thing. It was the exact sort of thing that she had to put up with when doing the host segments for those Mondo movies. She didn't care much for race politics, but sometimes the desire of white people for "novelties" was a little maddening, especially the way they treated "the Far East." It went beyond Fu Manchu and Wu Fang and Dr. No and all the rest. It was deliberate misunderstanding in pursuit of cheap, privileged thrills.

The truck ground to a halt for the last time, and the thin light of the nocturnal desert flooded on them again. Tamaron stood in the center of a small cadre of guards. "Hurry up," he said. "The Abbot is waiting, and since he's undoubtedly heard the truck he will be struck with a certain impatience."

Mrs. E contemplated how foul those words sounded in an American accent. Tamaron was too young to use such a pretentious tone—some American professors could make it sound good, but generally a British accent was more becoming. In any case, she and the Honduran walked down together into the desert. Before the truck there towered a mountain, and up its expanse, a path leading up to a weathered stone gate. Within, they could see a beautiful garden some kind. It really did look like a garden of a Japanese fashion, which went against the Tibetan implications from earlier. Another sign that this was all the construct of a non-Asian who fetishized cultures that weren't theirs. And they were wealthy enough to own property on this mountain, if they didn't flat-out own the mountain itself.

"Get moving!" Tamaron's voice barked.

And they obeyed his command, the five of them. The men were weary from days of starvation, torture, and travel, and she frequently had to help them along. Occasionally Tamaron would aid as well, but not out of mercy. They hardly noticed the faint emission of a thin vapor from the stony gates as they passed into the garden.

It was the Honduran's turn to collapse, but Mrs. E was at his side. "We're in the garden now," she said. "I'll look for a way out..."

But it seemed to take a long time for her to turn her head, and by the time she had fully done so the garden was different.

It was now an enclosed space, like an enormous cave, but made of repeating geometric patterns cut into reflective gems of blue crystal.

At first, it seemed almost like ice, so pale was the blue, but the air was as warm as any desert night. Mrs. E's pulse quickened, and she jerked away from the sudden new settings. Terror flooded her and only intensified when she noticed that she was being loomed over by enormous...shapes. Some of them were enormous dark cones, while others were more akin to cylinders. At each of their bases was a star of some kind, through which light could be seen. Somehow, through these apertures, or merely through their presence, Mrs. E felt like she was being watched.

"W-what are these things?" she asked, staggering.

"I believe they are called Xipehuz," Tamaron said, apparently seriously. "They are said to come from beyond our planet. They are astounding killers—evidently the Abbot is a great man indeed to have the authority to keep them as guards. If they aren't killing us, they're expecting us. Humanity met them once, at our earliest dawn, and surely it must have been the experience of meeting such bizarre beings that gave us the power of imagination. Which they say gave us the chance to become the top species on this planet..."

"It is indeed by my dominant power that they are restrained," came a booming voice. The confusing chamber, cut into crystalline patterns reminiscent of the Zippy-whatevers, amplified the intruder's voice. And yet he was not the intruder here. She could tell from his robes, so similar to Tamaron's, that he was the Abbot. There was a feature that stood out to her under the habit's hood, which was that he had a very offensive bowl-cut, lacking a proper tonsure.

"I am Peta Margong," he said. "I am told, Mrs. E, that you are fond of novelties?"

"O-on occasion," Mrs. E said then. Her focus was divided between the newcomer and the things that Tamaron had identified as living. He had to be lying about their alien nature. In the course of all her adventures, she'd never found proof of life on other worlds; even in the ancient lore of Ylana of Venus, Mysta of the lunar Mazan Dynasty and its Feline Legions, Nyah of Mars, and Duessa of the Ledan Atlantis colony. She ignored the runic tales of the Lithlux, or the Sorors of Daat-Nox of the Distant Galaxy, of the Craa-cult of Pythia. Those were just legends. Right?

"Well, my Abbey is a veritable museum of curios. We will take you among them immediately, for time is of the essence. We must make sure you see the right sights when your mind is in the right place."

She nodded, absentmindedly, only partially comprehending what he said.

Perhaps he understood this. "I am the source of many great curios myself. After all, meddling in history is one of my hobbies, when I get the chance to do it."

"What does that even mean?"

"Nothing, nothing. Now, let us visit our first marvel..."

"A-aren't we here to find out why Tamaron killed all those people...?" she murmured.

Tamaron was at her side then, even as the Abbot began to lead them into a passage into the shining lattice. She swore it hadn't been there before. "We already know why I killed the gentlemen's families. We need to learn why I killed Gabe Caruso."

"And that is why six of you are needed," the Abbot proclaimed. "One of you is the receiver of information—in this case my dear friend Mr. Tamaron. The other five will function as his senses. Only one of the senses will be stimulated to give you the answer. But it could be caught by the eyes, the ears, the nose, the fin-

gers, or the tongue. One of you will be lucky to share communion, and will experience a vast vision of the space I keep within my...Abbey."

And now they were walking down a crystalline hallway—the Xipehuz and their eyeless stares were thankfully behind them. The gems that composed the corridor were darker here, with the internal light that glowed in them being fainter. Indeed, the crystals emitted the light rather than reflected it. The passage wound down a long way, at least to Mrs. E's perception, but at once, the Abbot encouraged them to look instead through a doorway to their left. Inside was a crystal cave, but this one was paved with a rug of ruby pigments. On it was the most lavish bed any of them would ever see, Mrs. E included. On top of it was a topless woman of Laotian appearance. She wasn't entirely nude, instead wearing a thin g-string laden with tassels and fake jewels. It was incredibly tawdry, so tawdry in fact that Mrs. E couldn't help but feel revulsion. Playing off of a worn-down record player was some sort of jazz piece, probably decades old.

"This is pretty tacky," she said quietly to the Abbot. "I'm not impressed. A stripper routine? I've seen a billion of those."

"Oh, but she's yet to turn around, Mrs. E!" he squealed. And she did, slowly, nervously. She began to sweat when she noticed that she was distinctly *upset* about showing backside. But sure enough, this dancer turned, and when she showed her nude back there were the deep angry lines of whip-marks. Many hundreds of them. This, too, was something she had seen before. She wanted to step in at once, regardless of the consequences and regardless of her sudden lack of physical coordination. But Tamaron was in front of her then, glaring at her. She again made the mistake of looking in his eyes.

What lurked behind them was distinct from the harsh mathematical perfection of the crystal citadel. It was fluid, and *mushy*, like a decaying corpse—the eyes that windowed this pile of mush were as dead as a corpse's, black, and full of a chilling distance from what was familiar. If he had seen her for the warmth behind her eyes (though there was ice there too), then she could recognize him for his utter lack of life. That his spirit appeared as a *humanoid* corpse showed that he could still be corrupted further, or driven into a weirder shape, but in just a few decades whatever had once made him a human being had been pounded and tenderized, to make an outline for something else. What could have been the thing that did this to him? Was there something inhuman in his ancestry? Was there a tragedy in his family that made him lose hope? Mrs. E had the impression that if those were part of his history, it wouldn't matter. There was simply something intrinsically evil about him, and there had been from an early age if not from birth.

Perhaps he knew that she was looking at him in his way, but she knew he'd seen her in the same way at some point. Strong as he thought he was, he didn't know if he could take her. In any case, he seemed as confused as everyone else. He was not immune to the mind-bending scope of the Abbey.

"Now you've seen both sides of her, who still desires her?" the Abbot con-

tinued. "I ask purely...in scientific and statistical interest."

To her horror, one of the men slowly raised his hand. He hadn't spoken before, and she'd never hear him speak. He appeared to be quietly grunting. Inside, the girl continued her dance, wearily.

But before he could step in, the room vanished, as if it had never been there at all. For all they knew it hadn't been.

"Keep moving," the Abbot said then. "Pain is not your destiny here. After all, none of you have sensed anything bringing you closer to your goal—have you? Let us show you now some genuine pleasure."

The hallway still went on, but there were another room, this time to their right. This one the Abbot beckoned them to enter. Once they were inside, they found respite from the sharp edges of the ground. (Mrs. E only now noticed that most of the men didn't have shoes. Hector did not.) A plush carpet, soft as the bed they had seen so briefly, instantly relieved the burden, and they found themselves in both an open space and an inviting one. Scattered everywhere was a vast sea of pillows, and atop these pillows were a variety of women—free from scars. "These are my prize ladies, the ones with no blemishes," the monk said. "They will instruct you on how to access all dimensions of pleasure."

And suddenly, at the laps of these courtesans were a variety of dishes, not for eating but nonetheless for ingesting. There were some black lumps that Mrs. E recognized, that were meant for the pipe. The neat stacks of white blotter paper tabs couldn't hide their identities, nor could the bright, candy-like pills, the dried red mushrooms, or green cacti buttons; and there were more innocent adventures in the bowls of green buds. The light shone oddly on these things through the thin violet tapestries that hung along the walls.

Of course, as the men slowly set themselves down—some seeking the pillows, some the women, some the drugs, and some all three—men and women in fine, Western-style uniforms appeared, carrying dishes intended for digestion of the gastric variety. Chicken, pheasant, shrimp, and lobster, potatoes, caviar, clams, wine, and whiskey all emerged, and before Hector or Mrs. E could do anything everyone was quite besotted. Tamaron came up behind the two and urged them to join their fellows, and slowly they set themselves down next to a trio of women. They had water-pipes loaded with hashish, but they both declined. Mrs. E's weakness was only increasing. Occasionally, the women would vanish entirely, and there would just be the other prisoners writhing around moaning, in various states of ecstasy and un-dress, in what appeared to be a bare earthen room, perhaps a cave of some kind.

Hector refused everything except the food. But as he bit into a pheasant wing, roasted crispy, Mrs. E came close to him. "Food might be drugged," she said.

"We fall red Eben drugged," he replied. She had no response to that.

One of the women pulled herself close to Mrs. E. She was attractive, certainly—long and gorgeous blonde hair, a round and pleasant face, dark brown eyes, pale and fairly-sized breasts. Even though she liked her face there was an odd

expression across it. The concept of reality was doubtlessly foreign to this woman now.

"Are you human?" she asked.

Mrs. E laughed, assuming she was joking. "Most of the time, I think," she replied.

"I am not human."

Her voice had a strangely, childlike lilt to it.

"Oh? Then what are you?"

"I am a werewolf."

The grin, now, was becoming creepy, especially since Mrs. E realized her initial observation—that this woman had brown eyes—was wrong. She had blue eyes, but the blue was pushed out so far that it was only a faint ring of ice around a sea of black. Her pupils were horribly dilated. "I am a werewolf from the planet of the sugar-plum fairies," she continued, quietly. "A-and there are diamonds all around me."

Mrs. E was about to say "I see," but only got out something equivalent to "ice." "This lady here," and the blonde pulled a redhead close, "she's a vampire. She comes from the planet of devils and d-demons."

The adventuress looked nervously at the door, closely kept by her two enemies. "That's lovely."

"I need blood to live!"

Mrs. E turned. The redhead was leaning forward, a look of what appeared to be grief on her face. She had a thousand-yard stare and not just because of the drugs. Or maybe exclusively from them, from a bad trip. "I need blood to live!" she repeated, with an awful desperation in her voice.

And she jumped back, and huddled close to the self-proclaimed werewolf. Her head bobbed around like a snake's, as she stared greedily at her throat. The werewolf didn't notice.

"And my other friend, she needs to have her *tan'na* leaves." She gestured to a woman whose hair color was a mystery, as she was now wrapping herself in a variety of fabrics, including the wall-tapestries.

Mrs. E looked at Hector, who was staring at the "vampire." Suddenly her gaze had shifted to look as his neck instead. Mrs. E leaned close to him and assured him that if she tried anything, she'd snap her neck. And it seemed like the vampire understood this just as he did.

They glanced over at another mat, and there was a woman who had poured out a spread of navy-blue powder over a wooden tray. She had her fingers splayed out and was dabbing the tips of them in this powder with the rhythm of a child playing patty-cake. She looked enthusiastically at Mrs. E. "Have you ever tried 'blue-finger'?"

Mrs. E shook her head no.

"It is objectively the greatest high on Earth. To feel it...trickle and burn...

through your fingertips...is like lightning." She began to strain and bristle a little, moaning and squeaking quietly. "It's like lightning," she repeated, as Mrs. E saw the scars that lined her body. Places where it looked like different bodies were joined together.

Then she turned and looked away, choosing to focus on a lantern instead. Mrs. E was content with that.

But as they sat on the pillows, and the sounds of the men moaning in joy increased, they slowly heard another sound over it. They couldn't put their fingers on it for several minutes, but they could hear it better than all else even as the sounds of their room got louder. It sounds like a man screaming, but in agony rather than bliss. They weren't imagining it—she knew what she was hearing, and he could see she could hear it too, and he trusted her senses. Maybe this was the sign the Abbot spoke of, and they could just get out of here. Instead, the scream got louder, and they had to stand up and look for it. The women tried to pin them down, but they barely noticed their efforts. After all, there was an ounce-brick of hash in that water-pipe, and they had been puffing on it for some time. Mrs. E pulled Hector closed and they stepped over their comrades, noticing that Tamaron and Margong had thankfully vanished.

As they neared the left-hand side of the chamber, the screams got louder, though they occasionally cracked and broke as the voice wore itself out. Here, they could see a faint illusion—the pattern of the crystal that made this place had been printed onto a blanket, and hung over a small doorway. She crept in first, in case there were any traps. There weren't, but she wished she'd kept him back when she did see what this was.

Three more of the women were in here, and they were holding a man down. He wore the same uniform that they now realized they were wearing—it was some sort of skintight beige thing, leaning towards the cyan side during to the light of the crystals, which showed off legs and arms but didn't appear easy to remove. Because his arm was exposed they had an opportunity to plunge a syringe deep into the bulging veins crawling up his muscular forearm.

Immediately Mrs. E snapped into action, diving forward and yanking the spike from his arm. She hurled it against the ground but it didn't shatter. She set about dispatching his captors, swinging weak blows at them. They seemed to go down easily, as she proved with one of them, but before she could go further the prisoner's hand snapped to a tight grip on her arm. He looked her deep in the eye as he grunted: "I need it." Sweat dripped in his eyes, but he didn't blink.

And, without breaking eye contact, without losing an ounce of that desperation, he knelt to the ground and recovered the needle, and returned its tip to the bulk of his muscle.

"I *need* it."

Immediately, they returned to the other side of the blanket.

But when they emerged, it was already too late. The girls had seized their

guests and throttled them to the hard ground, wrestling them like professionals, but fighting dirty. Their screams were blocked out as their throats were seized and squeezed. Suddenly the pipes and bongs were gone, and in their stead were the same types of syringes that had buried themselves deep in the junkie's limb. Taking care not to be jabbed themselves, Mrs. E and Hector set themselves upon the women, using the element of surprise to hurl them back.

Shit, this was reminding her of Silling Castle all over again. All those decadent aristocrats in the musty old place. "Run, guys!" she yelled to all of them. They took her word seriously, no matter what degree of grogginess they were experiencing, and so with little struggle they evaded the women pawing at them, and followed the pair to the door.

When they were in the corridor, Tamaron and Margong were there again, smiling.

"Why did you do that? You said you were offering us pleasure," Mrs. E said, slightly winded.

"I offered what?" the Abbot said. His face looked seriously concerned, but she ignored him.

"Come," he said. "The time has arrived. One of your number has committed a serious error, and his trial must begin."

"Wait, what?" Hector spoke now, but his voice didn't come out the same as Mrs. E's.

"Yes. The charges will be announced when we reach the trial chamber."

Behind them, then, came the sounds of marching in lockstep. The hooded men who came down towards them, all nine of them, were wearing tall leather boots which struck hard against the crystal floor. Without a word they grabbed one of the prisoners, the one who had said that he would still sleep with the whipped girl. He struggled, but they continued their march upon seizing him, driving the prisoners and their captors down further. By the time the time they reached their destination, however, the nine guards had apparently found another passage, as they and the man they took were gone.

And suddenly, then, the corridor was the one to go, and instead, they were standing on a quartz balcony overlooking the largest space of them all. It almost seemed to take up the entirety of the inside of this mountain, and though the blue light radiated throughout the space, it was dispersed in the endless darkness of the cavern, and there were spots where was no blue, only black shadow. Had they traversed a hallway? Mrs. E couldn't remember. Now and then she would envision the peaks of distant structures—*buildings*, as if this mountain housed an entire metropolis.

The balcony they stood was near a concave wall, which had several platforms of the same nauseating quartz emerging from it. On these platforms stood men wearing the same robes as Tamaron and the Abbot, and they stared down at a singular platform connected to the wall. One of the prisoners—she didn't know

anything about him—was standing on this platform, handcuffed. It seemed he had real cuffs now, as his attempts to jerk on them led him nowhere. Of course, he may not have wanted to move far, lest he slip off his platform and fall into the abyss.

"As you requested, Mrs. E.," Abbot Margong said. "Novelties. This is what a trial looks like in our Abbey."

"But this isn't part of any real faith...and I know, I've been part of so many..."

"Just go along with it," Tamaron said. "He is just trying to get into your head. You will resist him, with your instincts. With that assurance...let go and enjoy what we've done to your mind."

The "justices" across the gap were speaking.

"You have allowed yourself to become aroused sexually within our temple," pronounced the man standing directly before the accused. "Let the speakers be deployed so that the whole of the sanctuary may hear your final screams."

The man suddenly spoke for himself. "Why did you offer us girls to fuck if you didn't want us to become aroused?"

They did not answer. And in places, the blue crystal yielded instead to a shimmering smooth surface—cut with circular runes, like the outlines of subwoofers. They vibrated faintly with sound as the members of the court, on their disk platforms high above that which served as the stand for the accused, began performing a strange gesture. They would pull their fists to their throat and jerk their arms outward, straightening them. It was a nearly convulsive jerk, and each time they did it, they made a deep-throated grunt. It seemed *angry* to Mrs. E. The subwoofers amplified these grunts, these thrusts of sound, and slowly, a bridge extended out to the platform that the crewman stood on. One of the monks began to walk towards him, carrying in his outstretched hands a black ribbon. He tied this around the crewman's throat, and began to imitate the gesture of the men up above. Each time he performed it, the ribbon thumped heavily against his neck. They began to leave a necklace of purple bruises, and at first the crewman merely gagged, but it became more and more painful, and the fear of death came upon him. Again, and again, a pull to the neck, and then a jerk down and out with the straightened arms. He screamed.

And his scream began to come out of those speakers—quietly, at first, but growing, as the microphones apparently scattered through the trial chamber picked up the reflected screams coming off the chamber's own speakers. For miles there was nothing but the tangible echo of a man screaming and pleading for his life. And somehow, above the droning white noise of this scream, came a voice: *"This is what will happen if you sin. All trespassers of the law will be subjected to horrible agony."*

What were the charges again...? She could have misheard when she said that they were killing him for having an erection. Her senses were reeling—and the screams were only getting louder...

But there was a whisper in her ear now. It was Abbot Margong, suddenly at

her side. "This has just been entertainment," he said. "Satiin holds the real answer."

There was a limit. Deep in the brain was a painful wall that the mind would be shoved against as it was pushed with ever so much stimulation. It was like TV static, burning hot and loud, and she was crackling inside it. Thank the goddess— she was finally passing out—

CHAPTER IX:

She didn't recall leaving the Abbey of the monk Peta Margong. They had probably all been carried out, though Tamaron may have had a chance to walk out—he seemed in control of his faculties. There was no way of guessing what talents he had to protect himself from the delusion that was that place, nor what benefits the monk may have given him. There were three men now. Somewhere in that mountain, someone had actually died.

Mrs. E told Tamaron what Margong had apparently told her, and she gave him the last known location of Prince Satiin. He had returned to his homeland after turning over control of the Devourers of Life in Brazil to her, making her into "the Divine One." If Tamaron *was* going to indulge her, and they were going to seek Satiin's counsel, they would be in Bangkok. And if she could make a break for it that meant she'd be home free.

After all, Bangkok also held one of the sanctuaries of the Order of the Madonna.

Shortly after the Devourers and the Madonna Order had their schism—her fault, effectively, for not properly guarding herself against Hazel Hexen's machinations—she had been a rogue agent, until she heard from one of her English girlfriends about a Madonna operation taking place in India involving Afghan Princes, clowns, and the woman who deposed her, the daughter of the infamous Major D. Smith. She'd ended up assisting the success of the Order's goals during this caper. The Order had taken her back and when Mrs. Smith retired she offered Mrs. E the position of Madonna. And the girls of the Order were her "friends." She didn't like to call upon them often, giving them freedom to run their own operations from their base on the island of Rhahl, out in the Indian Ocean.. They had taken it from Raba Khan, alias Prince Ranah, in the mid-'70s, who had stolen it from them some time earlier. Ranah had retreated to Rhahl after a raid of his previous headquarters in the '60s, and it had been Ranah's half-brother Chamal who was caught up in Mrs. Smith's 1981 jewel scheme, which ended with that tedious affair of Chamal's nuclear bomb.

God. She'd been a journalist once, hadn't she, informing the public about these complexities—? That had been long ago. She hadn't taken a photograph in ages.

With the Bangkok agents of the Order of the Madonna at her side, Mrs. E would no longer be just a movie star for porno smut—she was in command of an army. They would disable the enemy by any means necessary, trying not to kill until everything else was exhausted. That was their way, and she was glad it was so similar to her own.

Too much history. She didn't even like thinking about the hard details of the past. To her, the past was almost nonexistent—it was so inconsistent, running

parallel to itself and interrupting itself. Going on tangents. It was best to just ignore it.

They drove again, and during this time, the four prisoners slept. Any contact with the Order of the Madonna was still long ahead. When they slept, there was relative peace among them. It would not last.

After a few hours they stopped once more, and were exposed again to the air. The dawn was coming up quickly, and once again guns were waved in their faces. Tamaron was at the fore.

"We're at the airport," he said. "The flight leaves shortly. However, we only have tickets for five. I do not like spending tremendous amounts of money at once."

"That's good. After we—we lost that one guy back in that place, we're down to five," Hector said.

"I have thought it over throughout the night," Tamaron said then, "and I know I would feel more comfortable with two of my guards along. Therefore we can only bring two of you. Sorry."

And they shoved the two men back away from Hector and Mrs. E.

"Wait, what are you doing...?" Mrs. E choked out. She asked only as a pretense. She knew what was next.

"Sorry," Tamaron repeated.

They aimed their guns.

"Wait!" Mrs. E cried to the men, the ones being targeted. "What are you names?"

The guns rattled for a second and a half. The bodies were on the ground then, and the sand greedily soaked up their blood.

"Oh, Jesus fucking Christ," Hector gasped. He was crying—she knew she was, too.

"Be glad you're alive," Tamaron said. "I know that's what you're thinking, Mrs. E."

She *was* thinking such a thing. As long as she was *alive*, she had a way out.

"Let's go," the wizard said then, in a calm voice. And they kept following him. Again, they had no restraints on them. If they ran for it, he would kill them, and then he would kill every damn witness in the airport.

Indeed, it didn't take long for the flight to board, and to take off. Mrs. E sat next to Hector, and Tamaron and his guards had changed into formal business-wear, doing so in the airport restroom in shifts. They hid their guns in their luggage once they got to the airport, but they did so in the open and that didn't seem to raise any eyebrows. Presumably because the staff knew what was in store for them if they didn't oblige Tamaron and his men—they could be terrorists and out here it was better to simply indulge such people rather than risk a massacre. Most of the time, small businesses like this station weren't likely to end up targets.

Of course, this was atypical. It didn't matter in this situation. The flight took nearly ten hours, and by the end of it jet lag was the very last thing Hector

and Mrs. E wanted to add to their troubles. But still, they endured it. Mercifully, Tamaron had given Hector shoes—he needed them to get aboard the flight. Despite being full of vertigo and nausea, the two prisoners were loaded into a car that was evidently the property of some of Tamaron's followers in Bangkok. The Order of Draco had a reach that far out, which was a horrifying prospect to Mrs. E. But then, he had come to Greece just fine as well, with devotees there too.

They began driving to the city's outskirts. "Before we left Greece, I made a call to my followers here, and forged a deal with Prince Satiin. We can go directly to his estate, and he'll receive us just as the Abbot did. And through him, I'm sure we'll find the secret that we all seek."

They said nothing. Mrs. E—Mae—wasn't even angry anymore. Against the leather seats she pulled Hector's hand close once again.

She wasn't being a very good sexual detective. Her sex drive was strangely absent here—the danger wasn't exciting to her as it usually was. She didn't want to fuck Tamaron. He would turn her down if she offered, anyway, being only inter-ested in relationships if they furthered his goals. Despite his relative youth, he was already heartless towards love. Perhaps it was his youth, however, rather than his age, that made him cold.

These outer edges of Bangkok were indecisive in which class they wanted to represent. Here, rich men could be the neighbors of slums, and that was often the case. She wondered how the two classes interacted, if ever they met. It was nota-ble, of course, that while the houses of luxury and antiquity were distinctly Thai, the buildings used as capitalistic punishment borrowed architecture from buildings in America.

The palace of Prince Satiin was familiar to her, even though it had been fourteen years. Fourteen years to her was as yesterday—but she had etched this place in her mind, with the spiritual journey that she had undergone here. It filled her with nostalgia. But it had been nine years since she had last seen Satiin, and even then he had shown a dark side. The Devourers of Life had a history of murder, after all, and he had commanded them. As the Divine One, he had been their god. She knew she had to be prepared for anything.

The car parked, and servants of the Prince emerged in great droves. They were the same who had attended him fourteen years ago, their faces marked by age a little. They were Asians: Indian, Chinese, Vietnamese, Korean, and Laotian. Prince Satiin appeared to be a white man, with appeared being an operative word. He was played by an Italian when they did the movie, old Ivan, and he'd done a decent job. Determining how to rate the quality of one's performance was difficult in these movies, which would honestly never reach the audience necessary for them to im-prove. But then, people like Mathews and Anderson didn't want to improve, at least on the surface. They wanted to survive.

There were two modes of people, it seemed—those who lived and those who lived minimally. Sometimes it seemed like the real adventure was in scraping by,

paycheck to paycheck. It made the moments of peace, where things seemed to stop for just a few moments, not just good, but *glorious*. And yet, oftentimes the suffering was undue and unnecessary, and that was what put cruelty in privilege.

She'd been rich and poor alike across all her lives. She struggled with guilt in both.

Now she felt guilty for meandering. She would need to be as focused as possible if she was going to get away from the Prince.

Even if he was in league with Tamaron, and they were enemies now, he would probably desire to uphold his politeness. He was a Prince, after all, though not all Princes were gentle. Mrs. A, when last they'd communed, talked about Prince Ranah, the dictator she'd been a prisoner of. She said he'd once been known as Raba Khan, apparently the leader of a cult that carried out human sacrifice in an "ironic" sense—as a parody of real human sacrifice. That didn't matter. She enjoyed the company of Prince Satiin and she hoped she would again.

Hector, and Tamaron, to an extent, marveled at the internal architecture of the place. The floor was tiled black-and-white like a chessboard, but within each tile was a symbol resembling the yantras of the Tantric traditions. Mrs. E couldn't identify the glyphs, and perhaps they were too old even for the Prince himself to understand. But she doubted it. The man had always conveyed that he carried the weight of great age. Sometimes he was very good at passing as an ordinary politician. When they'd first met, she'd wanted him to let her photograph his father, the King, in exchange for some physical favors. Only later did she discover it was all a joke—there was no King, and the country he'd claimed to be from was equally fictional. She couldn't even remember the false nation's name. He was still royalty, he said, or at least he grew up in aristocratic wealth.

"This place was a shrine once," Tamaron said. "Observe the four pillars arounds, and how the walls are angled to draw your eye here..." He gestured to the grand staircase directly opposite the entrance, made of a golden stone, leading up doorway. Everything was *round*, and smooth, unlike the harsh crystalline shapes of Margong's Abbey.

At once, the doors of that doorway opened, carved mahogany flying fast through the air on hinges. At the top was Prince Satiin, unchanged in the years that passed. He slowly and elegantly descended the stairs towards his guests. Despite the intensity of his entrance, his devil-bearded face was mild. He regarded the two men and the guards who were with Mrs. E, and when his eyes settled on her in particular he managed a thin smile. "I wish to speak only with Mae," he said. "You others must wait. Mr. Tamaron, I will deal with you at the conclusion of our conversation."

Tamaron took no issue with this, and slowly, Mrs. E and Satiin climbed up. She shot a backwards glance at Hector, now entirely in Tamaron's custody. He looked brave and she was glad for that.

When they passed through the doorway, the immediate left led into the often-recalled memory of the Prince's study. The only object worthy of note, besides

the wide bay window, was the enormous bed, which the two of them had gone to again and again. Once more, however, she wasn't feeling like a sexual detective, now realizing that she wasn't feeling the second word of the title just as she didn't feel the first. She was struggling vainly in her attempts to detect, here and now. The Prince was good at hiding his feelings—he was either going to seduce her or kill her. Possibly both. Why he would do so, or what he wanted, remained a mystery.

Fortunately, he began to speak. "It has been a long time, Divine One."

"I don't go by that title anymore," she said. "Nine years ago, the Devourers went down in flames, and I've been running ever since. Fortunately they and the thugs who assaulted my stepdaughter seem to have shriveled up."

"Yes, it was a shame that the Devourers collapsed. I'm sure they would have found *actual* occult secrets at some point." They were both sitting on the bed now, but the situation was entirely without intimacy. "Of course," he continued, "there are stories that the Order of the Madonna survives to this day. They used exclusively female agents, didn't they? The Devourers accepted men after I took them over, but the Order mostly relied on a series of convenient marriages as far as obtaining male operatives involved."

"I'm not too sure. After all, the Order was the invading faction. I was loyal to the Devourers but eventually they lost their loyalty to me. I didn't bother learning about the organization that almost assassinated me."

"Did they attempt such a thing?"

She froze. He was acting very much like Tamaron now.

"Satiin, what's this about? You and I are old friends. I may have lost the Devourers, but they were unstable. I don't share your optimism—I don't think they were leading the way to true occultism. And I was partially to blame for that…"

"But aren't you familiar with the occult? In our sessions together, you seemed to recall all the rituals like you'd done them before. And you are not the only one to notice that, while you don't use it, you have the power to keep Tamaron back."

Now she was taken aback. That thought had been in her head hours ago, miles away. At once, she understood his threat—he was implying he could read her mind.

But still, she could count on their friendship. And she could count on his honor—

"I am now going to be direct with you, Mrs. E," he said. And he moved to sit closer to her. At once, his hand went to the back of her neck, under the pretense of massaging her. In truth she knew he could crush her vertebrae. "I am a man of great efficiency these days. My control over some of the occult orders of this world have cost me much of my personal fortune, which I've built up over the years of… making myself. These setbacks in my accumulations have led me to accept a bribe of sorts from our mutual friend Mr. Tamaron. He will bankroll some of our experiments in exchange for my obtaining a special secret from you. It's nothing person-

al—it is simply that I have grown fond of the trinkets I've picked over the years. In a life long passed, I made a pact with a great power, and when that power fell I fell also. Ever since, I have rebuilt that life, in its own way."

"What the hell are you talking about?"

"You are familiar with reincarnation, right?"

"I am, Satiin."

"Then you know that sometimes living people can possess several selves, too. After all, as we age, we effectively become different people. And sometimes, those other selves, from other lives, and spaces, and times, they live in the same place and time as us. As such, we as we perceive ourselves are just one piece of a larger whole. We leave echoes, and people see our lives in those echoes. I have had many faces, and though I've hidden them from you, some of them are—or rather are capable of—evil.

"And again, I will be frank: you *know* of this, Mae. I have investigated the Order of the Madonna, and I have learned of...the others. They also show up in films. They're *you*, but they're *not*, and I don't know how that can be, because you aren't like us."

"Us?"

"Peta Margong is like us," he hissed. "Today he is an Abbot, and a simple meddler, and in this, the seventh of his journeys through the circle of life, he is good, though he is too obsessed with loving the birds, as his name in Saxon suggests. His path has already begun in darkness and failure: no doubt he exposed himself to that which he exposes all his guests to, his vision of how the human mind works when confronted with a complete separation from reality. He often said that in order to construct this environment, he would have to commit a completely senseless murder, one intended to mix sheer bafflement with the horror of death. And yet it is the most materialist thing of all to want to separate yourself from reality. Materialism leads invariably to sin, Mrs. E, and it is sinful to ignore one's role in the world." His eyes sparkled, as if perhaps he thought the two of them still shared what they'd once had. "In the future the material world, and all the manias it brings, will consume him completely, and he will become a dreadful storm. But for now he is merely a clown, called Fugol'leofa, the aforementioned Anglo-Saxon name meaning 'Bird-Lover'..."

"Oh dear," she said.

"Yes, it's a mouthful, isn't it? He is also called Kurq'wes, his name in an even older language."

"And who are the others of this 'us'? I mean, you yourself are counted in that, right? Do you also have an Old English name?"

"If you must know, I am Wenan, again in Old English. In another language you would see that my original name, 'Cunning,' is similar to Sumuro, a name you used once if I recall correctly..."

"Enough about names. I want you to speak more rationally."

"Ah, but you see, I am Satanic, my dear, as my name implies. I am a Champion of Death, and I am not alone in that. Abbot Margong, in his guise of Kurq'wes, is also such a Champion, and you must understand that I also have a brother who shares the title, though he is Champion of something else. He was called 'Dreamer,' or in Anglo-Saxon, Ansyne. Our kind so often ends up in Britain, and a mutual friend of ours used Anglo-Saxon greatly in telling tales of us, so we honor the tongue."

"But...you and Margong appear Asian. Why don't you use a language like Tibetan or Vietnamese?"

"Appearances are deceiving, often. Were you to meet Ansyne he would look English to you. I have already had my time to use the language of Easterlings."

"Of...what?" She stood, breaking away from his "massage," and he stood as well. They faced each other, never breaking that eternal eye contact.

"No matter. Anyway, I wished to say of Ansyne, my brother, that he considers himself a Healer, even though his sign is Omega, The End. And someday soon, I will be his Master. He and I are both sorts of Angels, he being one of Order and I one of Chaos; he is Ohrmazd, and I am Ahriman. He is my greatest enemy, though sometimes I am his friend, and his servant, and he is mine from time to time, because he and I are one together, two sides of the same coin. Our battle has carried us to Algol and beyond...years later in another time I led the forces of the Iron Court against him.

"You don't want to hear about names, but to us, names are important, for we three consider ourselves to have important roles in your history. We are interested in you because you are like us, made of stories and events that can't happen, wrapped in the chitin of archetypes and ideas and legends and myths somehow brought to life. But you are still flesh and blood and there are many of you at once. What are you?"

She stayed silent.

"Do you even comprehend?"

"Old friend," she said precisely. "You are perverse and you can't speak straight. I can't stand bad communicators. You've let time mess with your head—claiming to be some spiritual being now, an alien, I guess, with a bunch of fantasy names from languages chosen from a hat."

"Now listen to me," he said, in a velvet-smooth voice. "I am a Prince, and once, when I dominated you, you called me Master. Now you will see fit to obey me. Tell me the secret of Mrs. E."

And then she scoffed at him.

"Like Hell."

And her leg swung up. Even though he deflected at the last moment, the blow to his thigh left a bruise, and he was temporarily crippled. She sprinted away from him, towards the window. Outside the palace was a faint ledge—to her left, below, was an awning. There was no chance it would support her weight, but she could

get along the edge, the supposed "no chance" was inherently a better chance than doing nothing. She had the distinct impression he would kill her if she stuck around. He was professing to be some sort of fiction-being, apparently, and that was the sort of thing one believed if one took psychedelics on a daily basis. Probably the sort of thing she'd warned Hector about when he had told her about his fears. Such an addled mind would hardly notice killing.

Thinking of Hector reminded her that she needed to find him in his mess, too. Poor thing. He would be okay, though, once she got him to the Order. Like Margong, Satiin spoke only tedious word-salad, in codes no one with a happy life would bother solving, but he did mention some truths now and then. From that, she saw that she had clearly done a poor job of hiding the truth behind the Brazilian schism. He had learned that she engineered it.

Again, it didn't matter. She looped around to the front of the palace, hoping that the Prince's servants hadn't bothered to lock the entrance. She also hoped that Tamaron trained his guards poorly enough so that they still had the limitations of ordinary human reflexes. When she burst into the door, her hope was answered— the guards were stunned by her sudden appearance, and before they or their Master could respond, she was pulling Hector back into the open air. On the stairs was Satiin, who did not share the hesitation of his comrades.

"Gun them down!" the Prince roared. But the door was closed then, and if they fired, Mrs. E didn't care. They were running again, running as she ran from prison twice over, running like she ran from the snuff film bastards. As they ran in the desert when those men were killed.

CHAPTER X:

There came a time when they had to stop running, because they were too thirsty to go on. By then, the sun was starting to go down. Hector was pale, now, and his feet, even with the shoes, were worn red with blisters and white with calluses. They would be lucky if he could move come tomorrow, even with water and sleep. She had pushed him too hard.

But all the same, hope still lived in him. "W-we did it..." he murmured. "Got away..."

"No, we haven't. I'm sorry, Hector. Prince Satiin told me his resources were diminished, but he'll still have access to the best trackers in the world. Tamaron's helping him, too. I just don't know why Satiin didn't just get what he wanted from me by reading my mind..."

"Wait, that guy could...could read minds? And...what is it he wanted?"

She laughed, absentmindedly. "He wanted...my identity."

"I see. And why was that important to him? You two were once lovers, weren't you?"

"Yes, long ago. And yet not that long ago. He wants my identity because my identity is particularly complicated. I'll...explain when we get there."

"Uh...can I ask where 'there' is?"

"The headquarters of...well, my family."

He chuckled. "Your family lives in a 'headquarters'?"

And she laughed too. "My family is an organization like Tamaron's. But we... do things better than he does, I like to think."

"I...see."

"You have no reason to trust me," she asserted. "I could be preparing to sacrifice you to the Terrible Dread."

"That's a name that doesn't bode well," Hector said.

"It's funny, the same name also means 'the Admirable,'" she replied. She considered how she had done well at lying to Satiin after all—she'd unraveled a few of his codes during their talk. They were irrelevant here, though. Satiin *had* lost a good deal of his power, by investing too much in cults, and even if he had good contacts his contracts with them would only be able to last a certain amount of time, before the fees attached turned his riches to rags.

They could rest for now. They were deep in the jungles of Thailand, and she knew where to head to find their way back to Bangkok. Thankfully a city like Bangkok could hide anybody. The Order had lived in the city for many decades now, unseen. .

For a few hours, however, she let Hector rest, and let the cool of the night heal her. Amidst the night insects, and the lizards and monkeys of the jungle, she found some water and fruit, and brought it back to Hector. When he awoke, he had

a canteen to drink from. He didn't ask what its origin was.

They sat together for a long time, and as he ate his vitality came back to him. Vitality, of course, is a complicated word in regards to humans, who frequently twist words in a barbaric and pathetic attempt to conjure up the sexual jokes of their youth. Since they still had some time together—and since, they decided, he should be kept off his feet anyway—they decided to enjoy a pleasant diversion. He didn't tell her that it was his first time going on such a diversion, but she did most of the work anyway, for the sake of her own pleasure. She absolutely *ruled* her lovers; but let them rule her too. It wasn't control in the ways of tyrants—it was taking care of someone else, awakening them to knowledge of their body and its natural abilities. To have great skill and knowledge of those abilities increased one's chance of spreading pleasure. True pleasure, born of feeling. Born of a living storm.

They slept again after that, and when they woke up they said nothing as they went back on the run again. Hector very much wanted to express himself but couldn't find the words: she was so confident out here, in a foreign jungle. Soon they were at the edges of Bangkok again.

"Those jungles seemed familiar to you. You took to them like Mi'Bassa to India," he said.

"Who?" she asked.

"There was a pulp writer in Honduras who wrote *Aventures de Mi'Bassa*. Mi'Bassa was essentially Tarzan with the serial numbers filed off, set in India instead of Africa."

"I see." She looked back at him, and grinned, and took his hand. "It'll be easy to get to where we're headed once we hit the market. In fact, it's right before the..." And she paused. "I shouldn't say it out loud."

"I get it," he said. "Let's get going."

It was early in the morning, and yet still the streets were packed. From experience, she knew that many of the people here were the ones who made the city work. They ran the businesses that fed and clothed people, and gave them treasures and tools and media. Probably half the businesses in the town were already open, or never closed. This was a place cut with blood and sweat, and probably not a few tears as well. Yet as strong and proud as these people were, they were unaware that below their feet was unspeakable beauty...and horror. Obviously this space didn't span the entirety of Bangkok, but it was vast all the same.

Before Hector could take in the life of this city, captured and etched in psycheogeographic and hauntological patterns, they were at the door of a house. Mrs. E rapped her knuckles on the wood five times, and upon the fifth knock, a panel slid open on the door. There was a person inside, Chinese from Hector's perspective, who examined Mrs. E closely. After a moment, the door was pulled aside, and they could view this person in all her glory. She was gorgeous, but time had caught up with her in a way that it hadn't done to Mrs. E. She needed little time to examine her guest—at once, the door opened. "Mae!" a voice said cheerfully. "Welcome home.

Come in, quickly."

She had spoken Mrs. E's name aloud, but to Hector there seemed to be a degree of understanding between the two. And though they physically looked rather different, he couldn't help but draw similarities between them in his mind.

Once they were inside they got a good look at their settings. Hector was confused at first, as he saw this house was drab enough to be completely inhospitable. There were no beds, not even a cot or a pile of cloth—there was nothing to store food in. There was just a rotten bamboo mat covering the floor. He had an idea of where this was headed, though.

"You've come at a fortuitous time, Mae." Her accent was heavy and beautiful. "Moira is here too."

"That's wonderful, Amy! I don't suppose *she* is here...?"

"A? No, and I would know. But let's get down, quickly. We'll need to do a background check on your friend."

"There's no time, Amy, I'm sorry," Mrs. E said quickly. "We're being followed. By...you know."

And Amy, as she had called her, closed her eyes—but so did she. When they opened their eyes, Amy nodded.

"Let's go. Welcome aboard, Hector."

Hector was stunned, but when they began tugging at the edge of the bamboo rug he helped them. As he expected, there was a hatch underneath, with a low, flat wheel residing in a divot so it was flush with the ground. Mrs. E set upon turning this, and soon it yielded to her, dropping inwards as the frame holding it relaxed.

The hatch led into a tunnel, naturally, with a ladder leading down. To Hector's relief, it didn't go down far. Once, on his father's farm, he had been climbing the ladder to the upper level of their barn, and it had become unstuck from the floor above, and fell backwards. Ever since, climbing ladders was a burden to him. Amy and Mrs. E went before him, and when he joined them (doing his best to pull the rug back over the gap before pushing the hatch back to its lock), they were already a considerable distance down the steel corridor now revealed to them. He had difficulty believing it. There were electric lamps lighting the length of this hallway, and he was taking that in when they stepped into a larger chamber. It was still a corridor, in a manner of speaking, but the floor they had to traverse was drastically different.

The wider space was to accommodate the sections of the floor, which shifted along tracks. To be more precise the floor abruptly ended as it spilled over into a pit, which was full of sharp iron spikes. Crossing this pit were three bars, and sliding back and forth, were a trio of steel platforms. Some sort of motor at the base of these platforms was moving them along the bars, but there were vast gaps between each of them, and there was different timing between the movements of these platforms.

"What is this, a video game?" Hector asked.

"This more recent mechanism was inspired by some of our younger members playing video games, yes. This is, after all, a temple of sorts, like those in games," Amy said then. "It is a physical trial, to slow invasions into this hideout, like the traps in the sacred places of old."

"I-is there a way around it?" he said.

"There is not. We will all have to cross."

"B-but how are you even powering this? How did you...fund a facility that could house such a trap?"

Mrs. E was the one to take those questions. "The Order of the Madonna has run a scheme for some time now where we seduce rich people and convince them to give us our money. We've been running off the Prouse fortune for some time. We have quite a few proud Mata Haris in our midst who have snaked their way in and out of not a small amount of profitable divorces." As she said this, Amy lunged out from the edge onto the first platform, and without halting made it to the second as well. Once Mae had finished she was on the other side. Hector knew already he wasn't that fast.

"As for power," she continued, "we have a set of miniature hydroelectric—"

"Maybe I should just wait here?" he interrupted suddenly.

She looked at him, and a sad expression crossed her face. She realized how tired he must be, how hungry and thirsty and in pain. It was safer on the other side of this barrier, but she could hardly carry or throw him across. Instead, she smiled and put her hand on his shoulder. "You can do it," was all she could get out.

And as she walked to the edge, she looked over her shoulder.

"Just watch me!"

And he did. She ran forward about four or five strides, and when she reached the lip of the drop-off, she curved her toes around like she was letting herself fall. In truth she was thrusting herself forward onto the first platform. She didn't lose any momentum as she simply angled herself and lunged for the second—and she continued with the third. In seconds, she was across.

"Take your time!" the two women called at him, and it was like their two voices were one for a second.

Mrs. E watched him as he sucked in a deep breath and ran at them. She hadn't noticed that he had a limp at this point, from all the running they did before—his posture was all wrong. He made the first jump, and landed it, but his momentum ran out. His landing twisted his angle, it looked like, and his grunts echoed down towards her and Amy. But he stood up anyway, and made the next jump anyway.

The angle was almost wrong. He was on the far left side of this second platform; both his feet made it and he kept his balance. There wasn't even a grunt this time.

But he took off for platform three without eyeballing the jump first. This

time he came up short, and with a small sound his fingers caught onto the front end of his goal. The tips of his shoes grazed the spikes that poked out like beast's teeth. He shouldn't have looked down, but he couldn't help it.

He saw then that the floor of this space wasn't solely adorned with spikes. It had a slight angle to it, after all, to allow certain things to roll to the extreme end of it. He obviously hadn't been paying attention, as he hadn't noticed the inevitable outcome of this sort of trap. The extreme end of this pit was full of the bones of the people who had fallen on the spikes.

She couldn't imagine what he was thinking, but she bounded back to platform three and grabbed one of his hands. When she went for the other, it darted back, and he started mindlessly, aimlessly screaming. Still, she was able to pull him up, and only just. Amy reached her arms across the gap, and though it bowled her over she was able to pull him onto the other side.

"We've been through a lot, haven't we?" Amy said then. At first Hector thought she was condescending to him. But he saw she was talking to Mrs. E.

His screaming stopped for a moment, but his voice was still panicked. "You—you're the same...the same person...aren't you?"

And they said nothing.

"What are you?" he shouted.

And she said nothing.

CHAPTER XI:

When Mrs. E told Hector that this place was a "temple" he was expecting the same grandeur, scale, and esotericism as Margong and Satiin's spaces, but
simplicity seemed to be the idea here. There were several doorways in the room they
entered from the passage, which probably led into the necessary facilities. Here was
a small room, with the natural earthen walls coming through—there was no steel
visible. Four stone pillars held up the cavern ceiling high above. Hector focused
on the pillars, which had an odd eclecticism to them. Two were painted a pale pink
(one sporting a long crack), but one had been painted rich brown, and the other an
olive-xanthic color. Maybe there was some significance to why they were painted
this way, but Hector was too shaken to take E's perspective and be a detective. At
the base of these pillars were five armchairs, and astonishingly, a fake fireplace. The
kitschy comfort of this den stood in contrast to the potential significance of the pillars, which he knew he would never learn, because he knew she wouldn't teach him.
There would never be time enough. A million thoughts went through her minds, but
foremost among them was assuring Hector that he was okay.

"The bones you saw were from intruders," she said to him. "I know it's all
subjective, but they were...evil. In the same way Tamaron was evil. The things they
wanted to do to the people we keep here were abominable."

He said nothing.

"This is one of my homes," she said. "When I'm not making movies, or
being a reporter, or whatever. From the beginning of this life, in 1950, I've served
the Madonna, or the Octopus of the Blue Rings, or the Octopus with Feathers. Or
the Divine One. Whoever we've deemed the leader—though there really isn't any
leadership to us. We're just a place where people can hide, and find a community.
And some of us go out on adventures, helping people. We all have astounding luck,
both good and bad, and we've picked up quite a few skills over the years."

"But you and—and Amy..."

"Amy Wong," Amy clarified, interrupting him.

"You seem to share a mind. L-like you're aspects of a single being."

"It could well be something like that. We share a deep bond, in any case, the
four of us—in each of our adventures, we picked up the name of 'Mrs. E.' It spread
like a virus, actually a bit like venereal disease, because we each gained the title after
fucking each other." Mae paused then, because his face had dropped low with surprise. But she had to keep going.

"I was a good friend of E. A****, the first Mrs. E, so I borrowed the name
from her as the 'Black Mrs. E.' And Amy got it from me, and the fans of her movies
called her 'Yellow Mrs. E.' And then it looped back around when an old girlfriend
of mine, Moira Larssen, became the 'White Mrs. E.' When we made our movies
we also met a bunch of other girls whose movies were retitled to seem like they

were sequels to ours. Sometimes they'd be dubbed over to have the Mrs. E name. It was all a cash-in policy, a weird side-effect of us deciding to act out our adventures again."

"Wait, wait, wait, is this entire Mrs. E subgenre marked by the main characters being played by the women who experienced the adventures? So they're all a bunch of autobiographies?"

"They are. Some of us are good writers, but not all. We were astonished to learn of each other's' existences, and knew we had to band together. We have many names, like Iris, Isabelle, Jennifer, and Clito. The Order of the Madonna offered to house us and bankroll our further adventures, and over time we became the Order's executives."

"So you can link minds, then, because...?"

"If people are close for long enough, they can blur into each other," Amy said, in a voice so uncannily like that of the woman next to her. "It happens commonly with women, though men can still do it too, these days. It happens in music bands, or the military. There's nothing magic about it—supernaturally magic anyway." And she paused. "Or, maybe we're actually hyperdimensional fiction beings who create multiple avatars when entering realspace, each with a unique personality but ultimately sharing one mind, entirely dedicated to creating *stories*, which are our source of nourishment, having adventures that we encapsulate in time as movies so we can feed and survive."

"Sh! Don't fuck with him, Amy," Mrs. E said, seriously. (In his mind, she was still Mrs. E, even if there were "more" of her.)

"Even beyond that, I'm having difficulty following...but maybe I'm just out of breath..."

"We're a bunch of people, living in harmony under a quasi-religious structure, who do what we want, generally for the purposes of making the world a better place," she said.

"Oh."

She wasn't surprised that he was having troubles. She was wondering why she had been complaining about the complexities of the cults of Margong and Sati-in, when the Order of the Madonna was a historiographical nightmare. It had a history dating back to the '30s at the very least, though supposedly in the 1890s a woman named Zalma von der Pahlen had run something like it, with her partner Natasha di Murska, after an inspirational visit to the elusive Herland. Even before then there were whispers of a Sister Agatha in Italy in the 1390s who built an organization like the Order, and a witch named Abigail who died at Salem who ran a coven of similar intent, and even an ancient tribe with their beliefs from the Stone Age kingdom of Wahn'go. And there were the clubs and brothels of Moll Flanders, of Frances Hill, of the sadist Juliette Paris. But the Order as Mrs. E knew it had been founded in the early '30s by the Great L'Lar, a descendant of a clan of pirates. The Great L'Lar had started the Order as a criminal enterprise, and it had operated as one several times

under Mrs. E's guises. Throughout the '50s and '60s she had absorbed gangs led by, empowering, or composed entirely of women, including the group that their best pilot, "Kitty," ran—in addition to these criminals, the women they brought in were former intelligence agents, like Colonel Metterstein, and some ambitious Neo-Pagans, like old Calixta. Both joined a couple years after "Kitty" did. There were still some rejects; their names had been Ilsa, Olga, Wanda, and Greta, who had abused women even though they surrounded themselves with them. And then there had been idiots: the Chiroptera Woman, who they thought had maybe once been Irma Vep but was actually just a scientist named Sheila Myra, who'd become the leader of a gang of acid-crazed idiots yanked off of Zarpa Mesa after some deranging incident involving the living dead. She wasn't even a relation of that other Chiroptera Woman who was wrapped up with the infamous Dr. von Schalkenbach. Among the morons was also the splinter faction that fled to specter-haunted Blood Island, who called themselves Goddesses of Love in imitation of their former peers. It was all so confusing and frustrating. Nowadays, as the leader of the Order proper, Mrs. E preferred to be peaceful, inclusive, and above all else, *intelligent*; while still taking in girls not afraid of getting their hands dirty, like the Black Alley Cats. The 21st Century was approaching, and progress was necessary. Murder was not the way of the future, though killing in self-defense was not inherently cruel...

"Can you hear me?" Hector said then. "Are you okay, Eman—?"

"Don't speak further," Mrs. E said suddenly. "I am fine. Sorry. I was distracted, which isn't good. A lot of people believe that distraction is the opposite of intelligence..."

"I was just wondering if I'm...if I'm going to stay here."

"You can, if you want to. I'm going to go after Tamaron...but first..."

"Mae!"

The voice that came from one of the doorways was livid with delight. Striding across the ground was a short woman with a bleached-platinum buzz cut. Her figure was just as remarkable as Amy and Mrs. E's, and Hector was able to say such a thing with great certainty because unlike the other two, this woman was bereft of clothes. Once again, with just a single syllable, he could hear the similarities between her and the others.

"You must be Moira, right?" he asked.

"I am," she said. "You're Hector, aren't you? Welcome."

He didn't reply, but was cut off anyway as Mrs. E embraced Moira's nude form. They ran their cheeks against one another, and when they turned away they kissed. It was a long kiss, and Hector heard Moira give a small squeak as Mrs. E's tongue entered her mouth. The latter enveloped her lover's curving buttocks with a forceful hand, and pulled her pelvis close. Briefly, Moira ground her bare labia against the front of Mae's pants. Then, they parted from each other.

"Rare that we're all in the same headquarters together, these days," Moira said then.

"That's basically what I told her when she came in," Amy interjected. "I just wish A was here."

"I always wish A was around," Moira said. "But I guess she's too good for us these days. Now, you'd better tell me what you and your guest are doing here before I just drag you back to my dormitory and keep you here for an hour or seven."

"Renegade Incomputare," Amy said then. "Tamaron, it sounds like."

"Great," Moira said, rolling her eyes. "Say, aren't we technically rogue Incomputare...? They started the Devourers, the Devourers split in two, making them and us, you recombined 'em, and then they split again because of..."

"Yes, yes, I know," Mrs. E said dismissively. "Forgive me, it's just this is all too active in my mind. History. It's such a tawdry thing now."

"You don't like history, and you don't like novelties...you're really changing, Mae," Moira said. And she took a glance at Hector. "We'll fix him up soon enough."

"This time, his pain is my fault. I should be the one to heal him—it's my fault, not the world's."

"We've all fucked someone up, Mae," Amy said. "It's no big deal..."

"It is this time," she said poignantly. And the other two froze.

"Listen, Mae," Moira said finally. "I've been raped, and I've been *killed*—or close to it, we could say. I know your pain. I know how much you *hate* that pain..."

"I know you know," Mrs. E said gently. "I'm just thinking of retiring. I didn't care. I didn't care when those other men died, and I didn't care that his body—that yours, Hector—was beaten up so badly. Because I've seen and endured worse, I couldn't identify with him. I can't identify with people who aren't like us anymore. Isn't that wrong?"

Hector took a step towards her, but was too timid, and she was lost in the embrace of Amy and Moira. He was still largely confused, but he knew that he didn't want to do her any unkindness, even if she had just taken the opportunity to largely speak on his behalf. He was in a great deal of pain, and he was terrified, but he trusted her when she talked about the nature of the bones in the pit. And she was not the one who killed his family.

When the two broke away from their compatriot, they turned to Hector, and stared at him, grinning. Mrs. E was also amused. Evidently there was some sort of understanding between the four of them.

"Where do we go from here?" Mrs. E said softly.

"We could entertain him," Amy said, in a more provocative voice.

"I mean, we *do* already know he's pretty great in sack." Moira's voice was boldest of all.

"I'd actually just like...something to eat, I think," Hector replied. "Alone. With you, Mae."

The others weren't offended. And Mrs. E hadn't been on a true date in a long, long time.

Taking his hand, they stepped back into the kitchen, to cook together.

CHAPTER XII:

Mrs. E pulled Hector's head into the curve of her neck and shoulder. Both of their respective sets of brown hair were suitably tousled, and blended into the rich red of the pillow. Their nude flesh was warm against each other, sticky with sweat. "That's all I wanted, I realize now," she said. "After all that running. Good food, good fucking."

"I'm glad I could bring you both," he said. "The others—the other Mrs. Es, that is—did they..."

"...did they experience what we just did through me? No—they can shut themselves out if they and I choose it. That's why we don't know what happened to Mrs. A, or where she is in the world."

"Watch as it turns out she's working with Tamaron."

She blinked. "I hope not. Her straits keep getting direr and direr, but I doubt she's that desperate. No, I think she has a unique destiny. She always has—she created us, and while our adventures ended up overtaking hers to some degree you can't ever do better than the original."

"I don't know about that. But that's because I can't imagine someone better than you."

She grinned. "Sometime I *will* have to let Amy and Moira have a crack at you. With your permission I'd feel you through them, and the three of us would climax all as one."

"I'm not sure I'd be up for that..."

"Group sex has some good surprises to it—surprises that make up for some of the shortcomings of its hype. But this is a place where only what is *allowed* happens. If you want me to be your only lover while you're here, then that's how it will be."

"Thank you," he said cheerfully.

All was well.

But then there was a rumble, one considerably more external than that which they'd just been through. At once, their faces paled. "Oh no," Mrs. E said, almost whimsically. But she looked back at him. "Get dressed. We may have to leave."

"May?"

"We can stay if we fend them off."

"Tamaron's mercenaries?"

"And Satiin's. We'll only be seeing the best of their men—the clumsy ones will be killed on the spikes."

"Maybe we'll be lucky and someone will have enough sense to knock Tamaron off the edge."

She said nothing, and in moments they were both dressed. When they came out they were surprised to find that Amy and Moira were in an opposite state: they

had evidently decided to engage in an encounter of their own. "Guys, what the hell are you doing?" Mrs. E barked. "We're under attack."

"Undoubtedly. I think they blew up the house up above," Amy said.

"And the tunnel to our dorm's collapsed. Our clothes are in there," Moira added.

"You left your close in your quarters and came out here to fuck? We're dead."

"We're not," Amy insisted. "We do have weapons here still. Handguns, rifles if you want 'em. They're just..."

"In the weapons locker. Which is past our dorms," Moira said, wincing. "I'll start diggin'."

"And I'm staying here. You may need to my help," Amy said.

"Nonsense. You're naked. You should get to cover," Mrs. E replied.

"Don't be ridiculous."

And that was apparently that.

Already the vestibule separating the trap corridor and the first chamber had been sealed off. A metal door, part of the environment of the corridor, had descended, but if Amy had spoken correctly that had "blown up" something, a slab of metal wouldn't stop them. There was the sound of chatter outside this door, getting ever closer as slowly, what seemed to be a tremendous crowd crossed the gap. Then, mere moments later, a red spot formed at the base of the door. It turned orange—yellow—and white, until it was a little white star that ate a constellation up to the height of a man. Hurriedly it cut horizontally, and then back down, until suddenly the door was useless. On the other side of the fresh gap were a number of professional-looking paramilitary filler—professional-looking in this case meaning they wore gas-masks. There was the impression that they were just going to gas them all and be done with it. Mrs. E noticed that neither Satiin nor Tamaron were wearing masks, nor did they keep them on hand. The aging beard that adorned Satiin's face was lifted up his face as he grinned, at the front and center of things.

"*Now* I understand why I killed Caruso," Tamaron said. "It was to lead you on this longer quest, to this sanctuary—to the remnants of Hexen's foul cult. She and I fought for years, did she tell you that?"

"If you refer to the Incomputare witch, I only met her briefly," Mrs. E replied.

"In any case," Amy added. "Hexen kept on leading her Devourers of Life for a time after causing the schism in the Order, and in time she changed the name to the Order of the Eight Gates. We haven't heard from her in all that time."

"You lie. You can't hide her," Tamaron said. "I killed Yulmer Purrlzig sixteen years ago, and Cyrus Sincodemius many years before that. After that, she still has the gall to challenge and bedevil me. You have three seconds to reveal her to me before I order Satiin to gun you down."

"Satiin is a Prince, and you should think twice before 'ordering' him," Mrs.

E said simply.

"You raise a good point, my dear," Satiin said suddenly. "Tamaron, be wary. You may be the bastard son of the Incomputare witches—the 'Uncountables' or 'Unfindables,' as that word means—but by disrespecting me you encroach on the realm of the gods. And the Incomputare, great as they once were, were never gods."

"The gods are living, if they exist," Tamaron said. "And since they are living, they are fit only to be receptacles for my essence. I've dreamed once of breaking free one of the old gods, and then *becoming* them..."

"Stop rambling. If we fight each other we won't get what we want. Speaking of which, my beautiful Mae, I want to know who your naked friend is. My intuition tells me she is a key piece of your identity."

"I'm not talking, and neither is she," said Amy.

"Very well. Since you've disburdened yourself of your clothes, you clearly show an eagerness to be the plaything of my men. It's been some time since they've slaked their urges, and once they've got you on the ground then..."

"Now you have to stop rambling." Tamaron was speaking, and his voice was firm and icy. "You'll do no such thing. I don't tolerate that sort of violence."

"And why is that? If you don't care for it, don't participate."

"It's childish, brutish, and stupidly human. If you're a real student of the transcendental you'll subject someone to tortures of the mind. You will break them on every level but in a way that has purpose. *That* never has reason outside of blind angry lust. Evidently the years have stripped you of your charms. Once you were a power of legend, Cunning One..."

Mrs. E had barely had to do anything at all. Satiin was showing how far declined he was now, and it was brushing up against Tamaron's own faults. Maybe his current form was simply succumbing to the "material" drives that he'd said would overcome Abbot Margong. In any case: to be a traitor to himself in that way was worthy of death. And thankfully he and his intended rape squad were at an end.

Moira was still naked when she came in with her rifle. It was a semi-automatic—it was true, yes, that Mrs. E hated such things. But now, the mercy that spawned that hatred was gone, and as the bullets flew and knocked the stunned mercenaries to the ground and to their graves, she once again felt nothing.

She still had to move, though. She grabbed Hector and darted back to where Moira was shooting from. She had excellent rifle training, and she didn't even come close to hitting her retreating friends. Gesturing, she pointed out a second weapon to Amy, and soon there were two women without clothing firing into the crowd.

Some of the men were retreating, and in any case, those who remained seemed uninterested in drawing their own firearms. Moira pointed again, to something softer than guns. "Got our wardrobe back, by the way," she said. Amy paused and seemed content to pull a long sweater over her body. Due to its length it was basically a shirt and a miniskirt simultaneously. She drew more fire while Moira

paused to put some pants on. She'd no reason to bother with a top, as by this point she'd seen hundreds of Vietnam movies where male soldiers fired at the enemy shirtless—and you didn't see *them* with any bras on.

In the chaos it seemed to Mrs. E saw that Satiin had been hit. Three times, in fact. He was on the ground, and Tamaron stood over him, refusing to retreat for some reason.

She only heard his final taunt to the dying Prince.

"Look at you. Now you are as weak and shapeless as you were when the Snake-Tongued Specter killed you in myths. Your power dies with you and I'm glad it's just another chunk of magic gone."

And Mrs. E knew that to be true. Dark days were coming. Satiin, in his previous identity, was a symbol of the previous Age of Magic.

There was something odd about Satiin dying like that. It was a pathetic death, as Tamaron said. But it was so *simple*, so *realistic*. She had expected more from him—a grand final stand, a mystic duel with great energies being flung as he was chased through the screaming, reeling dimensions. Or even just the illusion of such. His death was just another thing that was ordinary, worn dull, like the Abbey of Margong, or even Satiin's palace. Everything turning to "novelties," which at the end of the day were just shiny stones and baubles.

If the soldiers were retreating, Tamaron would likely go with them—he was no brawler, and his body would go down under the hail of machine-gun fire. But Tamaron was bolder than he first let on. He bolted forward, and with limited but unexpected strength he yanked Hector off his feet and started dragging him away. He moved so quick that Hector couldn't respond, and Mrs. E couldn't follow before it was too late. She called his name before there was another rumble from above. She heard the whine of twisting metal as the passageway partially collapsed. Whether this formed a burial cairn for Tamaron and Hector she couldn't tell.

And then it was over. The noise above stopped, and there was only silence. It wouldn't remain that way for long, though. If they had bombed the house covering the sanctuary, the authorities, military ones, would be arriving shortly. They would certainly recognize Moira Larssen for assassination, and Amy Wong for jewel theft. Their profiles were international at this point. Being found with infamous journalist Mrs. E, who had run a cult, and who had been to prison twice, would only aggravate matters. And that was before they found the bodies. She closed her eyes, and again passed on understanding to the other two. They were to obtain only the things that would reveal their identities—any non-essentials, like clothes or books, had to be left behind. Once they were fully dressed, of course.

Once they'd done that, they decided to try the corridor that led back to the surface. The eruption above had clearly been a nasty one. The entire passageway was twisted like an anxious intestine, and the platforms were in alignment due to the motors having burnt out, and gravity drawing them to one extreme.

So much for the trap. She had seen a touch of wonder in Hector's eyes—

such a mechanism *had* been like something out of fiction. An underground spike trap certainly had a pulp feel to it. But it hadn't proven to be truly useful in a pinch. And neither had her fellows, for when it really mattered. She realized that they hadn't had to do any fighting for years—in fact, they'd barely left this sanctuary in years. And already Mrs. E knew that that was because they were healing.

She was across the smashed gap now, and hurriedly climbed the ladder. Passing through the shattered hatch and out into the broken remains of the cover-house, she wondered what people would make of what they find down the hatch. She was sure that'd leave a nice urban legend—sometime soon she had to keep a tally of all the ones she'd been responsible for.

For example, an American citizen with some degree of infamy was about to be found gruesomely and mysteriously murdered. So much for Edward Tamaron, "Enemy of the Public" and "Wickedest Man in the World."

When they were all at the top, they could see the cars approaching. Emergency vehicles bore down on them, but without a word they ran. They were still near the outer edges of the city, after all, and soon the forests of Thailand were all around them once again.

With the other two there, Mrs. E's mental endurance was tripled, but she was still scared. It was only striking her now—as she was formulating her plan of finding Tamaron—that the Order of the Madonna could easily come undone when they found those bodies. If the Order came undone, she would come undone. They were synonymous now, for all the members were Mrs. E. She knew they were all professionals, and the sanctuary *had* been scrubbed clean, but she was a criminal. A compassionate criminal. It was almost a Christ-like way to live, and that was probably one of the reasons why it was called the Order of the Madonna in the first place (though Sumuro and her damnable ego hadn't helped). Guilt and conscience piled on her back like a cross. Even she was not truly immune to entropy and decay infecting a closed system—time was her enemy, no matter how much she opened up her system.

Eventually, they were a good distance from Bangkok, and the fires of the sanctuary were now behind them. They agreed to loop back around once again, to another part of the city. And along the way, they once more reverted to speaking aloud, though they did so quietly.

"I want you two to find 'Kitty'—you know her, right, Kitty Mucho?—and fly to Calcutta," Mrs. E said. "Hide on Rhahl, and send a general signal to everyone else to fall back there too. With Satiin dead, Tamaron has an army, or will once he gets his influence over Satiin's hired guns. I think that might have been one of his ancillary goals. In any case, he has the advantage, but the fortress on Rhahl can resist a nuclear assault. Not like I think it'll come to that...unless Tamaron finds *another* mad Soviet General or wicked Prince."

"We're coming with you to find that guy. You think we're just going to *hide*?" Amy's voice was hot with anger.

"Yeah! Don't forget, Tamaron fucked *us* up too," Moira added.

"No. If things don't work out, you two will be the last—with A gone and everything. I don't think the others in our keeping are ready for the title so soon."

"Now you're talking like you're getting ready to fucking *die*," Moira said. And Mrs. E said nothing in return.

Amy was offended by this silence. "Be serious, Mae."

"Mrs. E, please. I'm the incumbent leader, after all, for as long as A is missing."

"We're *all* the incumbent, you selfish bitch," Moira said. But her voice was jocular rather than angry. Her attempt to lighten the mood was dragged back down. "At least tell us what you're going to do."

"I'm going to check Satiin's palace, first. If Tamaron was in touch with him maybe there's some clue to another of Tamaron's bases. He said he 'called' Prince Satiin to strike a deal, but even then, deals between men with their profiles aren't struck so quickly. They must have known each other previously. I'll go from there."

And to get her point across, she allowed her eyes to close. From there her feelings were conveyed, and they stared bitterly at the ground.

"Please come back," Amy said.

"I can't bear to let part of me die again," said Moira.

She smiled at them. "I will. I love you."

They already knew.

CHAPTER XIII:

When they were gone, Mrs. E probably said something to the empty air about getting tired of talking to herself. Then, resigned, she returned to Bangkok. Amy and Moira were out of sight: whatever avenue they took, she didn't consciously know. She had shut them out of her head, and they had done likewise. She hoped they would forgive her if it turned out that her willingness to die was taken as a request.

This wasn't about Hector. It was about herself, and she flayed herself for that. She wanted to make up for dragging him in. And now, with that feeling taking root, she already knew it was going to become an obsession. Once someone is obsessed the first time, they're tainted forever—emotions are supposed to splash over the mind and be gone, but obsession is what happens when one doesn't hold back the sea.

God, now she was thinking of Melville. She hated him and she hated the sea. It reminded her of her tiny island. With her brother.

Her feet ached, but all the same she found her way through the winding streets of the city to Satiin's palace. An endless array of spices and incense, and fabrics of all kinds, surrounded her, but she took no notice of them. The city to her was a void, its beauty already etched into her mind. Maybe when she was older the color would knock her down again.

The palace was unguarded. She'd of course just now caught onto the possibility that Tamaron and his newfound army could have simply come back here, but they hadn't. Tamaron moved quickly, and she had no idea of his next step. He could choose to simply kill Hector—maybe he was already dead. In fact, it was probable he was already dead. But only probable. Evidence was all that mattered, and she had no evidence he had been killed.

And she was here for evidence. Immediately she made her way for Satiin's bedchamber, where the impressions of where they'd been sitting still remained on the bed's cloth. There was a sudden dullness and quietness here—it was all throughout the palace but it was centered here. She didn't want to stay long, because in that dullness she could feel that this castle had some secrets to it. Down below it probably had something inherently and stereotypically unsettling. A crypt. An abattoir. But in likelihood the temple chambers were down there. She hoped she could just stay up here, far away from whatever Satiin had set free in the depths.

She checked his desk and his shelves, noting that his papers were written variously in Thai, English (Modern and Old), Ak'lo, and something she didn't recognize. Nothing with Tamaron's name, though.

There was an interesting-looking diagram that was tucked behind *Paradise Lost* and *Moby-Dick*, and she wondered why it was hidden. It was relatively crude and she had difficulty making sense of it—it seemed to show a huge box, with

which was a diagonal line leading up and to the left, to a rectangle. Below all this was another rectangle, isolated from everything else. There was a thinly-scrawled piece of Thai script, next to this first polygon, reading "Pakarang bxna tenra." Crudely, "Coral Pond Dance."

"What the...?" And she said those words aloud. Then, she rolled her eyes. Of course. Coral Pond Dance—Correspondence. Sort of.

And she realized at once what she was looking at. The box was the palace, the slanted line the staircase, the upper rectangle the room she was in, and the lower rectangle the hypothetical nether chamber. It must be at the far left—or far back— end of the room where the "Correspondence" was. Perhaps this diagram was meant to be found in the wake of Satiin's death, to reveal key pieces of mail he'd kept over the years, particularly that which kept his organizations running. He did own or invest in a few businesses which sustained his fortune.

Under the desk was the answer. She saw that the foot of one of its legs was flush with the wood of the floor. Presumably a cable connected the leg to a panel somewhere. Sure enough, on the side of the leg there was an almost unnotice- able button, and when she pressed it, a landscape painting at the end of the room slid aside. Not the cleverest thing she'd seen, but all the same she went over to the now-revealed gap. Already she could see the outline of a manila envelope, and it was both weathered and thick.

She reached inside and found the space mercifully dry, but at once her fingers found that there was a vent at the base of this small pigeon-hole. There was cool air coming up through it, and she found that interesting. When she retrieved the package she stuck her head inside somewhere. She couldn't see through the slats very well, but the sound of air moving through it was a low hum in her ear. There was something else to that hum. Every so often, there was a banging sound, almost like the drum popping from heat in her electric dryer, and yet it wasn't metallic. She waited to hear it a few more times—there were long spaces between each sound- ing—and she was under the impression that it was fluid, somehow. Like the ribbit of a frog, or a bubble of gas through thick grease.

As she left the room she hurried to replace the painting over the storage pocket before opening the envelope.

The letters that didn't present themselves as valuable she made sure to replace, as she would leave this package in plain sight before calling the police. That would be the end of Satiin's remaining unsavory endeavors—his henchman would be tracked down when his charges were exposed. Each of the letters offered more incrimination than the last: he worked with wanted men as diverse as Peters, Andol- fi, and Murtagh. A lot of his goons would be shot on sight with all this.

But there was nothing marked with Tamaron.

Nothing...

What?

She drew one last letter from the envelope, having noticed that the post-

marks were becoming more and more recent. The handwriting responsible for this final piece was familiar, and she read it in greater detail. Slowly, the temperature of her blood dropped, when she saw the name that signed the letter, and the address it was sent from.

Moira and Amy would be gone on a different flight by now, so she could fly unimpeded. Her flight was bound back to Greece.

The flight was cold and silent, and when she was in Athens she took out 1.3 million drachma—or about $10,000—and bought an excellent-looking '79 Corvette L48. It rumbled even on the smoothest of streets, which was exactly what she wanted, and exactly why she went for the L48. You needed a car that *rippled* for this business, and she wanted him to know she was coming for him.

She felt nothing. She was nothing. The flesh vessel she wore was as immaterial as a cloud to the people of this world, as soft as stone was to her kind.

When she arrived she nearly broke the door off the car. The night sand punched under her feet, even as her legs begged to be seated. Everyone who saw her—technicians, accountants, cameramen—stayed out of her way. There was one tent in particular she was bound for, and she wasted no time in reaching it.

She drew back the entry flap and stepped into the generous space. Edward Tamaron and Jimmy Mathews were sitting beside one another in aluminum folding chairs, with Clyde Anderson nearby, and when she came in Mathews looked at her as if she was a secretary delivering coffee. Tamaron was still a coiled snake writhing in the body of a man, and in the corner, Hector was bound and gagged, and looking very exhausted.

There was a chair in front of Tamaron and Mathews. "Sit down, Mae," Mathews said then.

CHAPTER XIV:

"Not only is Satiin dead, but he's bad at hiding things," the director mused. Clyde Anderson stared at the ground uncomfortably. Tamaron merely grinned. "Come now, Mrs. E, you called yourself a detective once. Play Poirot. Summarize the terms of the crime before all parties, and say who is guilty."

She gritted her teeth. She did always appreciate the Poirot approach. She knew one day, in the long course of reciting the solution to her mysteries, someone would come up behind her with a knife and end it all. But not today—but with this recitation.

"The affair began presumably some years before I came once again to Greece." She needed the right tone, the right flourish, and "affair" was a good noun for that. "Maybe around the time I went to prison for the first time. There was collusion between everyone in this room. Except Hector and I didn't know that we were a part of that collusion."
"I'm not a part of it, either, Mrs. E! Please understand—" It was Clyde Anderson who interrupted.

"I know. I will get to that in time. For now I urge you to be quiet." He somehow shrunk even further into himself. "There were several goals that each of you wanted to reach. Tamaron's teleology was to take revenge on me for our previous fights—he's been behind more of my life than I previously thought he was. Prince Satiin, meanwhile, was a more passive party. At his age, he has to be, but perhaps, Tamaron, he mistook you for that old boyfriend of his, the Abhorrent Dread. Sometimes called Nodens, I think, Master of the Ring of Silvianus. In any case, Satiin's the villain in that hero-villain-trickster trinity he was going on to me about, with Peta Margong and, uh, the Dreamer. I don't even recall now if he gave me reasons for why he joined up with you, Tamaron...if he gave any, they were probably false. That's the problem with eternal evil...

"And you, Jimmy, you needed money to make this movie? Last one didn't do so well for you? I trust you, and you have paid me well: I don't think you would have sold me out willingly. Perhaps that's too much credit given, but you like me, Jimmy, even if I suspect that you *only* got the budget if I was involved. Now the question is whether or not they had to torture you to sign to those terms. You're a tough man, Jimmy, and so you could hide torture, I think, even if it was fresh. But let's leave that unanswered for now.

"Tamaron, your role is vague, even though you mentioned receiving advice from Peta Margong—and that's where I decide that Mathews here is the one on my side. He works for money, and thus his goals are entirely and simplistically material. Don't let that deceive you, Jimmy, slaving for material wealth is awful but I also say that as someone who doesn't have to do it. In any case, working for a living beats surviving as a theoretical concept, and trust me, I know. But you, Tamaron, you're

a wizard in a world that has to believe in the tangible. The Age of Magic is ending. Fifteen, twenty-five years tops. Maybe there's some desperation in you, which is sad for one so young.

"As for you, Anderson, you are complicit—but by accident. I can forgive you, because accidents should be forgivable. You had nothing to gain, it seems, but maybe I just haven't blown your cover yet."

She could feel him sweat.

"Remember. I served once as someone on the opposite end of detectives. No more illusions: it wasn't that I belonged to the same order as the criminal mastermind called the Great L'Lar, it *was* that I was the Great L'Lar, even if she operated two decades before I say I was born. And I am her successor, the Wicked Madonna called Sumuro, or *her* replacement, who made made the octopus theme sexy and played with Fabergé eggs—or the Great L'Lar's biological successor, her daughter Moira. Through all of those women I learned to deal with crimes both legal and mystical. And through that experience all of you are open books to me.

"In fact, there's a depressingly small amount of actual deduction involved. You two are guilty, to be sure, but it is now a matter of finding the gravity of your guilt. That's how I'll judge you. And unfortunately, Jimmy, the principal blame lands on you."

He said nothing. His eyes shimmered, even behind his sunglasses.

"After all, you have always endeavored to escape these scuzzy, low-down movies. Clyde, after all, is the one who relishes in them, bathes in their waters. Mathews, you do a good job of wringing emotion out of us, but it's easy to imagine you would want more. You want a real dramatic story to happen *around* you, by itself, instead of your having to put energy into it. Like any other director strained by their medium. Right?"

And at once, he cleared his throat. The voice that came out was the best he touted for interviews, spoken in his native Italian. "I fundamentally believe that the story we are making here, the story of Commodus, is a murder mystery. History is something filled with great clouds, and so we are unsure entirely of how, where, and why Commodus died, with only a little hyperbole. Perhaps the studio wants this and the studio wants that, with this budget—they want me to fill it up with the stuff that Igor Horwess had in his movies, with the rape and bestiality and orgies. I could not do a Commodus mystery without a bigger budget, and I could not do my Commodus mystery without a bigger budget.

"It is true. All of this has been my mystery, but after all this time of making all these movies with Nazis and nuns and Amazon cannibals and zombies and women in prison, I lost my vision. My focus. I could not complete this mystery before you could solve it. So yes, I am the guiltiest party, Mae. I am the guiltiest because I am a fundamentally good man who chose to follow his own selfishness at the expense of the people Tamaron killed. It was a mutually creative relationship. He had his victims, to motivate your tragedy. That you found a bond with one of

the prisoners added a twist I did not conceive, for I've never been good at romance plots to be honest. I just wish I had a conclusive answer. Mr. Tamaron tells me that he took you to see Peta Margong."

"He did. It was bizarre, by my standards, and not in a good way."

"Yes—and I am familiar with his status as a trickster, though your full explanation, Tamaron, does not go unappreciated. Actually, it is relevant that you met two of the three powers in that world. You met the villain and the trickster but you did not meet the hero, and that's probably where I made my greatest failure. But then, it is apropos, for I had a secret project with all this. You see, what I want is a mystery story that leaves codes and gaps and lacunae in it to create a mystery for its audience—they become the players, the detective, like in the American Choose-Your-Adventure Novels, or like in video games. This is perhaps the next level of filmmaking. Or it at least is a curio. And curios, like treasures, still end up in museums." Without missing a beat, he continued: "The blood of many people is on my hands now. Now, my story is coated with blood. I've become like my great hero. I knew I was good at film when I worked with the Great Montero, now two years gone, God rest him, but I knew I *loved* film when Montero showed me *Saga of a South Seas Cannibal*, by the startling cinematic hero Karl Denim. It was an accident, of course. Montero was something of a hack, but through him and his accident I learned the ways of that hero. I learned the brutal truth that you must go the full distance for your art—and I found art in the brutality that today's market lusts for. There is something *fine* about when you have to mix your obligations and your artistic drives, a nice flavor to the weird fusion-things it breeds. This time, I have gone wrong. Poor Gabe Caruso—my aborted Emperor Commodus. I hired him on originally because I thought he was an actor I worked with before. Gabriele Carrara. The greatest actor I ever had..." And she let him trail off gently.

"Since you are making this so easy," she said, "I want to know how you and Tamaron collaborated. If you encouraged him to butcher those men and their families, you will be one of my enemies as Tamaron is." But she didn't pause. "I already know, however, that you could not have inspired Tamaron to do anything—not due to a lack of creative vision, but because Tamaron already delights in murder." She looked now at the self-proclaimed sorcerer, eternally stuffed into his Hammer Horror robes, who now resembled a balloon losing air.

But he was on the rim of laughing, just to spite her. Purely, eternally, to spite her. "The guilt or innocence of Mr. Mathews does not matter," Tamaron said, "because I currently control the armies of Satiin. They are all around this tiny camp, just waiting for the order to bury all this under the sand."

"I wouldn't count on that," she said. "You never learn from your fights, because all you do is fight. You fought me, and Hexen, and all the other remaining Incomputare. You survive by fighting, and you are always doing just that: surviving."

And the spotlights lit up around the camp. They could see the silhouettes of the crew and other actors, with their hands in the air—the night was split with

their screams. Farther beyond they could see the shadow-shapes of figures holding weapons, encroaching on all of them.

"You can feel it, Tamaron. You know that those aren't men out there with guns. At least, not exclusively men—there are many women out there, and they're my women. You can wait to find out who they are, or you can run now and maybe stand a chance of avoiding the fate of your men. I know not all of them were here tonight, but we'll find them. Soon all you'll be left with again is your tiny cult of scared people."

"Like you're much better."

She said nothing. She already knew what was coming, because beyond the screams of the falling soldiers there was silence.

One of the figures was at the side of the tent now. Their outline was holding a knife, aiming it at the canvas—the blade poked through and soon the light flooded into the tent. Clyde and Hector flinched from it.

Standing in the new gap was Amy Wong, now wearing something considerably closer to the skin than her outfit from the sanctuary. Aside from the knife she had a simple revolver. She was already readying both for Tamaron. "Even with your mind closed, I can find you, Mae," she said casually. "We've all been together too long." And a look of slight regret passed her face. Moira came in behind her, saying nothing.

As they stared at each other for that solitary second, there was a loud bang, and even Mathews flinched. By the time she turned on her heels Mrs. E saw the last lingering traces of violet smoke dissolve in the air. Tamaron's chair was empty.

But his voice did not join him in exiting, at least not immediately: "I'll be back, Mrs. E. I always come back. I will learn your secrets one day, and then not even Kurq'wes Himself will stop me from learning the secret of how you squeeze your octopoid forms into fresh bodies."

Amy scratched the back of her neck. "Uh...these bodies didn't exist before they were ours..."

"Let him believe goddamn whatever," Moira said.

"Remember, I'm the reason you're here," Tamaron cut in. "I displaced Aleister Crowley—that's how I put it to that band I dealt with months ago, 'displaced.' 'Replaced,' I think, is a better word, even if it's not completely accurate either. I think smashing him and all his spells across the timeline like a fly ripped open the barriers between your world and mine. Why else would all these fictional characters be popping up all over the place...?"

He was grumbling now, like a defeated child.

"None of this matters in the long run, Mrs. E. So a victory of four decades prior has turned to a defeat. I have succeeded now—I have the Mirror, Dagger, and Eye of Serpentis even if I've spent all my other gains. I am the premier Sorcerer of this world now, and you are fading quickly. We'll meet again soon."

And then the voice was gone.

"He's just a punk kid," Moira cut in again, "trying to think he's smart, tying a bunch of unrelated things together. He'll never really learn anything."

"Who's Aleister Crowley?" Amy asked. Mrs. E blinked at her, realizing what Tamaron's words meant. People were already forgetting; *she* was already forgetting. By the Goddess, he *was* a terror—he'd ripped a real-life wizard out of reality...no doubt that had spattered chaos-magic all over the timeline, and no wonder there were cracks opening up into fiction.

She stopped herself there. That train of thought was too far. She didn't want to make those cracks worse; she'd skirted close to the limits of her own self-awareness and there was no need to get closer.

Back in reality, Clyde Anderson was helping to free Hector, having gotten his gag off.

Mrs. E continuing gazing at where the smoke had been. "Now he slips away, like some..." and the start of an "f" sound caught in her throat, "...Fantômas."

"What's a Fantômas?" Hector coughed.

"Someone who gets away from consequences every time...a little tediously, if I remember."

Mrs. E turned to face the other two women. And she didn't look them in the eye—her own eyelids were pinched shut.

Once more, they understood. Hector was close to them now, and stepped forward and hugged Mrs. E tightly. Both of them, at the same time, whispered something in her ear, but he wasn't close enough to hear it. Even as they spoke at the same time, at the same rhythm.

And then they left. Hector never saw them again.

Mrs. E turned to face the director and the writer, then. Mathews was nonplussed, as ever, and Anderson had settled into an imitation of such. "I suppose you're going to tell us what will become of us now," Mathews said.

"You'll keep on making movies, I expect. As for Clyde..."

"I resign," Clyde said. "You have paid me in advance for the scripts for those Vietnam movies, that *Aliens*-cum-*Terminator II* ripoff, and whatever the hell *Three For One* was. So you can have them. I'm off to make movies of my own. Mrs. E, would you like to help me with these films? I know that once upon a time you were a costume designer."

"Certainly. But first, I need to take you to a sanctuary while my agents take care of scrubbing you and Mr. Mathews out of Tamaron's records."

"You won't need to hide me, surely," said Mathews. "It's not as if Jimmy Mathews is my real name. So few people today know my real name."

"Enough with the mysteries," Anderson replied. "In any case, my real name isn't Clyde Anderson. And Tamaron barely noticed me. I think I'll be okay."

"A shame. On Rhahl you could have met some of our head scientists. Like Dr. Zan. She ran her own all-female gang in the late '60s and now tends to the octopi. We have to keep a close eye on her, though—she's still got a little fatale streak

in her. She kidnapped some of the Tcho-Tcho dwarves of Tibet and attempted to create an army with them at one of our labs in Utah. Some of them escaped, and that led to what the first *Mrs. E called Mrs. E and the Goblins.* We haven't filmed that yet..."

"Goblins? What are you...?"

"Ha, ha—Clyde, you have much to learn. We had to create a new religion for these goblins, to steer them away from Dr. Zan's machinations. Their faith involves a Samhain cult from Stonehenge..."

He was smiling at her now.

"Go," she said to the two of them. "I'll catch up later. Tell the crew to start tearing down."

When they left, she and Hector were alone in the now-ruined director's tent.

"So what do you do next, huh?" he asked. "I bet you're going to spend the next few years hunting down Tamaron."

"No, I'm not. Being a costume designer sounds like a nice placeholder for now. My agents, and my...components, will keep up the hunt and the fight. But *I'm* going to stop. I can't push it," she said. "The first Mrs. E did that, and she started crumbling. She's still going out long after the burnout. My burnout is *now.* I've lost my vision, same as Jimmy—I don't believe in being a sexual detective anymore. My adventures have been turned to porn, and I'm just a fantasy now more than ever. That means I need a ground. I want to be a professor, instead, like Sappho. Gentle in the classroom, but teaching the next generation to be warriors, for when the storm comes 'round again. And so my closing-down has to happen now." She grinned. "So there won't be any *Mrs. E in the Days of Commodus*, or *Mrs. E and the Goblins*, or any other films with me, for that matter. At least not directly. Whatever happens, I know that my mark on this world will remain."

"It will. I saw those other women. They were magnificent, and not just in the bedroom."

"The movies we're in end up being sex flicks because of people. It's like how religions are bad when faith isn't. At least, I hope so."

"I know what you mean." They took each others' hands.

She pulled him close and he bent back at little. "So if we're going to be serious about this, and I'm going to keep you in my bed," she said, "we should be on a full name basis. What's your family name?"

"Manuel, my love," he replied. "Hector Manuel, at your service."

Manuel? Well, if she put their two names together, it made...oh! Now that was a fun coincidence.